MIDLIFE MAGIC

Not Too Late Series, Book 1

by Victoria Danann

Published by 7th House Publishing, Imprint of Andromeda LLC

Print Edition

Read more about this author and upcoming works at

VictoriaDanann.com

Prologue

I WOKE AS crashes of thunder shook the house, to track the strobe effect of rapid flashes of lightning against my bedroom wall. My husband slept as if it was a lullaby and not a storm of storms.

I'd been dreaming about such a night in a place I didn't recognize. In my dream I'd awakened to thunder-strikes accompanied by the sounds of snarling. Not at me. At something outside my window.

Even in my dream I recognized that it was odd to have a pair of wolves in my bedroom, but my sense was that they were a comfort and not a danger. When I rose to open the shutters, the creatures parted to make room for me but didn't back away. If anything, their protests became more aggressive when the subject of their alarm became visible.

A woman with long, dark hair was standing statue still

in my front yard just inside the white fencing. She was being drenched by torrents of rain but seemed not to care. She was familiar. And threatening enough for me to feel a cold panic course through my blood, even in my sleep. The wolves' intent to break through the window seemed to escalate in direct proportion to my rising fear. As if they knew what I was feeling.

As is so often the case, the dream vanished into smoke and was forgotten when I woke.

In time it would be recalled, but not until years had come and gone.

Chapter One

Journey

My name is Rita Hayworth. If that makes you laugh, it tells me that you have a few gray hairs underneath that fabulous color you're sporting. My paternal grandmother was a super fan. She told me that she gave my granddad a chance solely because his last name was Hayworth. My father would've been the moniker victim, but he escaped on the grounds that Rita isn't a boy name in any generation.

Never one to give up, my grandmother talked Mom into making me the lucky recipient of her devotion to "Put the Blame on Mame". It's hard for daughters-in-law to say, "Not in a hundred years," when their mission is to maintain family peace and tranquility. Knowing how persuasive my grandmother can be, I'm choosing to give

Mom a pass.

If you're not an old movie aficionado, here's the skinny. Rita Hayworth was a forties movie star in the days when a sex symbol could be sexy and mostly clothed. She was the consummate vamp. Not vamp as in vampire. Vamp as in a pretty woman with a sultry air, stripper hair, and bright red lipstick who uses charisma, charm, flirtation and a strangely pointy bra to manipulate men.

This is *so* not me. First, I wouldn't be caught dead in red lipstick unless my daughter hands it to the funeral director between my passing and my disposal. She's just mischievous enough to do it. She might put me in a leopard bikini while she's at it. Thank the gods I will've vacated this body before it becomes the *ample* butt of a joke. And, second, I have no charisma, no charm, and even less interest in manipulating anyone. I might've known something about flirtation between pubescence and marriage, but those skills are so long forgotten they've rusted all the way through.

As I said, Rita wasn't a popular boy name, but it wasn't a popular girl name either. At least not for my generation. In fact, I've never met another. Maybe that's not an upside. Maybe it just puts punctuation on the weirdness. But none of that has anything to do with this story.

What *is* relevant is the reason why I've just landed at Heathrow Airport, London. First time out of the U.S. A few weeks ago I couldn't have imagined this. But life is strange. Way stranger than you think.

The day after my forty-third birthday, my husband announced he was trading me in. His words, not mine. What he said precisely was, "I'm trading you in on two twenty-two-year-olds," and then laughed. When he realized we weren't sharing the joke, he added, "Seriously. I need to free up because this isn't working for me and I've found somebody who *really* gets me."

I could only guess that *really* 'gets' him meant that she was into watching him look at his phone during dinner out, was good at pretending to like football, and could field snipes about her appearance without resentment. More likely, these details are discoveries yet to be revealed. And endured. Good luck, sweetie.

THE NEWS THAT I was transitioning to single was unwelcome at the time, but honestly? I needed a good goosing to get up and find my way to the exit, just like love had a couple of decades ago. Why did I stay? It will have to remain one of the great psychological mysteries of the ages because I don't know. Maybe laziness. Maybe the benefits of combined income. None of the answers I come up with paint a flattering picture.

If not for the financial component, I might have been embarrassingly elated. But living in a state not friendly to discarded wives, I was also relieved of the financial 'security' I'd spent a lifetime accruing. Did I mention that Cole wasn't the sort of guy who was into sharing when he saw no benefit to himself?

I'd be reduced to my sixty-eight-thousand-dollar-a-year job as a claims adjuster for National Farm & Neighbor. I wouldn't starve, but I wouldn't be going on vacation to Las Brisas either. *Sigh.* Nope. The 'trade-in' would be enjoying a pink jeep, a private pool overlooking Acapulco Bay, and salads with flowers in them. *Sigh.*

SO. STARTING OVER? I didn't plan on it. Didn't see it coming. But pulling a sheet over my head and waiting for the end didn't seem like my style. Granted, I wasn't sure what my style was because I hadn't thought about freedom of expression since I was twenty.

Yeah. I'm over the hill. I'm over that and a world of other annoyances I kept quiet about when I was younger. But what's the point of packing on a few years and a few pounds if you can't speak up when the spirit moves you? Or gooses you in the ass.

Okay. Full disclosure. (Translation: *Partial disclosure.*) To the consternation of both my parents, who'd hoped for demure, I never was what you'd call closed mouthed. But I did manage a modicum of restraint until the recent, surprise announcement that I was about to undergo a 'status' change. In my present state of being disyoked from an overly-opinionated husband, I feel personal anarchy blossoming to life.

I CHECKED TO make sure the little stash I'd squirreled away was safe and secure at the Peoples' Prosperity Bank. There was enough for meager living quarters for a few months until I could figure things out.

I set aside everything that didn't fit into two rolling

bags for storage and made my way to the corporate residence, which was what we used to call a studio apartment. I left the bags standing in the living room, looking as lost as I felt, and let myself fall onto the tweedy sofa without thinking too hard about whether I needed to view the fabric through a black-light filter.

My boss was reservedly polite when I called to say I'd be taking a couple of weeks of personal time. I knew it was short notice, but I had time accrued. If sick time was counted, I had *a lot* of time on the books because I'd been fortunate to be healthy. And with no hobbies, and one child who was extraordinarily self-sufficient, I could work or watch Telemundo. I chose work.

I was sitting there, trying to summon the energy to go to the grocery for provisions to stock the galley kitchen when there was a knock on the door.

I looked through the peephole before opening. It was the cheerful kid from the desk.

"Something for you, miss."

"Gods bless you for calling me miss. Are you sure it's for me? Nobody knows I'm here yet."

He looked at the big, black lettering on the front of the

envelope. "You're Rita Hayworth. Right?"

I nodded dumbly. Hayworth was my maiden name. My head hadn't yet cleared away the shock of being told by my husband of twenty years that I was old news. I hadn't even thought about whether or not I would keep his name or reclaim my own. I hadn't yet called a lawyer, talked to my daughter, or decided to get rid of the navy-blue sedan Cole had insisted was 'classy' and just perfect for me.

"Well, then," the afternoon clerk said, pushing the envelope a couple of inches closer.

I took it. "Thanks." And began looking for my purse to give him a tip. "Just a second."

He waited while I fished out my wallet. I was clueless about the going rate of tip for delivering what seemed to be documents, but I didn't want to be thought of as a cheapskate by the afternoon clerk. So, I pulled out a five and handed it over. By the smile on his face I knew it wasn't too little. Whether or not it was too much was hard to tell.

I closed the door, set the envelope down on the cheap veneered coffee table and waited for a voice to tell me what to do next. Open it? Take a nap? Go get wine first? The last option was the only one that resonated emotionally.

"Wine it is," I said out loud to myself. When I realized I was speaking to no one, I added, "I've been not-legally single for a day, and I'm talking out loud to myself."

I grabbed my keys and set off on quest for wine and food that needed no more preparation than a couple of turns in the microwave. While learning the layout of a market I'd never seen before, because I was on the opposite side of town from where I'd lived my entire adult life, I received calls from the animal shelter where I volunteered, the exterminator, and my daughter. I told the first to leave me off the schedule for a couple of weeks, told the second to cancel the account, thinking that insect infestations were the least my soon-to-be ex deserved. Last, I assured my daughter, the college junior who'd heard the news from her father, that I was going to be fine.

Through all of that, I never stopped thinking about the 'package', as the clerk had called it. By the time I returned to my (hopefully) temporary digs, I was tired of waiting. I set the two-and-a-half bags on the little countertop and went straight to the envelope.

I ripped the cardboard zip free and removed the contents expecting it to be a notice of intent to divorce. After all, who besides Cole knew where I was? Come to think of it, I hadn't told anyone, including Cole, where to find me.

IT CONTAINED A letter of summary and introduction, several legal documents and a printout of travel arrangements in my name. *Paid* travel arrangements that included a first-class, *one-way* ticket to London. I spread the papers out on the coffee table and stared for a few seconds before deciding that there was only one reasonable course of action when approaching a rare mystery such as this. Pour wine. Drink wine. Then read.

Congratulating myself on the foresight to pick up a wine opener at the store – because of course there were cheap wine glasses in the cabinet, but no opener – I poured three inches of deep red liquid, intent on feeling neither pain nor guilt. I moved the envelope's contents to the dinette and switched on the swag light that hung above.

After getting as comfortable as dinette chairs allow, I took a drink of black blend. Not a sip or dainty taste. I enjoyed a full-on gulp with no shame and no one to critique my choices.

Dear Ms. Hayworth,

You have inherited a fine retail property with residence in the Eden of England, Cumbria, and funds sufficient to cover your personal needs and ensure maintenance of the property for your lifetime.

Enclosed you will find documentation of air transportation, a passport, a bit of currency, and a credit card in your name. After clearing customs, kindly look for a sign that reads 'Hayworth'. We will have a man ready to escort you to a vehicle suitable for completion of the journey. Your auto will be equipped with navigation and programmed to guide you safely here.

Feel free to overnight en route to our picturesque village of Hallow Hill. The choice is entirely yours. We look forward to your arrival.

Sincerely,

Lochlan Jois, Solicitor

This could be better than winning the lottery. Or it could be the opening scenes of a horror movie. There was only one appropriate response. I reached for the wine glass and downed all that was left in the goblet. My head was swimming. Granted, more wine wouldn't add clarity to the situation. But dammit. I deserved an illogical minute now and then.

I didn't know which mystery to focus on. How did Lochlan Jois know I was at the Southside Residence Inn? How did he know I had just become available for travel? Perhaps the biggest mystery, how in the name of all that's holy did he manage to get me a passport and credit card without my signature? Annnnnd, what is a solicitor?

The passport took priority for pressing questions. I opened it to find a recent photo that I don't remember being taken. It wasn't horrible. Just bad enough to be believable. And, yep. There was no question about the fact that the signature looked authentic even to me. There were two possible explanations. Late-developing somnambulism or incredible forgery.

Needless to say, everything about the event screamed fishy, fishy, fishy. Because I didn't really put any stock in the late-developing somnambulism theory. But was that going to stop me? Probably not. A woman stupid enough to marry a man like my soon-to-be ex is stupid enough to fly first class into the great unknown.

I looked at my bags, still standing where I'd left them like dutiful sentries, and wondered if I had the right clothes for late September in England. Even in the midst of bizarre and unexplainable events, I never lose sight of priorities.

The plan crystallized. I would take both bags. If it all turned out to be a gift from fate, my reward for surviving marriage to Cole, then my daughter could send the rest of my things in between semesters. With sufficient bribery, of course.

AFTER CLEARING CUSTOMS, which made me curse myself for bringing two large bags, I looked around for a sign with my name. Standing in a row of guys with handprinted cardboard signs was an ancient fellow grinning ear to ear, white hair going every which way. The sign said 'Hayworth'.

I walked toward him and, when I was close enough to

be heard, said, “That’s me.”

“Oh, yes, I know,” he said. “I’m Eckert. Right this way.” He took control of both bags. The fact that they were each four-wheeled made that possible.

“I can get those,” I said.

“Wouldn’t hear of it, Madam. I will see you to your automobile and get your luggage squared away.”

I wasn’t crazy about being called ‘madam’, since I was on the way to shedding that title for good, but he meant well. So I refocused on the airport’s sights, sounds, and the less desirable aspects of overseas travel.

We stepped outside into crisp, Fall air.

“Right over here,” he said, pointing to a very shiny red car waiting at the curb right in front of us.

“How did you get a parking place like this?” I asked. “I thought this kind of thing only happens in the movies.”

He chuckled. “The movies,” he repeated. “Think of yourself as a *very* important person. More important than movies.”

“Well, that might take some doing.” The man reached into the car and retrieved a clipboard from the passenger seat, which was on the wrong side of the car from my perspective. "This is a gorgeous car. Are you sure this is the rental they got for me?"

He chuckled again as he handed me the clipboard and a pen. "This is not a rental. It's yours. Just sign right there."

"What do you mean, mine? You mean…?"

I took the clipboard and looked at the first few lines. There was my name. Rita Hayworth. Owner of a brand-new Alfa Romeo Stelvio Quadrifogio purchased for… That's when I almost dropped the clipboard onto the sidewalk. Somebody had just bought me a car worth £85,700.

"This can't be right, um, Eckert."

Pointing at the signature line, he said, "Right there. Everything's in order, Madam. Saw to it myself." He looked at the vehicle lovingly. "A very fine auto this is. Will hug the curves between here and Hallow Hill like a lover."

Unsure that I felt comfortable with the reference, I opted for, "No question that it's a very fine auto. I'm just trying to process that it's intended for me. This car costs more than I make in a year."

"It's yours. I've programmed the GPS to take you right to the shop in Hallow Hill. If you decide to stop for the night, don't worry about the car. It's burglar proof."

After turning that over in my mind, I said, "I don't think there's any such thing, Eckert."

He laughed as he took his copy of the paperwork and put my copies in a beautiful leather-bound satchel that also contained the owner's manual. "Well, if you won't be needing anything else, I'll put these bags in the rear and leave you to get to know your new car."

"Three things. Let me fish a jacket and scarf out of the bag before you do that. And, could you make sure I know how to turn on the GPS before you go? And how far is Hallow Hill?"

"How far? Or how long to get there?"

I rethought what I really wanted to know. "How long?"

"A little less than five hours. GPS audio is on and it's what they call interactive? That means that you can talk to it, ask questions, and it will answer."

I wasn't sure whether to be more suspicious of Eckert's assurances or the car itself. The idea of Q and A interactivity with a car was a little too sci-fi for my tastes. But again, I let it go.

I STARTED THE car and decided that it couldn't hurt to try the interactive thing.

"Car."

"Yes?" The car had a nice male voice with a very pleasing accent and the slightest hint of Italian. "You're welcome to refer to me as Romeo, Madam."

"Okay, Romeo. I prefer Rita to Madam."

"First name basis it is then."

I was trying to decide how I felt about sitting in a car that could converse as well as most people I know when someone behind began honking. It seemed the enchanting parking space had a lifecycle.

"Um, Romeo."

"Yes."

"Do you work with the GPS? Can you tell me how to get where I'm going?"

"Indeed I can, Rita. I can even drive for you if you wish."

I blinked. "You can drive this car?" Under my breath, I

muttered, “I’d like to see that.”

“So you shall.” The car sounded ecstatic.

Before I could close my self-sabotaging mouth, the car had leaped into the traffic flow and was racing toward the airport exit. To my credit, I did not scream. Although that may have been in large part because my vocal cords were frozen from fear.

I had no idea how to retake control of the car and couldn’t make my voice work to ask.

The first quarter-hour was terrifying because of the alien aspect of sitting in the front right seat while driving on the left side of the road coupled with the fact that we were in heavy airport traffic. By the time the traffic thinned out, my nerves were shot and I was longing for a place to stop. The good news was that my voice had returned. I verified that by clearing my throat.

“Okay. Romeo? That was a marvelous demonstration of self-drive car. When we leave Greater London, is there a nice inn on the way where I could eat and spend the night?”

“Yes. We’ll be there in less than an hour. The Spotted Hare. Good pub food. And they have a rare ensuite room available for the night."

"How could you know that?" Silence. I decided to try another question. "Do they have wine?"

"The establishment does serve wine. In fact, they have your favorite black blend."

"Are you omniscient?"

Silence.

I wanted to enjoy the scenery, but I was too preoccupied with survival to look away from the road until I felt the car slowing. We, meaning Romeo and I, were approaching a white building just ahead. The colorful hanging sign depicting a spotted hare was a sure giveaway that we'd arrived. The parking lot was crowded, but Romeo scored a spot near the front door, put the car in park and turned the engine off.

"I regret that I can't help with luggage, Rita."

"That's alright. You've done quite enough."

After transferring what I needed for the night from luggage to tote I used the fob to lock the car, but suspected Romeo could take care of himself. And my belongings.

AS THE CAR had said, there was a nice ensuite room

available.

I'd left home at dinnertime and eaten on the plane. First class overseas will set everything you've ever heard about airplane food on its ear. It would have been lovely if I'd had a long stretched-out nap on the plane. The convertible seat would allow for it, but for whatever reason, maybe excitement, I didn't sleep.

At home it was too early to get up. At the Spotted Hare it was just after lunch time and I hadn't slept. That meant that I looked dreadful, felt worse, and was irritable, wondering what sort of hairbrained broad would throw caution *and* common sense to the wind.

"How can we help you?" said the rosy woman behind the bar.

"I was told you might have an ensuite room for the night?"

"In fact we do. American, are you?"

"Yes. It's my first trip and I've just arrived."

"Well, I hope you have a lovely stay. You'll be paying with a bank card?" I nodded as I began the fishing expedition. First the purse within the tote, then the wallet within the purse. "And a quick look at your passport as well, please."

I handed over the card and the passport. "I see you're still serving lunch?"

"All afternoon. Will you need help with luggage?"

"No." I lifted my tote. "I got it."

She handed back my card and passport along with an old-fashioned metal key. "Number 21, right up those stairs."

"I don't suppose you do room service?"

The woman laughed and shook her head.

After consuming a ploughman's special like I'd never eaten, I fell into a deep sleep, still in my clothes. I woke hungry just before midnight. It would be hours before food would be available. So, I rummaged through the tote and found two protein bars that had been stowed sometime in the past. I didn't check the expiration date because I didn't want to know. I'd rather deal with the consequences, whatever they were, than be hungry.

The fact that they were still good probably meant they were more preservatives than nourishment. So much for health food.

Satisfied that would tide me over until… I looked

around for some kind of literature that might mention when breakfast would be served downstairs. The drawers were empty, but there was a flyer-style info sheet framed and hung on the wall. Seven o'clock. A little over six hours. I told myself I could make it if I kept myself distracted and drank the entire two-liter bottle of water that had been left as a thoughtful touch – for an additional five pounds.

I brushed my teeth, pulled out the clean clothes I'd planned to wear in the morning and, by that, I meant when it was light outside, and looked out the window to the parking lot below to make sure Romeo was okay. He was fine. I suppose I'd decided that Romeo was a *male* obscenely expensive and gorgeous car because of the voice. I reread the letter from the solicitor several times while questioning what in holy schmoly I was doing.

Then I turned on the TV, lowered the volume, and began the search one channel at a time. Talking heads and "Torchwood". I didn't know anything about "Torchwood" but I knew I wasn't in the mood for world news in the middle of the night.

By six o'clock I'd found that, indeed "Torchwood" had

been a distraction, and I was a guilty-pleasure-type fan.

A bath and fresh clothes went a long way toward making me feel presentable. Hopefully, breakfast would top me off and give me the confidence I'd need to complete the drive to Hallow Hill, with stops on the way for snacks. Lots of snacks. I'd learned a valuable survival lesson. Never be caught away from home without portable food.

At six forty-five I was sitting at a table by the parking lot window waiting for the breakfast bell. I had scrambled eggs with tomatoes and coffee. I'm not a connoisseur, but still, I wished I'd skipped the coffee. I said, "This bread is toasted on both sides."

The server looked blank, but said, "Yes. Isn't that the usual way?"

I said, "Not according to Sting. 'Englishman in New York'."

"Hmmm," he said and moved off.

At seven thirty I returned the key to the pub bar and headed for the door with my tote over my shoulder, wearing the kind of thick black jeggings that hide a history of good times, an oversized white knit sweater that fell to mid-thigh, and a long aqua scarf that people say brings out the turquoise in my eyes. I was more nervous than excited, but eager to see what the day would bring.

"Good morning, Mad… I mean Rita," said Romeo, as I got behind the wheel.

"Hey. So. Who's driving? You or me?"

"I'm very sensitive and fun to drive on two-lane roads, but if you prefer to sightsee, I will drive."

I decided I could test out Romeo's sensitivity another time. Since he'd done such a good job of getting me thus far, I said, "You drive."

"Excellent choice."

"How far is it?"

"Four hours. Some of the roads are narrow and what some would call off the beaten path."

"Carry on then." I don't know if Brits actually say that, but it felt like going native to say it out loud.

Half the trip was spent on the kinds of roads I'd only seen in sports car commercials. Curving and narrow blacktop flanked by gray stone walls cut across undulating hills complete with grazing sheep and buildings that looked like movie sets in period films. By eleven, we were pulling into the village of Hallow Hill.

It was a fairy tale. I found myself in amusement-park mode thinking what a marvelous job they'd done of recreating a charming English village and had to remind myself that it wasn't a knockoff.

The center of the village was a large cobblestone circle surrounding a green with a garden in the center. The fact that there were no cars in sight added to the nineteenth-century look.

Romeo didn't answer, but came to a stop in front of Hallows Antiques and Treasures.

"Would you like me to ring Miss MacHenry?"

"Um. Yes?"

"I should really park in the rear. Autos aren't allowed here at the village center."

Before I had a chance to answer, an Irish woman said, "Hello?", in a charmingly pronounced accent.

I waited for Romeo to answer since Romeo had placed the call. When he didn't, I finally said, "Hello. I'm Rita, um, Hayworth. I'm here about…"

"Oh, I know what you're here about. Come in. The car can park itself in your garage."

A series of short dashes indicated that the call had

ended. I decided to bring my purse and leave the rest. After all it was headed to "my" garage.

"Romeo," I said. "Do you know where, um, my garage is?"

"I do."

"And will you be able to park there without any further assistance from me?"

"I will."

"I'm taking the key fob thingy."

"Very well."

"That's not a problem for you?"

"I don't require the… key fob thingy to follow your instructions."

"That's kind of amazing." I gave myself a mental shake when I realized that, in less than a day, I'd added talking to a car like it was alive to talking to myself. I wasn't sure which was worse. "Alright. Watch my luggage."

"Your luggage is safe with me."

Not sure why, but I believed him.

I STOPPED AND looked at every item in the display window then tried to see into the dark store beyond. It wasn't huge and may have been made to seem smaller because it was crowded with all manner of collectibles. But my attention continually returned to the red shoes in the front window.

They were bright and glittery and seemed completely out of place, more like they belonged in a party store. Maybe that's why they drew my attention.

"Mrs. Hayworth." Turning toward the voice from the car phone, I saw a woman a few years older than I open the shop door and step out onto the sidewalk. "Welcome. Welcome. I'm Maggie. How was your journey then?"

"Very nice," I said. "It's, um, *Ms.* Hayworth."

"Oh sure. Sure. O'course 'tis."

"But it doesn't matter because I'd rather you call me Rita."

"Very well. Rita's a fetchin' name. That scarf makes your eyes look very blue."

I wasn't sure whether to say thank you or not because saying my eyes look blue wasn't necessarily a compliment. "That's the consensus," I said and hoped the correct response wasn't thank you.

Waving me inside, she said, "Well, come have a look at your new life."

That brought me up short.

Wait.

I agreed to take a plane ride and see what this was about. I didn't agree to a 'new life'. Granted, I did accept a one-way ticket. But I reasoned that I had enough socked away to get myself back in coach class, probably in a middle seat between two large smelly guys with advanced cases of armrest and leg spread entitlement.

I stepped in. Antique shopping wasn't a hobby, but I had been in stores with old things. None like this. I didn't have a dealer's eye, but I did have a degree in art history that has done nothing but gather dust. *God. It seemed like that was a hundred years ago.* Some of that education must have soaked in because I felt like I could sense that some of the inventory items were were real treasures. Expensive. Rare. Unique. Maybe even all.

"Well. What do you think?" Maggie asked with pronounced pride, hands on hips.

"I'm overwhelmed," I said truthfully since I'd really expected something more along the lines of flea market wares.

She beamed. "'Tis just the time difference talkin'. In

no time at all you'll be regular whelmed."

I smiled. "I couldn't help but notice the red shoes in the front window."

"Oh. Those are no' for sale. They belong to you."

"To me?"

"Oh aye. So much to tell. They were more or less put there as a beacon. Consider them a welcome home gift. Just let me close the front door. Would you like to see your house first or should I put the kettle on in back?"

I wasn't sure how I felt about the references to my garage and my house. The terminology sounded alien when my brain tried to process it.

"Tour first then tea. If that's okay with you?"

"Well o' course you want to see what there is to see. Let me lock the shop and we'll have a quick look."

"Oh. I don't want to cause you to lock the store." It was a lame protest because it was a lie. I totally wanted her to lock up so I could get my tour.

"Do no' fret a bit. Tuesdays are slow as sap." She locked the front door, turned the CLOSED sign around, then headed toward the back. As she passed by me, she said, "I'll bet you're full of questions."

I nodded. "I am. First question. Who's the buyer? These things," I gestured toward the shop, "are amazing. I'm no expert and even I can see that they're extraordinary."

"Well we don't have a buyer per se. The stuff just shows up."

I blinked slowly. "Just shows up?"

"Oh aye. 'Tis part of the shop's charm it is."

"So you, um, I mean we don't pay for what we sell?"

"No' in the Queen's currency. No." She shifted an item a quarter of a turn and stood back to assess something I could not see as she said, "Tonight we're to have dinner at Lochlan's house. He's eager to transfer ownership to you."

"Lochlan? He's the one who wrote to me. A solicitor?"

"Oh, aye. Looking forward to meetin' you he is. You'll like him. He was a heartbreaker in his time," she said wistfully. Then added, "Though a bit studious."

"So he's older?"

An unreadable expression flitted across her face, but she recovered her bright demeanor quickly. "He is mature. Aye. Make a list of questions if ye wish. We'll have a lovely meal with Q and A. He has a fine cook. Envy of all who eat."

All who eat? Wouldn't that be everyone?

"And mayhap," she continued moving toward the rear, "we'll get to know you a bit better." She stopped, turned, smiled and winked. "The supper's sure to be accompanied by a fine spirit or two." With an abrupt about face, she ordered, "Come this way."

I followed Maggie's curvy figure toward the back of the store. Her shoulder-length hair was wild and fly-away and the color left some faded clues that she must have been a bright redhead before the white began its campaign to take over. Not that I could talk. I touched up my own mahogany tresses on a regular basis. So no judging about physical evidence of time passage.

By the time I took the fortieth birthday grand scale ribbing complete with headstone cake and Geritol as a wrapped package, I'd come to terms with the fact that the only way to escape the march toward pallor of skin and hair was death. I'll take option number one. Thanks.

It was impossible to nail down Maggie's age on looks, and that was made harder by the fact that she 'seemed' young. You might call it an attitude. Or an air.

My eyes fixed, as they had again and again since I arrived, on the pendant she wore at the end of a braided silver chain. It was a stone that appeared to be a light aquamarine, the size of a child's hand. It picked up and reflected light and color every time she moved. Of course, it couldn't be a real aquamarine. If it was, it would be worth more than the entire village.

I saw that she'd caught me staring. So I owned it.

"Your necklace is so unusual. I've never seen anything like it and just can't seem to stop staring."

"'Tis unusual. The only one of its kind. 'Twas a gift from a cousin. Long time ago." With a hand wave to her right she continued the tour saying, "There's a little office here for cataloguing new inventory and officey kinds of things." She motioned to the left. "There's a little kitchen here for tea or whatever you prefer. 'Tis good for breaks and havin' lunch. You do no' have to worry about missin' customers."

"Why not?"

Maggie pointed to a bank of monitors above the door that connected the back rooms to the store. I could see the shop from every angle.

"Oh. That's very, ah, modern."

Maggie chuckled. "'Tis indeed." She leaned closer to whisper conspiratorially. "'Tis also fun to watch people when they do no' know anyone's lookin'." Her eyes sparkled with such mischief that I couldn't help returning her naughty smile.

"No' much more to tell about the downstairs. The proprietor's residence is through there." A cherrywood door with arched top sat at the end of the hall. Maggie fumbled with her jumble of keys before pulling three free. They hung on their own hammered silver ring, a Celtic dragon chasing its tail. "This one is for this door that connects the shop to your house. This one is for the front door that faces the lane beside us. And this one is for your garage."

With outstretched hand, I accepted, then rubbed the silver between my fingers. It was heavy and intricately ornate. "This is beautiful."

"Oh, aye. We have a silversmith in the village. Exceptional fellow. You'll meet him." She glanced toward the door. "Go on then. You do the honors. After all, 'tis your house now, isn't it?"

With a long look at the door, I said, “So when you said proprietor’s residence, you meant me.”

She laughed. “Well, o’ course. Who else might I be meanin’?”

“Honestly I’m still processing all this. Three days ago I had no idea I was related to an English shopkeeper.”

“Who said ye are?”

I was dumbfounded. “The letter I received said I inherited property.”

“Perhaps ‘inherited’ is the wrong word. ’Tis more like you were chosen. A great stroke of luck to be sure. You must be Irish.”

“Not that I know of. What do you mean by ‘chosen’?”

“I don’t know all the criteria that goes into the process of choosing, but I’ll tell you that ’tis always a person who’s deservin’. The last owner was a lovely man. Lived to be over a hundred and was still doin’ most things for himself. I think there’s somethin’ about the place that promotes long life. Happiness maybe.”

My skeptical and cynical sides were screaming at me to not be seduced by the prospect of happiness. From the outrageous talking car to the wares that ‘show up’ I was feeling more like Alice down the rabbit hole than the luckiest soon-to-be divorcée ever.

"And the former owner passed away?" I looked at the closed door. "Recently?"

Maggie's features softened as if she understood my reticence. "No worries, lass. The spirit of the last owner passed on in peace. I have it on good authority. The space is full of goodness and nothin' else. If you e'er decide to turn the key and step in, you'll see. It's been made ready for *you*."

I was half decided that I was going to look and leave, but I'd come too far to go home without looking around and, at least, having the Q and A dinner. With Lochlan, the solicitor.

Holding up the key that I thought she'd said opened the door, I ventured, "This one?"

"You know. On second thought. Perhaps you'd rather begin with a front door entry. Let's go 'round the buildin' and come in through the front. Personally, I do no' put much stock in Eastern mysticism, but there're some things about Feng Shui..."

She left that thought unfinished, but I took her meaning. "Well, if you…"

"Sure then. Do no' know why I did no' think of it sooner. Come along. We'll walk 'round."

As we locked the shop door from the outside this time, I found myself wishing I could be both as decisive and sure of myself as Maggie.

The walk was short. We arrived at a green door set in the stone facing of the two-story building. There were two large casement windows accessorized by window boxes with blooming flowers. And I had to admit it was a warm and welcoming touch. The number on the door was 18.

Maggie pointed across the street. "Your garage is just there. No need for garages when the house was built you know. You might say 'twas an afterthought."

I nodded.

Maggie stood waiting patiently for me to remember I was holding the keys. "Oh. I have the key." I laughed nervously. "Sorry."

"No need for sayin' sorries. I'm sure the circumstance would have most people feelin' upside down."

I turned the key and opened the door, half expecting some horrible odor, must or incense or mothballs, to send me running. There was no smell. Just the way I like it and an auspiciously good sign. So I swung the door open all the way.

The sight that greeted me couldn't be described in any way except by one simple word. Perfect.

I'm not particularly imaginative or creative, but if I was, I'm sure the townhouse living room would be what I'd choose. Down to the smallest detail. The walls and floors were light. The fireplace was blackened with two hundred years of history and cheery fires. The furniture was covered in English floral prints that, while perhaps not in style, were pretty, homey, and welcoming. On the far wall there was an elegant French writing desk facing out toward a small garden.

I stepped in and turned in a circle. Again, I'm not especially intuitive or sensitive to energy, but the house had a vibe that could only be described as good.

"This is…" I started, while Maggie closed the door.

"Is?" she asked me to finish.

"Lovely." It was whispered almost reverently.

"Well," she chuckled. "Should be. 'Twas done just for you."

"You mean the decorating?"

"Oh aye. Everythin'."

"But how could you know what I'd like?"

She ignored the question. "Kitchen's over there." She pointed. "There's no formal dinin', but the table is plenty big for company."

I was pulled in the direction of the kitchen like it was a magnet. Again, it was a dream. Old-world brick and stone with modern appliances and a wood-fired brick oven. As she'd said, a large rectangular table sat in the middle of the room that could double as an island.

"I'll let you go explorin' upstairs on your own." She checked her watch. "Take your time. When you're done lookin', you can spend the day gettin' settled in, look 'round the village, or have a nice toes-up. We're due at Lochlan's at six fifteen."

"Alright. How far is, um, Lochlan's?"

"Three minutes afoot. Maybe four on a wet day. If you need anythin' at all, you can go right through there to the shop."

Following her line of vision, I saw that the arched shop door was at the end of a short hall off the kitchen, just past the pantry on one side and the 'powder room' on the other.

"Thank you, Maggie."

"No need to thank me. I'm just the help. I'll mind the store until you tell me to do somethin' else. Now there's a deadbolt on the shop door you can lock from inside when you're home. For privacy, you know."

Hearing the door close, I took a deep breath. It was very quiet, but not in a bad way. I did lock the deadbolt on the shop door before slowly walking the kitchen, trying it on for size. I ran my fingertips over the shiny new commercial appliances that included a fully stocked wine column – a luxury I'd never imagined owning, admired the copper sink and looked around for the way into the small garden that could also be viewed from the kitchen window.

Access was just off the living room in a small alcove at the base of the stairs. Go right up the stairs or left to the garden. I chose garden first. It was surrounded by stone walls on four sides, which gave it a feeling of safety and security. An overhang formed shelter for a small patio that would allow for sitting outside even on rainy days. The centerpiece of the little courtyard was an blood orange tree with dark glossy leaves and fruit the color of persimmons. My first thought was to think it might be my new favorite place on earth.

My second thought was to wonder how they'd managed to bring oranges to ready-to-pick stage at that time of year. The process was a mystery, but I was in love with the result.

I don't know how long I sat in the garden, admiring the blooms and trailing vines in large planters and pots, or how long I spent reflecting on my life thus far, but I know the time was well spent because, by the time I was motivated to continue exploring, my spirit felt restored. Maybe not to pre-marriage. But somewhat.

Baby steps.

Dog.

I'd always loved dogs. Always wanted one as an adult, but my ex wasn't an 'animal person'.

What if I'd stumbled into a pot of happiness at the end of a rainbow?

On reentering the house, I once again noticed the writing desk that faced the garden and thought how nice it would be to enjoy that view when on my laptop. I went directly upstairs to find a space that was easily three times as large as the downstairs. It was, apparently, above both the living room, kitchen, and store.

The master bedroom was enormous with a fireplace that shared a chimney with the living room below. Light, bright and outfitted with furniture covered in real handmade crewel. The kind that comes from India and sells for two hundred dollars a yard. I know because I'd lovingly caressed it in the fabric store a few dozen times, certain I'd never own anything so extravagant.

I snorted when an image of Romeo came to mind.

The adjoining bath was large and luxurious, outfitted with odd, but modern fixtures. The rest of the space was comprised of two rooms and another less dramatic bath. I supposed that, if I stayed, my daughter might occupy one of the rooms from time to time.

Though I'd spent an hour imagining myself in that house, I was surprised to hear myself think, *if I stay.*

Should I stay or should I go? Yes. I heard The Clash's answering ten chords in my head.

It was not a decision that would be made in a day.

First, I'd 'try on' the new life. See if there might be a fit. But I had to admit it was a hundred times more promising than the temporary residence inn and no idea what I would do next.

THE KEY TO the garage was a remote. The door responded immediately with a rolling noise and I was relieved to see Romeo. He'd done an excellent job of parking himself and the deep polished shine made me wonder if he was somehow able to bathe himself as well.

Without being asked he popped the latch so that I could drag my luggage out. It wasn't going to be easy to get those babies upstairs, but hey. I wasn't really over the hill. I was just well over forty.

"Thank you, Romeo," I said, just because I was kind of getting into the joke of talking to an auto.

"You're welcome, Rita."

"If only you could carry luggage upstairs."

"Shall I call someone for that?"

"Who?" Silence. "No. If I can't handle it, I'll ask Maggie if there's a strapping young man about who'd like a tiny tip." Realizing how that sounded, I was just as happy that Romeo persisted in his newfound silence.

The street between my house and my garage was the width of an alley and one way. I got the impression it didn't get much traffic, which would be more than okay with me. It didn't escape my notice that I thought, *my* house and garage.

I'd just reached the door when I heard a gravelly but friendly voice.

"Mrs. Hayworth! Here. Let me help you with those."

I turned to see a small wizened man. He wasn't physically attractive, but had a contagious grin.

"Uh, hi. It's, uh, Ms. Hayworth. Or no. I mean Rita. It's Rita. And you are?"

"Bradesferd Skeech. At your service." He pointed to my keychain. "I'm the silversmith."

I looked down at the ring in my hand. "Oh, Mr. Skeech. Your work is phenomenal."

"Go on. I'm too old to blush. But since you've offered your given name, locals call me Brad."

I grinned. "So I'm a local? For that matter, how did you know my name?"

"Oh. Everyone knows your name. We don't get new

residents often. You could say you're a celebrity."

He treated me to a good-natured laugh then looked pointedly at the bags. I didn't want to hurt his feelings or his masculine pride by suggesting he was too small and too old, but I didn't want to be responsible for injury either. "Are you sure, um, Brad? They're very heavy."

He smiled up at me. "I'm stronger than I look."

"Okay," I said, opening the door and stepping back to give him room.

He lifted the two bags like they weighed nothing and set them down just inside the front door. "Upstairs?" he asked.

Since I'd become a believer in the idea that you can't judge strength by looks, I said, "That would be wonderful. If it's not too much trouble."

"None at all, but the staircase is narrow. So I'll take one at a time."

I waited in the living room while he carried one then the other upstairs. He returned showing no sign of exertion whatever.

"Is there anything else I can do for you?" he asked.

"I already owe you a favor for this. If it was a hotel, I'd

think you were entitled to an extra tip."

"I'd be insulted to have you think of such a thing. We look out for each other around here. We're glad to have you take over the Hallows. It's very special."

"Do you have a shop on the circle?"

He nodded. "Shop and workshop. Just across on the other side of the green. The Silver Braid. You can see it from your front window. Drop by any day around two. I usually stop for tea."

"I certainly will. If I stay."

He gave me a quizzical look. "If you stay?"

I dodged the question and said, "I wouldn't think you'd get a lot of customers. Hallow Hill seems kind of out of the way."

He smiled. "We get just the right number. Not too many. Not too few."

"Well, who could object to an economy like that?"

He turned to go. "I'll be off then."

"Thanks again, um, Brad. This really was very much appreciated."

I STOOD IN the bedroom trying to figure out where to put

things because there were no closets. Eventually I figured out that the wall with a bank of four triple rosewood armoires was there for a reason.

I heard myself say, "Duh," out loud.

Each of the armoires had space for hanging clothes on either side of a stand of drawers with pretty brass pulls and there was no smell of decay that sometimes accompanied old furniture. Someone had thoughtfully provided a selection of wood and felt-covered hangers.

I was committed to one night. I fished out clothes to wear to dinner, shook them out, and hung them up. Everything in my luggage had that strange travel smell and I wished I could launder it all. It was a nice day. So I decided to take the dress and jacket I was planning to wear to dinner down to the garden and hang them out in tree branches.

The scene of my clothes hanging from the trees brought a smile to my face. It struck me as fanciful and fun and I was sure they were having a better time than they ever had with me. I was thinking that, since the space was walled in, there would never be a breeze, but when I turned to go back inside, I felt a breeze ruffle my hair.

"Huh," I said out loud. Again, talking to myself as I was trying to imagine how that was possible. Science hadn't been my favorite subject in school, but I was pretty sure that air didn't make a habit of moving around in an enclosed space without cause.

Chapter Two

Jodhpurs and Jugular John

KEYS IN HAND, I decided to lock up and walk around to the front of the shop as opposed to going through the door that connected the store to the residence. I slipped the keys in my pocket and cinched the scarf tighter around my neck because the air had a little more chill than earlier. When I turned the corner, I couldn't help but notice a striking bay mare tied to a hitching post by the green. Her coat gleamed like it was someone's full time job to brush her.

I walked into the store. Maggie was nowhere in sight, but the place wasn't empty. A man turned when I entered and closed the door. He was bona fide, daytime series, tall, dark, handsome, and wearing a riding costume. His face was a sculptor's dream and as void of expression as if it had been carved in stone.

"Hello," I said with a slight nod.

He stared but made no reply.

After an awkward pause, I said, "Are you a customer?"

"No," he replied.

His eyes were so dark I couldn't discern where pupil ended and iris began. They were also hypnotic, so much so that I almost missed the fact that I was in the middle of an awkward pause. After a slight internal shake, I said, "Do you need help?"

"No," he replied, continuing to stare without blinking.

My exasperation was growing in direct proportion to my self-consciousness and the rate at which I was running out of questions. It had been a long time since a handsome gentleman had found me mesmerizing to the point of being speechless. Okay. So that had never happened, but what's imagination for?

I decided the best course of action was to call on snippy Rita. I didn't know why he was staring, but it wasn't a prelude to flirtation. The phrase 'out of my league' came to mind. Because the man was odd, but devastatingly attractive.

"Well, perhaps you'd tell me why you're standing in the middle of the shop?"

At long last he blinked, which was a relief because I was getting worried about his eye health.

"Perhaps. Perhaps not," he said in English, but with a trace of accent that gave away foreign origin.

I didn't especially care for that answer no matter how Valentino he might be. "The thing is, this is a business. We sell things here. So unless you want to buy something…"

"What if I simply required help with directions?"

"Do you need directions?"

"No."

"Is this a game?"

His face might have altered to allow for a ghost of a smile, but it was hard to tell. His eyes finally left me long enough to scan the premises and come to rest on the statue of Eros.

"How much for that?" he asked, pointing at the archer.

I hoped there was a price tag since I didn't know any more about it than he did. A quick check and I found it hanging from one of the love god's wrists.

"Twenty-five thousand. I guess that's pounds."

"What else would it be?" The challenge was accompanied by a second hint of smirk.

His eyes wandered back to the life-size bronze statue. At least it would have been the likely height of a god in the days of Ulysses. Now it was more the height of a typical fourteen-year-old boy. He, Eros that is, was notching an arrow, appearing intent on a target. His upper body was half bare, the rest tastefully covered in a short toga with leather belt. I had to admire the man's taste as well as his looks and, by all indications, money.

"I'll take it," he said. "I'll send someone around tomorrow at eleven. Will that do?" As he spoke he removed a flat leather wallet from his jacket breast pocket, selected a Coutt World Card and extended it in my direction. "Here you are then."

Since I had no idea how to process the card, I wrote down the information and asked for his name.

"John David Weir. Mrs. MacHenry knows my address."

My eyes met his when I handed back the card. "Nice to meet you, Mr. Weir. And thank you for your patronage."

"And you are?" he said.

"Rita Hayworth."

That time I was certain a smirk had flitted by. He couldn't possibly be old enough to know the name, Rita Hayworth. Apparently he was satisfied that the exchange was concluded because he turned and left without looking back. I drifted toward the front window and watched as he mounted and rode away looking every bit the nineteenth-century gentleman.

Maggie emerged from the rear. "Oh. I see you met the vampire."

I turned slowly. "The what?"

She looked like I'd just caught her in something very naughty, but her expression changed quickly. "Oh," she chuckled. "'Tis what we call him because he's secretive and lives alone."

"He's strange, you mean."

"Well… I suppose that could be said. But it might also be said of any of us."

I couldn't help but smile at the generous spirit behind that remark. "True enough."

"He probably just wanted to get a look at the new proprietor." She paused. "Nice enough lookin' fella."

I smiled because it sounded like she was fishing. "Oh? I didn't notice." She chuckled. "He bought that." I pointed at the Eros statue. "I didn't know how to process so I wrote the info down. He said he'd send someone to pick it up tomorrow. At eleven?"

"Seems you're good for business. Luck has already turned our way. That'll make book for the month to be sure."

"I didn't do a thing except ask him to buy something or leave."

Her face fell. "You did that?"

"He was just standing in the middle of the store. Still as a statue. I asked if he needed help. He said no. The conversation went downhill from there." I took in a deep breath. "But he did end up buying something." I eyed the Eros statue. "It's a nice piece. Do we, um, put a sold sign on it?"

"O' course we can. 'Tis high unlikely some other gentry or out-of-season tourist will wander in and ask to buy it before tomorrow. But we have nothin' else to do at the moment. So why no'?"

"He must live close by. Since he arrived on horseback?"

"Just a few miles. Has a good-sized place. Old manor estate. Keeps tenant farmers like the glory days."

"Glory days?" I repeated dumbly. It seemed like I was doing a lot of that.

"Downton Abbey and all that. 'Twas no' so glorious for the people doin' the work. But 'twas glorious for the idle rich."

I nodded. "He's right out of central casting."

"Central casting?"

I smiled about taking turns with Maggie, repeating the end of a sentence and turning it into a question.

"It means that, if I was casting a character for that part in a movie, I'd pick somebody just like him. He looks the part."

"That he does."

"I think I'll have a look around the village then."

"Oh, well, sure. If ye get hungry, the pub will be servin' a decent Shepherd's pie. Or some roast chicken with peas and carrots. 'Course they'll have a fillin' potato soup with leeks."

"Stop or I'll never get back into my goal jeggings."

She blinked. "Do no' know what this is."

I laughed, realizing that there's more separating me from Britain than an ocean. I chose to change the subject.

"Is there anything in particular that I should look out for?"

"On your stroll about the village? Aye. Avoid the little goblin at the boot shop. He wears a nasty humor like a prize waistcoat. If you're in the market for a custom-made pair of boots, that's fine. He does know his way around a length of leather. But if ye have no need of new boots, pay him no mind."

"I didn't really mean look out for in the sense of avoidance. I meant is there anything in particular I should seek out?"

"'Tis a distinction it is." I nodded. "We get some tourists now and then." I immediately began calculating how the village stayed afloat with anything less than a steady stream of tourism. "They like to take pictures of the mill wheel."

That did pique my interest. Flying my turista colors proudly, I asked, "Which way?"

"River's a few strides downhill. Go past your front door, keep walkin'. You'll run right into it." She chuckled. "Do no' recommend that. The water's already coolin' off, gettin' ready for winter. I have a distant cousin who…"

She looked away quickly so that I didn't hear the end of that sentence as she busied herself moving things around.

"I didn't hear the end of that. You have a distant cousin who what?"

"What? Oh. I think I hear the kettle." With her cheeriest smile so far, she began walking away, saying, "Have a nice outin'. Get yourself settled in, but be back 'round for dinner on time."

I felt dismissed, but not in a bad way. The day had turned even cloudier, but I didn't smell rain. I buttoned my jacket that was more stylish than warm, thought about going back to the house for something more substantial, but decided that would be wimpy, even for me.

The cobblestone circle was deserted. No cars, pedestrians, or horses.

Looking across the way I could see The Silver Braid sign. Perhaps I'd get a ring to replace my wedding band.

I'd invested so many years in the nervous habit of turning it over and over that ringless made my left hand feel naked.

The shop directly next door to the Hallows appeared vacant, but the one on the other side of that had a pink neon sign in the window that was out of place and keeping with the 'vibe'. As I drew near, I was thinking I would have made it illegal if I was on the city council. The store's name was Notions and Potions.

The door opened and a woman in her early thirties emerged to lean against the door jamb, almost like she was waiting for me.

I nodded and said, "Hello."

Her response was a smirk. "G'day."

Huh.

I walked on, evaluating the possibility that I might be misjudging. Maybe that was just what her face does when she thinks she's smiling.

Sitting at the head of the circle like a state building, The Hung Goose was the focal point of the Hallow Hill business district. It featured a large hanging sign with a portrait of a handsome gray goose that, thankfully for my appetite, was alive, well, and sporting a red bow tie. I'd been thinking about Maggie's verbal menu ever since she'd described what might be expected for lunch.

I took a slow turn around the circle, peeking in windows, but not opening doors. The shop that called to me was the florist. Stands of blooms, made all the more attractive because they were out of season, almost lured me into the shop to buy an orchid for the writing desk. Then I remembered I hadn't yet decided to stay.

The storefront on the next corner was the smallest bank I'd ever seen. The sign said loans, exchange, currency storage. Notary upstairs in solicitor's office. There were two deserted intersections on the way to the pub, meaning places where I might encounter cross-traffic. I looked down the narrow streets at what appeared to be row houses. They were old and timeless, but pretty and colorful. Not in a graffiti sort of way, but in a flower box sort of way. The streets were too narrow for four-wheeled vehicles to park, which added to the charm.

Continuing on, I took note of each business. Apothecary. Silver shop. Market. I would have called it a grocery store, but that's just me.

The next shop of interest was the Magic Spindle. There was a large display window on either side of the deliberately distressed blue door. Each window featured an antique spindle as the focal point in the center. "Hand-weaver" was painted on the door in gold script and, certainly, it would be easy to believe the pieces in the window were created magically. They were *that* beautiful. One was an oversized shawl in greens, blues, and mixed media of wool, silk, and bits of soft suede latigo laced through like ribbons. It was beyond gorgeous, a timeless piece to hand down to a daughter, and would probably be out of my budget even if I hit the lottery. Which was impossible because I'd never bought a ticket. I stood and stared until I saw an opaque outline of a feminine figure inside waving for me to come in. I smiled politely, shook my head, and continued on.

Book store.

Boot shop. I was too busy admiring the boots in the window to give proper heed to Maggie's admonition. I plead guilty to being a shoe person.

Like an adolescent with faulty self-control, I pulled the door open, stepped in, and closed my eyes as I breathed deep the intoxicating scent of tanned leather.

"What do you want?"

My eyes flew open at the challenging tone, which made the words sound more like accusation than question.

A smallish man sat on a stool in the rear in front of a worktable surrounded by bolts of leather in various textures and colors. He had a bald head, huge ears, a strikingly low forehead, and arms that appeared to be a tad too short for the rest of him. I could see why Maggie had called him a little goblin and, while the idea might fit, it seemed kind of a mean thing to say.

"Are you deaf? I said, what do you want?"

"Do you always talk to customers like that?"

"Bah," he said, losing interest in me and turning back to his work. "You're not a customer until I agree to sell you something. Come back when you want boots. Go someplace else to waste time."

"Wow," I said.

"Wow," he mocked with a goading smile.

"This is the last place I'd go if I wanted boots."

"Good," he said. "The door's behind you."

Deciding that taking the exchange any further might end with one of his tools coming in contact with his unusually shaped head, I satisfied my pride by choosing the more mature response and left, heading straight for the pub while thinking I should listen to Maggie's advice more, impulses less.

The day had grown colder and windier and I was rethinking what I'd planned to wear to the solicitor's dinner. I was also imagining living in the tiny picturesque village that looked like a feature of Disneyworld.

All of a sudden it felt like life was moving too fast.

I happened to turn my head to the right and see the Hallows Antiques and Treasures sign. Inexplicably, I was overcome with a warm feeling of pride and proprietorship.

It was only eleven thirty, but I was hungry. Probably more so because of the chill creeping underneath my jacket and scarf. Hot tea sounded good. Hot soup sounded good. I hoped they were open.

Just a few steps from the door a forceful gust of wind blew my hair into a tangle and caused me to gather my scarf in both hands to keep it from being blown away. As I reached for the handle, a man came around the corner with a big smile and pulled the door open for me.

I ducked in and, when the door was closed, said, "Thank you."

"You're most welcome, Mrs. Hayworth. I'm Fie Mistral. I'm happy to meet you and welcome you to our village." He waved his hand. "And the pub."

He had black wavy hair, flawless latte-colored skin, and cognac-colored eyes that gave the impression of maintaining a perpetual twinkle. Like everyone I'd met so far, I'd be hard pressed to nail down his age. Some things about him made me think young. Some things about him made me think old.

His clothes indicated that his days were occupied by some kind of business, albeit not a formal one. He wore boots that were, no doubt, made with loving care by Thomasin Cobb, jeans, a mock turtleneck, and tweed jacket.

"Thank you. It's, um, Ms. Hayworth."

"Of course. My mistake. Please call me Fie. Are you here for lunch?"

I smiled. "Yes. Maggie MacHenry recited enough of the menu to make me want to live here."

He laughed. "Please. I'm eating alone. Will you join me?" I hesitated. "Just neighborly lunch. I have gossip."

"Just lunch and gossip?" I grinned. "Well then. I'm your girl. And please call me Rita."

Fie Mistral looked toward the bar where a couple of rustic-looking gents were engrossed in conversation. They were turned toward each other, standing, each leaning an elbow on the bar, mug in one hand and one foot on the rung of a barstool. I had the impression that they were farmers.

He nodded to a woman walking behind the bar.

She smiled in return. "Good noon, mayor?" she said, but her eyes had immediately glanced off him and fixed on me.

"Molly," he said, as if that was an answer to her question. "This is *Ms.* Hayworth."

The two patrons stopped their dialogue and turned to see who'd arrived. "No. Please. That's way too formal. I'd rather be thought of as just plain Rita."

Fie took command of the room. "First names all around everybody," he announced.

Fie pointed to the two at the bar. "Jack and Ebon."

Putting myself within handshaking distance only required two steps. So I closed the space, shook hands with both of them, and was treated to warm smiles in return.

"And that's Molly," he gestured to the tall brunette behind the bar. She looked close to my age and beyond the stage of caring what people thought. I liked that.

I chuckled. "I guessed that when you called her Molly earlier." I hoped he knew my teasing was good-natured.

A smiled played on Molly's bow-shaped mouth. She was clearly enjoying the joke. "How's your day, Rita?"

"Good so far. Hungry."

"Then you've come to the right place at the right time. Sit anywhere."

I looked at Fie. He smiled and said, "Ladies' choice."

Since I had a thing for tables by windows, I motioned in that direction and he nodded. Sitting down I looked out at the circle and noticed that pedestrian traffic had picked up some.

"So I have the honor of lunching with the mayor?" I asked.

With a soundless laugh, he said, "More a nickname than a title. Hallow Hill doesn't actually have a mayor."

"There must be some reason for the nickname."

He wagged his head from side to side. "We do have a local idea of community, loosely organized, and a shared treasury. Such as it is. I guess people thought that, since I'm the banker, it made sense to put me in charge of the money."

I laughed.

"What?" he said.

"Well..." I was sorry I'd laughed. "Promise not to take offense?"

"I do."

"In America, most of us would think a banker would be the *last* person who should be in charge of money belonging to the commons."

He grinned. "May such distrust of bankers never catch on in Hallow Hill."

Molly arrived with a menu for me. It was printed on paper designed to look like parchment and housed in a leather cover. It gave the impression of being old, but that was obviously what was intended.

"You'll know it by heart before long," she said. "We do change the soup daily. So, if you're interested, just ask."

"Okay. What's the soup today?"

"Winter white." I glanced at the cold fireplace. "It's the name year-round. Potatoes, carrots, leeks, cream."

"Sounds good."

"That what you're having then?"

"Maybe. I want a chance to explore options."

Molly looked at Fie. "She means give us a couple of minutes with the menu."

"I'll be back."

When she was gone, I said, "She really needs to learn to say that Terminator-style."

He squinted. "What do you mean?"

"Um. Nothing. It was silly. American pop culture from the eighties. Never mind."

"So what do you think of our little village? Did you go down to the river? See the mill wheel?"

"Not yet, but I was told it's a hit with tourists. So how long have you been here?"

"I'm not from here, but I've been here long enough to feel like a native."

"And you like it."

"I've a feeling I've been promoted to ambassador for

the village. At least for the duration of this lunch." His eyes traveled down the menu I was holding. "Know what you want yet?"

"What are you having? No. Wait. The better question is, what's your favorite thing on the menu?"

"Bangers and mash."

"Ew. No. Never mind." He chuckled as I looked down.

The door was opening and closing every few minutes and the pub was beginning to look like it might be busy for lunch.

"Yes," I said. "I'm having fish and chips. If I'm still here tomorrow, I'm having Guiness beef stew. If I'm still here the day after that, I'm having the roast chicken."

"You've already ruled out the soups? Without hearing what they are?"

"You didn't ask about the soup."

"Because I already knew I was having bangers and mash."

"Do you ever have the soup?"

"No."

"Not the most outstanding recommendation. Why not?"

"Because soup is not manly."

I stared for a couple of beats before laughing. "You're joking, right?"

"Hard to say."

"What do you mean, hard to say? You don't know whether you're joking or not? Be careful how you answer. Hallow Hill cannot leave its treasure in the hands of a person who doesn't know whether or not he jests."

The corners of Fie's mouth twitched. "I simply mean that, I would eat soup if it was served at a dinner party. To be polite. But I would not select it deliberately from a list of nice alternatives."

"Because you don't like it."

"Because slurping from a spoon is not 'eating'. It's drinking."

"Not if there are chunks of things that must be chewed."

"The soup here doesn't have chunks of things that must be chewed. They call that stew. Not soup."

"You're very particular for a person who's concerned with manliness."

"Are you disparaging my masculinity?" He said with

mock astonishment. "We've barely met."

I was shaking my head when Molly returned.

"He's having bangers and mash," I said. "I'm having fish and chips." She nodded and started away, but I added, "It's good. Right?"

"It's the best in the county." She hurried away before I could question her further. "That's good, right?" I said to Fie. "I mean, for all I know there might not be a single great place to get fish and chips. 'It's the best in the county' isn't necessarily a great review."

"Do you always give so much attention to lunch?" he asked, sounding genuinely curious.

I sighed. "No, I… Uh. I've been dieting. Fish and chips is a cheat. It's a cheat I might be willing to take for *really* great fish and chips. But if it's mediocre, I'll be sorry I wasted a big chunk of calorie allowance on something unremarkable."

"Gods let me never incarnate as a woman."

I nodded. "It's an invocation you should repeat often. I guarantee you'd think long and hard about bangers and mash. And not for the reasons that made me say 'ew'."

He laughed.

We spent the rest of lunch talking about Hallow Hill, Cumbria, and the village's level of dependency on tourism. He recommended a variety of local sightseeing trips in between cheerfully introducing me to locals who stopped by the table to meet the new kid in town. I knew there was no prayer I'd remember half their names. I had three big takeaways. First, if I moved to Hallow Hill, I would be close to great pub food. Second, it appeared that I was welcome. And, third, the unofficial 'mayor' was well-liked, witty, and good company, even if he was a banker.

BY THE NUMBER of people out and about I was getting the idea that Hallow Hill residents were late sleepers. Nothing wrong with that. I had a penchant for both laziness and sack time.

I strolled back toward the house, but when I arrived at the front door, I kept going. The next time somebody asked if I'd seen the mill wheel, I wanted to be able to say yes.

Five minutes later I was standing in a spot that looked like a fairy tale. The grass sloping down to the river was as green as Ireland. Or what I imagined grass in Ireland would look like. The river was pretty and still as glass, reflecting every color and light in the vicinity. No wonder it was the pride of the village. I had no trouble imagining myself frequently sitting on the bank of the river with a book, or a picnic lunch, or a thermos of wine.

I lingered until the chill began to feel damp and then headed back up the hill.

Chapter Three

Jest and Jargon

After a short nap and an hour of changing my mind about what to wear, I stepped out the front door and locked up. Perhaps, if I stayed, I'd get used to going through the door that connected the shop and residence, but at present, it was an architectural intimacy I just wasn't ready for.

I glanced at the garage after having the totally irrational thought that I should check on Romeo. Maybe raise the door a crack and say, "Hey. How you doing in there?"

I turned away, taking a stand, refusing to indulge in a moment of cray cray. The Romeo phenomenon simply meant that, when high tech begins to sound like a person and perform functions that only humans should be able to do… like drive, I've aged out of the times. The proof is in my impulse to want to look in on Romeo and make sure he's not lonely or afraid of the dark.

I'd finally settled on a thick knit, red, pencil-shaped dress over boots that would probably earn a scowl from Thomasin Cobb, but it was, in my opinion, too cool for even a few inches of bare legs. I'd topped the dress with a plaid jacket and red silk scarf the same rich scarlet as the dress.

The light was fading when I pulled open the door to the shop.

"Oh there you are!" Maggie pronounced as if search parties with hounds had been combing the hills for me.

"Um, yes. Here I am."

She made a rather dramatic show of whirling a houndstooth cape like a bull fighter before guiding it to settle just right around her frame. "Ready." She smiled.

"Are we, um, riding? Or walking?"

"He's just o'er there." She waved in the general direction of the hills as she stepped out and locked the shop door.

"So how was business today?"

She chuckled. "Well, I'll tell you this. You practically

set a record for sales within minutes of arrivin'. We do no' move items that precious often enough to make us rich."

"No? Well, that's disappointing. I guess this situation isn't right for me then."

Maggie stopped and turned toward me, looking stricken.

I laughed. "No. I was just kidding. Great excessive wealth never was one of my dreams."

With a smile, she relaxed visibly. "This way," she said as we resumed walking past the circle toward one of the cobbled streets that ascended the hill. "So, what are your dreams?" A bark of a laugh erupted from my solar plexus without permission. "'Tis funny? Which part?"

"I guess I'd been thinking I'm too old for dreams. But here I am walking in the most charming English village and possibly inheriting something better than I could've dreamed up."

"There're worse lots, to be sure."

Hearing that made me curious about Maggie. "Tell me something about yourself. You're Irish?"

"Oh aye. And old as the hills."

"Single?"

"Ne'er had the slightest inclination otherwise. Although I've enjoyed a tryst now and then." She winked. "I've worked at Hallows for a very long time. 'Tis a good life. Good people. Good work."

"Aren't you worried about me disrupting your routine? Maybe you wouldn't like working with me. Maybe we wouldn't get along. Maybe you should've inherited the shop instead of me." When that last sentence babbled from what had evidently become a free-range mouth, I immediately regretted saying it.

With a low chuckle she said, "I have what I need includin' a lifetime appointment workin' at the Hallows. You can no' get rid of me if that's what you're thinkin'."

I shook my head vigorously. "That is not what I was thinking."

"Besides. 'Tis nonsensical. We already do get along." She pointed. "There 'tis. Just ahead."

You might say the solicitor's house was located on the outskirts of the village if you wouldn't feel silly talking in terms of 'outskirts' when the distance could be traversed on foot in five minutes. It was a gray stone house. Not large. Not small. Surrounded by a stone fence and 'guarded' by two border collie mixes who were beside themselves to greet us.

Despite the enthusiasm, they were well-mannered dogs. They ran in circles and leaped in the air, but did not jump on us.

"Well, Angus," Maggie said to one of the dogs, "'tis always lovely to be greeted with such a display." She turned to the other dog. "And how are ye this fine evenin', Aisling?"

A wide smile had formed on my face. Partly because of the show the dogs put on and partly because I liked the way Maggie talked to them. If I stayed, maybe I would get a dog.

Maggie took hold of the large brass doorknocker and gave it three firm taps.

Within seconds, the door swung open wide and the dogs zipped by our legs to run inside past a gorgeous young blonde with a heart-shaped face and dazzling smile.

"Maggie! Come in!" Her enthusiasm was so palpable it made me feel like I'd failed as a hostess every time I'd greeted visitors, throughout my entire life. She immediately turned to me. "Mrs. Hayworth. Such an honor to have you in our home and welcome you to Hallow Hill."

"She does no' go by Mrs., Ivy. She prefers Ms.," Maggie told our hostess. To me, Maggie said, "This is Lochlan's wife, Ivy."

When I stepped toward Ivy to offer my hand, I was treated to a variety of scents that were nothing less than olfactory delight. Ivy smelled like a garden.

"Please. Just call me Rita."

Ivy had a megawatt smile. "What a beautiful name."

I returned her smile while searching my memory. I could have sworn that Maggie had said Lochlan was advanced in years. I'm not completely naïve. I know that people don't always marry someone their same age, but Ivy looked twenty years old.

In the cheeriest tone, she said, "You're having some sort of roast animal for supper." As we followed her deeper into the house, I realized that it was much larger on the inside than would be guessed. "Don't mind the dogs. They're such scallywags."

She led us into the living room, which was an eclectic hodgepodge of dark polished wood and furnishings from different eras. That approach to décor isn't easy to pull off, but Lochlan and Ivy had managed to do it and have the result be more shabby chic than mess.

"Please sit," she said as she breezed through without stopping. "Lochlan's here and will be in right away." Aiming the bright intensity of her gaze at me, she said, "Please know you're welcome. I will love to learn more about you after you've settled in."

It was a little confusing, but I gathered this meant she was leaving. "You're not staying?"

"No." She smiled. "Your inheritance is a private affair."

That caused my head to swivel to Maggie, who read the question on my face.

With a chuckle, she said, "I'm included because ye might say I'm part of your inheritance."

That may have caused a slight scowl to form on my forehead, meaning two vertical lines between my brows that frequently ask, "Will you or won't you botox?"

When I turned back to offer perfunctory dinner guest gratitude and a genuinely regretful goodbye, Ivy was no longer there. I opened my mouth to voice the first question on my ever-growing list to Maggie, but was interrupted by a male voice so upbeat it rivaled Ivy's for cheerfulness.

My first thought was that they, Ivy and Lochlan, belong together.

My second thought, upon turning to acknowledge his entrance, was that Lochlan was an octogenarian at the very least.

My expressive face has been a lifelong bane of my existence. You could rightfully call it a curse. People have every right to be selective about what they will and will not divulge. I can't imagine how wonderful it must be to be unreadable. My kisser is a constant source of tell all. That means the only way I can make friends or win an argument is to try to be an *authentically* good person. Because whatever I'm thinking shows on my face like a Chyron running across my brow. And, ugh! It gets old.

Honestly. There are times when I would love to be able to plot murder while staring at my intended victim, who is completely clueless because I effortlessly maintain the friendliest, most believable, richly sociopathic smile. *Bond. James Bond.*

If I was offered three *real* wishes, not like in the fables where the poor recipient ends up worse off than before, I would definitely ask for non-revelatory facial expressions. Sigh.

All this is to say that I didn't hide my surprise quickly enough or well enough when eighty-something Lochlan entered a few seconds after twenty-something Ivy left. His pale blue eyes lit with amusement.

"Ah. You're wondering how a codger such as myself won the heart of someone so young."

Maggie'd been right. It was easy to see that Lochlan had once been a babe. Even with age, he was tall with an upright posture and a body that gave the impression of being hard under his clothes. He moved easily, like a much younger person, and had a thick shock of white hair, longish around the ears, still dark at the sideburns.

How I wished I could lie with plausibility. But alas. The jig was up.

"Ivy is young and very beautiful, Solicitor. She made me feel welcome." That was the best I could do and I hoped it was enough. I called him 'Solicitor' mostly because I didn't know how to pronounce his last name and was afraid two goofs in sixty seconds might be record breaking even for me.

"Ah, well, a diplomat you are then. All the better." Lochlan nodded slightly as he sat down in an oversized, overstuffed, rust-colored velvet chair.

"Ivy's a bit of a flibbertigibbet," Maggie said, "but she's perfect for our Lochlan."

"Maggie, my dear," he said, "how are you on this fine English evening?"

"Safe, sound, and single," she replied.

He regarded her with obvious affection. "I've been telling you for…" there was a slight pause as his glance flicked to me before jumping back to Maggie, "a long time that I have eligible cousins."

"Aye. 'Tis true. But you know I'm no' a suitable companion. I'm… what do they call it? A workaholic."

His chest heaved as he took in a deep breath and turned an enigmatic smile my way. "Mrs. Hayworth. Would like a before-dinner drink? Wine, perhaps?"

"Thank you. That would be nice. And please call me Rita."

"If you wish." He angled his head toward the back of the house, but didn't raise his voice. "Maisie. Would you bring Mrs., I mean, Rita a stem of black blend?" A reply came from deeper within the house, so soft it was almost inaudible, but apparently it was heard by Lochlan. "Yes. That will do. Thank you."

"Rita had lunch at the pub today," Maggie offered conversationally.

"Did you?" Lochlan smiled. He trained his attention on me in a way that made me feel like I was being assessed for a position with the NSA.

"Yes," I said. "I'm sure you already know the fish and chips are to die for. Speaking of food, I'm smelling something that's making me salivate."

Maisie, or at least I presume so, walked in with a tray that held a glass of wine, a Scotch whisky, and what looked for all the world like a bottle of blood. Maisie, a middle-aged woman in a blue jean skirt, flowered shirt, and hand knit cardigan lowered the tray to me with a smile.

Having overheard me, she said, "It's pot roast with carrots, roasted potatoes, three kinds of onions, brown gravy, and sugar snap peas on the side."

"That sounds heavenly," I said. As I reached for the wine, I let my gaze slide to the label on the dark red liquid.

Lindisfarne Red Mead.

Maisie set the opened bottle and glass next to Maggie. "Shall I pour, Mrs. MacHenry?"

Mrs. MacHenry?

"For all the charms no," Maggie said. "I can still heft a full bottle."

Maisie and Maggie shared a brief laugh that almost seemed like a private joke before Maisie proceeded to deliver Lochlan's Scotch. "Dinner will be served in fifteen minutes," she told the solicitor. He nodded. She left the room.

"So," Lochlan began after what appeared to be a satisfying sip of Scotch. "This is your first trip to Britain."

It wasn't a question, which raised a question. "It is, but how did you know that?"

"You're inheriting a substantial legacy, Rita. I've been entrusted with the duty to keep that legacy intact and thriving. Naturally, I must properly vet the recipient."

"How can inheritance be 'vetted'? Unless it's conditional? And who exactly is the benefactor? I didn't know I had relatives in England."

"So many questions." He smiled. "And who could

blame you? We'll linger over dinner until all your questions have been answered. Feel free to ask anything."

"I will. So, you had me investigated."

Maggie sat back with her glass of dark red liquid in a way that suggested the conversation had become a dialogue from which she'd withdrawn for the time being.

"I did," he said without apology or hesitation. "Did you meet the proprietress of our pub?'

"I did." I answered in kind. "And I had lunch with Fie Mistral. Some people called him mayor, but he denied that it's a real title or office. Am I still being investigated?"

"Oh, no. Not at all. Just making conversation. I'm curious about your trip."

"I'm curious about what you learned about me. And why you thought I'd reassume my maiden name when my divorce is final."

"I learned that you're an extraordinary person who has lived an excruciatingly ordinary life."

My mouth fell open. "Wow. Don't pull any punches, Lochlan."

"As to why I thought you'd prefer the name, Hayworth? My wife was adamant about that. She could not think of a single reason why you'd prefer to bear your late husband's name if you had a choice. She was sure you'd shed that burden at the earliest opportunity."

I blinked. "He's, um, not my 'late' husband. He's not even officially my ex. Neither of us has filed divorce papers."

"Of course. A slip of the tongue. Was Ivy right? About your name?"

"Well… yes."

"There you have it then. I'd love to hear thoughts about your journey from London to Hallow Hill."

"So would I, but I was too terrified to form thought."

"Terrified?" He looked confused. In my peripheral vision I saw Maggie's interest rally.

"I've never been in a self-driving car before and, even if I had, I'm pretty sure the way Romeo speeds into curves instead of slowing down is the stuff of nightmares. Then there're the trucks…"

"Lorries," Maggie corrected.

"Whatever. Things on wheels that are way too big for these little narrow roads and speed by so close that you'd better have your side mirrors tucked in if you want to keep them. Speaking of speed. Romeo thinks it's Nascar out there. Did I mention the honking at the roundabouts? Good gods. It's worse than New York. Everybody's honking. You have no idea who's doing it or who they're honking at. If you go, they honk. If you don't go, they honk. Nerve-wracking is the phrase that comes to mind, but it just doesn't rise to the occasion. Nerve-*stripping* maybe. Perhaps we passed pristine idyllic countryside with pretty black faced sheep happily grazing their days away like a postcard. I wouldn't know. You know why? One word. Terrified."

Lochlan regarded my rant with the sort of noncommitted expression I'd die for. After a brief pause, he said simply, "Who's Romeo?"

WITH NO SMALL degree of embarrassment, I described when and why I called beautiful car Romeo. When there was no immediate response, I added further the high points of my conversation with the car and how bizarre it was.

Maggie cleared her throat. "I had no idea. You seemed so put together when you arrived."

I started to argue and then realized she was right. "Well. To be fair. I did stop for the night. I'd slept, had breakfast, and there wasn't as much traffic on the last leg of the trip."

"I like your dress," Lochlan said out of nowhere. "She likes red, Maggie."

Did I just have a petit mal seizure and miss a block of conversational context?

Maisie poked her head in. "Dinner's ready."

"Excellent," Lochlan said, rising from his chair with the ease of a thirty-year-old.

On the short walk to the dining room, I said, "It would have been fine with me for Ivy to join us."

"That's kind of you, but she had some function or other. And she doesn't eat meat. Just, you know, green things."

The dining room was rustic and cozy with a small fire burning at one end. The distressed table looked ancient. It would seat eight, but it would be a tight fit. Lochlan sat at the head of the table and gestured for Maggie and me to sit on either side.

The place setting matched the décor. Pewter plates on

wood chargers and large red napkins made from thick linen. A low centerpiece adorned the table, a mix of five different kinds of red flowers.

"These are gorgeous," I said with a wave toward the arrangement. "Did these come from the floral shop on the circle?"

"Yes," he said. "They can get almost anything if you ask a couple of days ahead."

Maisie set a large covered roaster on the table, lifted the lid, and held out her hand. Presuming she wanted my plate, I handed it over.

"That smells even better up close," I said.

"It was chosen with you in mind," Lochlan said.

"Because you guessed I like pot roast?" I ventured.

"Because I *know* you like pot roast," he countered.

"Come on. What kind of service is going to dig that deep? And how would they know?"

"The kind of service that's thorough. A couple of times a month you dine out at a place called The Mason Jar and you always get the pot roast," he said.

My lips parted, as much from astonishment as from anticipation. Because I'd never been in the presence of a pot roast that smelled more tempting.

"So you didn't just, um, look into me. You had me followed."

He looked dumbfounded. "Well certainly. How else could I be sure what sort of person I was investigating?"

"Well. Since I've never 'investigated' anybody, I guess I wouldn't know, would I?" I smiled, tickled that I'd just found an appropriate way to end a statement with a question the way English people do.

Lochlan handed his plate to Maisie. "I suppose I've been doing what I do for so long, I've forgotten that other people do other things. Sign of getting old I suppose."

"Since it happens that I'm not a criminal, or a bad parent, I don't particularly object to being looked into. It's just unnerving. The idea of somebody knowing how often I eat out, where, and what I usually order."

"Always order," he corrected.

"Okay. *Always* order. The service you use must be really good." I narrowed my eyes. "And really expensive. Who paid for that?"

"It's both. Really good and really expensive and a budget for transition was built into the prospective transfer of responsibility. So payment didn't come out of your estate if that's what you're thinking."

"It did occur to me."

"I like a woman who knows how to look after her bottom line."

"Well, that's nice, Lochlan. If I was such a woman, I wouldn't be my age with nothing to show for it but some modest label clothes, half a mortgage, and a silver Acura SUV with eighty-five thousand miles on it."

Smiling he said, "Your luck has taken a turn for the better." He took a bite of roast beef and I suddenly remembered I was hungry, too.

I guided a fork with beef and a white pearl onion into my mouth and groaned with unladylike pleasure. "Oh. My. God. This is the best thing I've ever tasted."

I spent the next few minutes more intent on testing the carrots, potatoes, sugar snap peas, and grainy artisan bread before coming back to the beef. All thought of goal jeggings was long gone and far away.

"Did Maisie make this? Whatever you're paying her, it's not enough."

"Probably true," Lochlan said. "So you wandered past

the floral shop and you had lunch at the pub. Did you meet other villagers?"

In between bites, I said, "Yes. John David something."

"Weir," Maggie supplied.

"Right. He bought a really expensive thing at the store."

"Rita came in when I was in the rear," Maggie said. "She told him to buy something or leave."

Lochlan's jaw dropped. "She did not."

Maggie giggled. "She did."

Wondering if I'd been out of line, I said, "He pointed to the most expensive thing in the place and asked how much it was. I read the price from the tag. He agreed. Now why are you both acting like that's the most remarkable thing ever?"

"Mr. Weir does no' talk a lot," Maggie said.

I nodded. "Yeah. I guessed that."

"Who else have you encountered on your brief, but eventful time here?" Lochlan asked.

"Brad from the silver shop. Thomasin Cobb, the bootmaker." I saw both her dinner companions roll their eyes at the same time.

"Do not let that little scamp lure you into buying new boots," Lochlan said.

"I'm very sure there's no danger of that."

"Did you happen down to the river?" he asked.

"Yes. And I see why everybody asks that. It's a post-card scene that you hope too many people don't find out about."

"Indeed."

WE TALKED ABOUT the area and its economy while we finished dinner. Tourism. Farming. Maisie cleared the table and asked what else she could do before leaving.

"More wine?" Lochlan ventured.

"I don't suppose you have coffee? If we're going to talk about serious things, I do best without brain fog."

"We have a coffee contraption. What sort of coffee do you prefer?"

"Dark Kona or with Kona if you have it. Cream or creamer."

"I'll have some, too," Lochlan said.

Maisie looked at him strangely. "You will?"

"No' me," said Maggie. "This very fine bottle of mead

is all I'll be needin' for the night."

IN A SHORT time, Maisie returned with coffee in big-handled mugs, creamer, and dogs. The one named Aisling wiggled over and put her head on my lap.

"Aren't you a precious flirt?" I asked as I petted the silky hair on her head and ears. To Lochlan and Maggie, I said, "I'd love to have a dog someday."

"That can be arranged," said Lochlan. "Aisling's due to whelp in a few weeks, give or take."

I looked down at intelligent brown eyes, full of reflective light, liquid with adoration, intent on trying to communicate some mysterious canine thing. And I knew I could do worse than be the recipient of a puppy.

"Thank you. If I stay," I said without looking away from Aisling, "I'd be lucky to get a puppy."

As if she understood, Aisling raised her head and wagged her tail.

"You'll have to pay what anybody else would pay." Lochlan said sternly.

"Why ye old penny pincher!" Maggie said. "Just make her a bloody gift of the dog."

Lochlan stared at Maggie for a few beats, took a sip of coffee, made a face, then said, "I don't know what you're thinking, Margaret. You know it's against the rules. You also know she can afford to buy a dog." I couldn't help but feel a tingle of excitement thinking about having a dog like one of Lochlan's two. He turned to me. "We will think on it and decide, should you stay."

I was nodding. "Fair enough."

"Well ladies," he said. "Maisie's gone for the night. Shall we get down to business?"

"By all means," I said.

Lochlan looked between Maggie and myself then said, "Before we begin, I must have your promise that you will hear me out in entirety. There's a tale to be told and you may find the subject matter unusual."

"'Tis a tale as old as time." Maggie nodded as she said with grave seriousness.

I stared for a few beats trying to decide if I should laugh, but receiving no visual cue that she was kidding, I moved right on to the scowl that was rapidly freezing deep crevices between my brows. Sometimes known as WTF lines.

Since I'd been complimented on my diplomacy, a precedent had been set. Now that I had a reputation to maintain, I couldn't be as forthright as I wanted to be. So, I chose my words carefully, staking out a position that was agreeable with not much commitment behind it.

"That's a strange beginning. I've come a long way to see what this is all about. So, of course, I'm going to hear what you have to say."

Lochlan nodded, seeming satisfied with that. "I'm holding you to it."

"Very well."

He turned to Maggie. "See? No reason to tie her up." Thanks to my very expressive face he saw the shock that registered and laughed. "Be at peace, Rita Hayworth. It's merely my offbeat Yorkshire sense of humor." Seeing the light in his eyes I relaxed slightly, but not completely. He turned to Maggie again. "Did you bring the shoes?"

Without a word Maggie pushed her chair back, rose, and left the room.

"How have you been enjoying your life so far?" It was question posed far too casually for the very profound subtext.

"Well. It's had its ups and downs. Honestly. I'm trying to decide if I'm in the middle of an up or a down."

"What if I told you that your understanding of reality is only half complete?"

"I would wonder what you're selling for $19.95."

"What?" He squinted.

"Never mind. I guess you have to be American."

He nodded. "The fact is that everything you think you know about the world is about to change. Tonight. Over coffee."

I looked around the room as I muttered, "But wait. There's more."

"I beg your pardon?"

"Nothing."

Maggie returned carrying the red shoes that I'd admired in the shop window. The ones she'd said were mine.

This was not beginning the way I'd imagined. I'd thought a staid and stuffy lawyer would read the terms of inheritance while I sat up straight and tried to appear smarter than I am. My mind was racing, trying to find a connection between glittery red shoes, inheriting a shop and residence in a pretty English village, and having my world rocked; the last dependent on Lochlan making good on his promise to upend my view of reality.

"Look…" I began.

Lochlan raised his hand just enough to stop me before I said whatever I was going to say.

"Do you believe in magic?" he asked.

I looked from him to Maggie, who'd reseated herself across the table from me. Whatever was happening, Maggie was definitely in on it.

"Like Mickey Mouse having a broom carry water?" I ventured.

Lochlan looked at Maggie as if he needed an interpreter. She shrugged as if to say she was every bit as clueless as he.

"I do not know the reference, but I suspect my meaning isn't that," he said. "What I mean to have you understand is that there are people and creatures you probably believe to be myths, or fiction, that are as real as you. Living right alongside humans with humans none the wiser."

I was trying to estimate how quickly I could get from my chair in the dining room to the front door when I remembered that I'd promised to hear the man out. Not that a promise should necessarily be my bond. I'd once promised my parents I'd never smoke a joint of demon weed. I'd promised my soon-to-be ex that I wouldn't go over the budget he set for our daughter's prom dress. When I stopped to think about it, my life was a path strewn with broken promises.

Oh God. I was a terrible person.

"Rita?"

Caught not listening, I jerked back to the moment at hand.

"Here," I said dumbly as if Lochlan had been saying 'Bueller' over and over.

"Are you following so far?" he asked.

Several heartbeats passed while I grappled with how to answer. When nothing brilliant arrived on my mental horizon, I went with, "Not really. No. I came here for what I thought was a semi-legal meeting, but the evening has taken a bizarre turn. Conversationally. Magic? And creatures living among us? This has all the ear markings of a prank. But I don't know anybody rich enough to spend this kind of money on a joke." I looked around. "Are there cameras? Is this being recorded? If you're going to want to know if I'll give my permission to use this on TV, I'll tell you right now. The answer is no. So let's say the jig is up and you can tell me the truth about all this."

Lochlan sat back with a deep sigh. "I miss the days when I could light up a pipe after dinner."

"You can still do that," Maggie offered.

"No," he said. "Times have changed." At that he brightened a little, as if he'd had a brainstorm. I wasn't the only one with an expressive face. Looking at me eagerly, he said, "You had lunch with Fie Mistral. Would you be more likely to have an open mind about extranormal topics if Fie was to join us?"

I was sure my forehead crevices would never smooth out again. "What is this? A cult?"

"Saints preserve us," Maggie said.

"Since when are you Catholic?" Lochlan asked Maggie.

"I'm no'," she said. "But sometimes the references just fit. You know most of my people are believers."

I stood up. "I'm going."

"You can't go without hearing us out. Promises were made," Lochlan said. "It won't hurt to listen and, if needs be, we can offer proof to back up all our claims."

Saints help me. And, no, I'm not Catholic either, but Maggie's right about the lingo.

"You have proof of magic? And creatures?" I said.

Lochlan gestured toward the chair. "You've come far. Indulge us with an hour of your time. What's the harm? More coffee? Perhaps with Baileys? And we have some of Maisie's famous bread pudding."

"I'm not a fan of pudding," I said slowly. Then looking between them I added, "But I am a fan of Baileys."

Maggie practically jumped to her feet. "I'll do the honors."

Lochlan gestured to the chair again. "Please." I sat. "Rita, this is not a simple legal transaction. You've not inherited the Hallows and residence and the sizable assets that go along with that..."

"Sizable assets?"

"Well, yes."

I'm not greedy. At least I don't think so. It's just never come up before. But the idea of 'sizable assets' beyond the store, the house, and Romeo, had me thinking there was no reason why I couldn't spend an hour listening to lunacy next to a cheerful fire with Baileys.

Lochlan picked up the story at the point where I'd interrupted.

"In all the world you're chosen to be the next magistrate. The last judge passed away a few weeks ago. A marvelous fellow. Fair. Measured. Served for forty years." I had nothing to add to that except to wonder how long it would take to make a fresh brew of coffee. "He'll be missed. Anyway, it's a lifetime appointment with perks. The store. The house. The car. And money."

"How much?"

"Have not looked lately. A good bit."

"Enough to pay for my daughter's education? Even if she wants grad school?"

He chuckled. "Oh yes. Plenty enough for that."

For a second I'd been lured into a state of starry-eyed dreaming about writing debt-free checks for tuition. Then I came back to earth. "I can't be a judge. I don't have a law degree. I barely managed a B.A. in Art History. And, even if I did have a law degree, I wouldn't be able to be a judge here. In England. I can't think of anyone less qualified." I immediately realized how ridiculous that statement was and amended. "Okay. I can think of *lots* of people less qualified. But that doesn't make me the right person for the job. Judges don't have names like Rita. They have names like Judy." Even I knew that was arguably the stupidest thing I'd ever said. For that reason, I sincerely hoped I wasn't being recorded.

"You are the *exact* right person for the job, Rita."

"Who says?"

"The Powers That Be."

"Oh here we go," I said.

Maggie returned with a tray laden with a silver pot of coffee, a bottle of Baileys, fresh mugs, and what appeared to be lemon crisp cookies. "Here we go." She repeated my last words cheerfully without realizing I'd just said that... in a much different tone.

"The position offered is not one of presiding over mundane courts," Lochlan went on. "You'll decide disputes between parties who are part of the magical world."

I took in a deep breath and received the unintended benefit of a nose full of fresh, dark Sumatra blend coffee. It was the perfect distraction. I glanced up at Maggie and said, “Thank you,” as she poured.

“Leavin’ two fingers at the top for Baileys,” she said.

Two fingers sounded like a lot to me. But what the hell? I might be needing a lot.

I nodded, took the bottle, poured one finger, then decided to add a splash before recapping the bottle.

“Is there more?” I asked Lochlan.

“I believe so. Maisie buys these very large bottles.”

I shook my head. “I’m sorry. I didn’t mean is there more Baileys. I meant did you have more to say on the subject of a shop, a house, a car, and a judgeship.”

“Court convenes eight times a year on solar and seasonal festival dates. It’s taken very seriously. When in session, everyone in the magical world will defer to you.”

“Honestly, Lochlan. Even if every word you’re saying about parallel universes or whatever was true, do I strike you as the sort of person who commands that kind of respect?”

Lochlan was shaking his head before I finished. “We’re not talking about parallel universes. The magical world is right here. Right now. All around you. It’s simply protected from human view.”

"Uh-huh," I said drily.

"And yes, Rita. You do strike me as the sort of person who will make an excellent magistrate."

"Why is that?" As soon as the words left my mouth, I heard my grandmother's voice. *Curiosity killed the cat.*

"For one thing, you're not gullible. Not blinded by charm. Because who's more charming than myself?" he asked. I wasn't sure if that was rhetorical, so I left it alone. "It's an important quality because charm is cheap and plentiful in the magical world. For another thing, you ask pertinent questions that go directly to the heart of a matter." He took a sip of the coffee Maggie had delivered, which reassured me greatly. "That's no doubt due in part to your insurance work. Over time you've developed a kind of sixth sense for when folks are forthright and when they're shaving the truth. Wouldn't you say that's true?"

True? That's an understatement. It was spot on. After a while I did kind of 'know' whether to take a claim at face value or look a little deeper.

"Could be," I hedged, "but if what you're saying is true, I wouldn't be evaluating, um…"

"Humans?"

Every part of the question sounded wrong, wrong, wrong. But the answer was, "Yes."

Lochlan chuckled. "Indeed, it is true. We can be a wily bunch. But that will serve to keep life interesting for you. The Powers That Be are never wrong about the choice of magistrate."

That sentence was dripping with lawyer double talk. It made me wonder what sorts of things the 'Powers That Be' are wrong about.

"Just for giggles," I began. "Let's say this is on the level and everything you say is true. Why would the, um, Powers That Be choose a human to sort out disputes between magical, um, people?"

Lochlan beamed at Maggie then at me. "An excellent illustration of pertinent questioning. The magistrate is always human because it's the best way to ensure impartiality. And magical people would never agree on anything else. We're a contentious bunch. You'll see."

"Now Lochlan," Maggie said. "Do no' scare the girl away."

I turned my full attention to Maggie. "Do I have reason to worry?"

She hesitated. "Worry?"

Uh-oh. My inner lie detector caught the 'tell'. When a person who's not hard of hearing repeats a question, it means they're stalling for time to craft an answer that's more advantageous (to them) than the whole truth. And a crafted answer is always a *partial* truth.

"What aren't you telling me, Maggie?"

Lochlan interceded. "Your personal economy is funded for life. You'll never have to be concerned about finances. Your personal safety is guaranteed. You'll have the whole of the magical community sworn to protect you."

"But?"

With a sigh, he said, "It's not a *worry* per se, but some may try to curry your favor in view of prejudicing a future ruling toward their side. As said before, magical people can be very charming. We can also be persuasive." He smiled. "You may be forced to maintain a bit of cynicism."

"That's it? The downside is that I need to maintain a healthy cynicism?" They both nodded. After letting that sink in, I laughed silently. "If a skeptical outlook is part of the job description, it would make sense that an American would be the best candidate. We're squarely in the middle of an age of cynicism. But you do realize that means that I'm not wholesale swallowing what you're selling. Right?"

An enigmatic smile passed over Lochlan's face. "I suspected you'd be wanting evidence."

He pulled his phone out of the pocket of his open cardigan and appeared to send a text while Maggie and I looked on. He then gestured toward Maggie.

"Maggie's brought shoes that will help you see the entire world, mundane *and* magical. After you've settled into your role as magistrate," he paused to add, "if you accept, eventually the magics will adopt you and you won't need anything external to see. But if you want proof now, put the shoes on."

I couldn't help a grin. "Okay. This really is when somebody pops out to say, 'Gotcha. It's the new 'Voyeur Video' show."

Neither Lochlan nor Maggie gave anything useful away. My super claims adjuster powers were silent as the grave.

At this point I wasn't sure if I wanted it to be a hoax or if I wanted it to be true. What I *really* wanted was validation one way or the other.

"Alright," I said. "I'm going along with this just so I can say I fulfilled my promise to hear you out in exchange for an entertaining evening and the best pot roast I've ever had." I looked at Maggie. "Give me the shoes. I hope they're a size nine."

She handed them across the table. "They'll fit like they were made for ye."

I took the shoes which, I had to admit for the second time, were beautiful; glittery and glitzy. That alone should have told me something was odd. I'm not typically attracted to glittery and glitzy. They appeared to be made of fiberglass or something equally uncomfortable, like a glass slipper for instance, but they were soft as suede to the touch.

Turning away I pulled my boots off and set them aside. I was wearing some black lacey socks that were as thin as stockings. That meant that, if the shoes were true to size, they'd still fit without me having to try them on with bare feet.

With no expectation other than going along to get along, I gingerly slipped first one foot, then the other, into the shoes as if I was Cinderella. They were a fit so perfect they might have been custom made by the best shoemaker in the world.

"Who made these?" I blurted, looking over at Maggie.

"Why, Thomasin Cobb, o' course," Maggie said. "He's irritatin' as a goblin can be, but he's also the best shoemaker in the world. How are they feelin'?"

"Perfect," I said. "They actually..."

I looked over at Lochlan and received such a start that I almost tipped my chair over. Reflexively, I grabbed the table edge to restore balance, all while never taking my eyes away from my host.

The 'person' sitting where Lochlan had been was wearing the same clothes, but appeared to be closer to thirty than eighty. His white hair was reddish blonde. His skin was smooth and flawless, his eyebrows not so thick and curly. That was the least of the shocks. The truly astonishing change, the one that would render even my Aunt Brigid speechless, was the pair of rather large, very pointed ears. Shocking and handsome at the same time.

I supposed the facial structure was basically the same. And he was wearing the same clothes. But the telltale clincher, the thing that caused me to know for certain that I was in the presence of Lochlan's true form, was the laughing blue eyes that were the same young or old.

"Lochlan?" I rasped.

"Indeed," he said. "It is I." We heard the semi-distant sound of a door closing. "And that would be my wife come to help with your orientation. Ivy's a pixie who spends a bit of time in her more magical form each day."

"Pixie? Like, um, Tinkerbell?"

With a laugh, Lochlan said, "Yes, my dear. Now and then mundies get something right. Would you like to see?"

Did I want to see a real pixie? Do bears bare? Do bees be? "If you mean what I think you mean, then yes, Lochlan. I want to see."

"Ivy!" he called.

Within seconds I was holding onto the table's edge again. A four-inch-tall woman flew into the dining room leaving a trail of yellow pixie dust that disappeared within seconds. Her wings were moving so fast they were a blur. Like a hummingbird. She hovered between Lochlan and Maggie.

"If you hold your palm up, she'll land there," Lochlan

said.

I wasn't at all sure I wanted that, but didn't want to be rude. So I raised my palm and Ivy landed. When her six-inch wings quieted, they were striking variations of blue and green and reminded me of peacock feathers. She was light enough to be a butterfly. Beautiful. Magical. And, unless I'd been drugged, I was no longer wondering if I was the butt of an outlandishly costly joke. "Why is it that the sound of our voices so close isn't breaking her, um, eardrums?"

Lochlan smiled. "Magic."

Even more astounding was that I could hear Ivy as well as if she was speaking with the vocal cords of a full-sized person. "Hello again, Rita," she said.

"A very long time ago, I met Ivy as I was passing through the region on holiday, a detour on the way to see His Majesty's Courts and Tribunals in London."

"*His* Majesty?" I said.

He cleared his throat. "As I said, it was long ago. Anyway, I encountered Ivy and was struck by love surely as if Eros had aimed an arrow at my heart."

"Awwww," Ivy said.

"Do not pretend surprise that I'm romantic." Lochlan smiled at the pixie before turning back to me. "She was tending a flower garden at the inn where I'd taken a room for the night. She was born here in Cumbria, which is known as the Eden District. The ley lines form an Isosceles triangle from here at Hallow Hill, to Derry in Northern Ireland, and Inverness, Scotland. It's not the only magical place on earth, but it's known for frequent intersections between the mundane and magical worlds.

"Ivy has strong familial ties. So I moved here." She zipped up and away and landed on Lochlan's shoulder. "It's one thing I've never regretted."

I was dying to ask about the things that he *did* regret but decided that would be off topic. So, I filed it away for another day. That's when I realized I'd made a decision to stay. There'd been no formal admission, no sense of crossing a line. It just sort of happened without conscious agreement. *Huh.*

I pushed my chair out a bit, crossed my right leg over my left and removed my right shoe. Lochlan was eighty-something and Ivy wasn't there. I put the shoe back on. Young elven-eared Lochlan had taken the place of the older-looking human and Ivy sat on his shoulder, wings moving slowly.

Repeating this twice more, not because I needed further confirmation, but because it was just cool, I said, "This is amazing."

"And you accept the post?" Lochlan said. "I have papers for you to sign that make it official and give you ownership of the estate."

My head was shaking no without my conscious direction. I took that as a sign. I remembered a phrase I'd heard watching depictions of courtroom dramas and thought it was appropriate.

"I need to take this under advisement. Let me spend a night, find out what it feels like to wake up here. Walk around the village in the, um, shoes. Am I going to see something different if I do?"

"Hallow Hill is home to a community of magic kind. That's one of the reasons why we're off the beaten tourist path. We own land far and wide around so that people don't see us as their center commerce. We don't get unwelcome residents because there're no jobs available for humans. Present company excepted. Of course."

"Of course," I repeated drily. "You're saying that, if I stay, I'll be the only human."

Right after Maggie nodded affirmation, I felt my eyes widen. "Oh my God! When you said, 'I see you met the vampire', you *really* meant that he's an actual..."

"Vampire," Maggie finished the sentence. Then her own eyes grew wide. "Oh, but there's no worry. When he needs to feed, he goes to Carlisle where there're no doubt plenty who're willin'. He'll no' be bitin' *you*. Rest assured."

"Um. That's good to know." As I processed this, my mind began to catalog the other people I'd met. "So, if I'm the only human resident, that means the silversmith..."

"Dwarf," Maggie said.

"You mean like in *Lord of the Rings*?"

Maggie looked at Lochlan, who nodded. "Just so. Are you a fan?"

"If you mean fan as short for fanatic, then no. But I like the story."

"You have good taste," said Lochlan.

"Thank you," I said. "Thomasin?"

"Goblin."

I pressed my lips together. "I need to take you more

literally, Maggie. You said the bootmaker is a goblin and you said the guy in jodhpurs was a vampire. I just assumed you were being… colorful. As Irish sometimes tend to be."

She laughed. "Can no' deny that. Storytellers we are, to be sure. What do they call it?" She looked at Lochlan.

"Hyperbole," he offered.

"That's it," Maggie agreed cheerfully.

"Molly?" I queried.

"Nurture nymph."

I shook my head. "I've never heard of that."

"Well," Maggie said, "there are nature nymphs and nurture nymphs. Nurture nymphs are at home takin' care of things that sustain. Like food and drink."

After trying to process that for a few beats, I continued down my list. "Fie?"

"Now there's a story," Maggie said. "As you probably guessed he's not originally from 'round here. Immigrant wind devil from someplace in the Middle East."

"Wind devil," I repeated, remembering the gust of wind that almost blew me over just as I was entering the pub and encountering the unelected Mayor Mistral. I looked at Lochlan. "And you are…?"

"Elf." He smiled when he said it as if he'd won a prize.

I looked at Maggie with raised eyebrows.

"Fae," she said.

"I'm going to need to brush up on my magic." Which was a wry overstatement since I'd never had enough magical knowledge to 'brush up'. "Notions and Potions?"

I hadn't noticed that Ivy had left, but I turned toward the door when I heard light footsteps. She joined us, tall, wingless, but just as beautiful.

"Aoumiel? The witch?" Ivy asked.

I turned to Ivy. "Is that what she is?" Ivy nodded. "And by that you mean she's a magical entity?"

Ivy nodded again. "Why do you ask that?"

I looked at the other three faces around the table. "Can I be frank to the point of gossip?"

The eagerness on their faces led me to believe I had carte blanche to dish the dish.

"Some people where I'm from use the term 'witch' to describe a person who's cold or unfriendly."

"Well, that sounds like our Aoumiel," Maggie said. "She fits the bill whether you're talking magical or mundane."

"The things she sells though..." I began. "They're, um, mundane, is it? Fit for human consumption?" Lochlan, Maggie, and Ivy all looked suddenly busy studying the wall paneling or pulling at threads on clothing. "Are you saying she gives actual real charms or curses or whatever to humans?" The silence persisted. "Do they know?"

That got Maggie engaged. "Oh no. If they knew, we'd be gettin' a far cry more tourist traffic than we're wantin'."

Lochlan jumped in. "You'll not be needing to adjust any insurance claims on her behalf." He chuckled at his own joke.

I didn't laugh.

"But these things don't harm anybody."

"Oh, noooooooooo," Maggie said in a way that was far too insistent to go unnoticed. "No one who does no' need a wee adjustment or two."

"I don't know what that means and I don't like the sound of it." I looked around the table. "Do you have a system of rules, or laws, or best practices maybe? Something that governs your behavior beyond disputes with other, um..."

"We do no' have laws like mundies if that's what

you're askin'," Maggie supplied.

"I'm guessing that's short for mundane people? That's what you call humans? Like me?'

"Well," she said, "'tis certainly no' what we call *you*. You've been elevated above the lot of us. Whate'er you say is what goes. For as long as you live."

"You really sidestepped my question. Other than disputes, does the magical community have some kind of code that regulates behavior?"

"Yes," Lochlan said. "But there's not much to it. It's mostly along the lines of 'do as ye will so long as ye harm none'."

"I see." I reached for my mug, but it had gone room temperature.

"Would you like a warmup?" Maggie was already reaching for the pot.

I looked at the coffee in my mug.

"Let me get you a fresh one," Ivy said and hurried away to the kitchen.

Truthfully, I was feeling like taking the cap off the bottle of Baileys and chugging it straight.

"The magistrate doesn't function as enforcer, Rita,"

Lochlan said. "The magistrate decides disputes and..."

"And what?" I demanded.

"And punishment," he said quietly.

"Okay. There have to be guidelines for that! Right? Like, a hundred dollars for every ten miles over the speed limit? Something like that?"

Ivy giggled. "We don't do dollars."

I looked at her thinking she'd missed the point as artfully as a teenager. "Sorry. I meant, um, pounds."

"We're not quibblin' over currency, Ivy," Maggie admonished.

"I know," Ivy said. "I just thought she'd like to know that people will look at her funny if she says dollars. Sorrrrry."

"What's worrying you, Rita?" Lochlan asked.

"That I'm completely unequipped to be judge..."

"Sit or preside as judge," he corrected.

"And listen to disputes."

"Hear complaints," he corrected.

"See? You're making my case!"

Everyone else laughed. The legal reference sounded like a joke, but it was unintended.

"Please believe me, in time these things will seem so insignificant as to be irrelevant. The Powers That Be are never wrong about the choice of magistrate. You're the right person in the right place at the right time." He glanced at Ivy and Maggie before retraining his attention on me. "Take a couple of days to give your answer if you wish. Tomorrow night have dinner at the pub. And wear the shoes. Not everyone who lives in and around will be there, but enough turn out of a night to give you a sampling of life here on the Hill. You'll see that you're a celebrity. Hallow Hill is the seat of magical justice for the British Isles and all of western Europe."

"Oh, God," I said, getting that woozy feeling I get when I've given too much blood. "All of Europe."

I had a history of stage fright in public speaking situations.

"*Western* Europe," he corrected. "After a couple of nights in your own bed the answer will come to you. The magistrate's house has good stuff. Sweet dreams."

What a salesman. *How could anybody predict sweet dreams?*

"And you like red!" Ivy said, clearly trying to be helpful.

I looked at her and blinked.

Maggie gestured toward my dress. "I think she means you must like red or ye would no' be wearin' this dress tonight. The reference is to magistrates' robes. They're red, about the same value as that fetchin' smock."

I sighed. "Um, yes. I do like red and I think I need to mull all this over. Sleep in the house."

"Aye." Maggie looked hopeful.

"Did you say you discourage tourism?" I asked.

"Well, no, we didn't say so. Exactly," Lochan answered. "But we don't encourage too much of it either."

"Because you don't need the money?"

Lochlan grinned. "We don't need money. But like all creatures, we need purpose. Lily isn't masquerading as a florist. She's providing flowers to locals and to humans in towns throughout Cumbria. Nothing gives her more pleasure. The same could be said for each of us who is engaged in commerce. Ebb and flow are on our side. We get our share of lookers in the summer months. We have to hire humans from Ambleside to help with parking, since we don't allow vehicles on the circle. We provide parking at the bottom of the hill and valet service for a reasonable fee. And they get a taste of the world pre dot-com."

"I knew it," I said. "Hallow Hill is a recreation of an amusement park." No one got the joke, but I wasn't surprised.

Lochlan forged on as if I hadn't said something that the three of them were unlikely to understand. "As for the times between high tourism when we get a nice trade from Mundies and Court Meets when we get a nice trade from the magic kind community? Well, we like our quiet ways." I didn't miss Ivy's snort even though she made a halfhearted attempt to do it quietly.

Twice now I'd made an exit speech and started to leave, only to linger for one more question. "You said eight times a year." Lochlan nodded. "When's the next, um...?"

"Court."

"Yes."

"Normally it would be about a week from now, but circumstances being what they are, with the magistrate's post in transition, we're pushing the docket off until

Hallowstide."

"Like Halloween?"

Lochlan smiled the way he would if he was being patient with a child. "Last week of October. Maybe a little longer next Meet because we missed the last one. People will come from far and wide. Most of the houses you see on the lanes that lead off the circle are here to house guests."

"Well that explains why there are so many houses and so few people about. And you think seven weeks would be sufficient time for me to prepare?"

With a little chuff, Lochlan said, "You worry like an old woman, Rita. There's plenty of time. The Powers That Be…"

I finished the sentence for him. "Are never wrong."

"Right you are!"

"Tell me, how long has this system of employing a human judge been in place?"

After rubbing his smooth jaw with a long-fingered hand, he said, "At least eight hundred years. Maybe longer. Has been a boon to us, it has. Before Merle…" He stopped and nodded at me. "He's the resident mathemagician."

"He's a genius, he is," added Maggie.

Lochlan began that thought again. "Before Merle came up with the idea, the magical world, our world, was becoming endangered. We argued and fought, refused to compromise, and were on the verge of killing ourselves off. You're providing a service to our kind and, in the ways that count most, you're elevated above monarchs, since you could put them in prison or even have them executed and all."

"Executed?" I squeaked. "I don't believe in capital punishment."

Ivy leaned into Maggie. "Does that mean killing?"

"I think so," Maggie whispered back to Ivy.

"Well," Lochlan said, "every magistrate makes their own way. You'll do the same."

"Execution is out."

Lochlan shrugged. "Up to you. You're the magistrate."

"Not until I accept the job," I protested. Lochlan splayed his hands as if to indicate that goes without saying. "Did you say Merle the, um…?"

"Mathemagician."

"Did you say he *is* a genius? Not he *was* a genius?"

"Aye. Sharp as a razor's edge," Maggie said.

"And you also said he came up with this idea?"

"Aye." Maggie nodded.

"So, you're saying he's eight hundred years old?"

Lochlan cleared his throat. "We may've not got around to mentioning that many of us are long-lived, compared to humans. But while we're on the subject, magistrates tend to live longer than most humans."

"Maybe somethin' about bein' 'round magic," Maggie guessed. "Seeps into the essence, it does."

Ivy nodded. "Maybe."

"One last question. Then I'm going." My announcement sounded final enough this time that I'd feel like a dweeb if I didn't follow through. "Has there ever been a magistrate who, um, quit?"

The three looked at each other with mutual shaking of heads.

"No," Lochlan voiced the consensus. "Guess what I'm going to say next."

"The Powers That Be are never wrong." I stood then turned back. "Okay. This really is the last one, or two, questions. I have a daughter. In college. She's grown. Or almost grown." Since no one took that as a cue, I went on. "If I stay, she might visit sometime."

"And welcome she would be," Lochlan said.

"Indeed," Maggie added. "So long as she does no' stay." I looked to Maggie for clarification of what sounded like an unfriendly thing to say to a person's mother. "'Twould be very hard to keep up appearances permanently, you understand. With a human in our midst."

"Right. Well, she's not the sort who'd want to live here. Quiet life is not her thing."

"What's the other question?" Lochlan asked.

"I'm going to be involved in a divorce proceeding."

"We have people to handle that. You'll not be troubled with such annoyances. We've also taken care of permanent work visas and such. When you're ready to give your final answer, tomorrow or the next day, I'll have you sign papers for ownership and bank accounts, and give you the code to the safe."

That was interesting. "What will I find in the safe?"

"Hmmm. Mostly journals of magistrates who've gone before. Some kept written records of the more interesting cases. Might be enlightening reading. But there's also the magistrate's seal. It's a big deal."

"You're a poet and didn't know it."

Without hesitating, he said, "You made a rhyme. You'll see your fellow before bedtime."

We both laughed. It would be hard to not like Lochlan.

Certainly, I was intrigued by the idea of journals and halfway wished I could take one or two to bed with me that very night.

"Reading some first-person magistrate history could help me with my decision. And my continuing education. If I stay."

Chapter Four

Jutting and Jaunty

I went back to the townhouse expecting that detached, slightly uncomfortable feeling you get when sleeping in a strange place. Particularly with it being an entire house all to myself. I withdrew a sleep shirt from my bag, not wanting to make a commitment beyond the night. But gradually I succumbed to the vibe of the house, which was as soothing as a loving hug.

Lochlan was right. I enjoyed the best night's sleep in memory and woke without a single indication of advancing age. No creaks. No aches. No grogginess. Just joie de vivre. I wasn't even feeling lingering effects from the time change.

I made coffee in the French press, noting that someone had taken the trouble to note my taste and stock my favorites, pulled the wool throw from the sofa around my shoulders, and took it out into the garden. The beautiful blood orange tree was gone. In its place was a pink tulip tree in full bloom. I reached up to rub a leaf between thumb and fingers, confirming that it was real. It was.

Twenty-four hours earlier such an experience would have had me running for the hills. But that was before I saw an eighty-year-old man become a thirty-year-old elf. Not to mention Ivy and her pixie dust.

After congratulating myself on taking all of this like a champ, I made toast, sat down at the desk, and opened my laptop to check email. I'd left it charging when I went to bed, right after texting my daughter to let her know that I was enjoying my vacation to England. She'd taken the news about the divorce better than I'd expected. Perhaps she'd known for a long time that her father and I weren't madly in love, but rather in a perpetual state of barely tolerating each other. She replied that all was well at school. She hoped I'd have a good time and added that I deserved it.

Two minutes into the email project I was forced to confront the fact that my life back in the U.S. was incredibly, well, mundane. I mean, 'how you gonna keep 'em down on the farm after they've seen an elf, a pixie, and a – *shudder* – far-too-handsome vampire, among others?

Every email I scanned seemed either too lackluster to warrant response or something was something unpleasant, such as the notice from my new attorney that divorce papers had been filed and Cole had been served. It was news to me that I was the originating party, but good for me. I was divorcing his ass. Not the other way around. Lochlan had said it was being handled and I had to hand it to the elf. He knew how to get stuff done, competent to a fault as my grandmother would have said.

Did that mean that I was seriously considering abandoning everything familiar to begin a new life judging non-humans? Surprisingly, the answer was yes.

What I lacked in confidence about whether or not I was up to the task was made up for by others who were convinced that I was the perfect new appointee. Who wouldn't be flattered?

Even the day job at the shop, which would be *my* shop, appealed to my first love, art history. I'd never worked in retail but talking to people about treasures didn't sound half bad. Looking around, I realized there weren't any curious goods in the house. Nothing that I would guess had been for sale in the shop.

I'd been staring at the tulip tree while these thoughts circulated in my head and made a mental note to ask Maggie how often the tree changed form. I glanced back down at the email inbox, noted the time, and shut the laptop. It was nine o'clock local time.

When I asked myself what I wanted to do next with my "vacation", the answer was clear. I found myself eager to get dressed, go to the shop, and have Maggie do the deeper dive tour regarding how things run.

AT TEN I stood in my kitchen trying to decide whether to go through the interior door or walk around to the Hallows entrance. At length I chose my front door. Using the 'owner's passage', as I thought of it, would seem like a thing to do if I'd gone all in and formally committed.

Opening my front door meant that I was staring at 'my' garage door across the lane. After locking up, I took two steps toward the shop before turning around and heading back to the garage. When the door completed its lift, I spoke to the car. "You okay, Romeo?"

The response was muffled, coming from inside the car, but audible. "Excellent, madam. And yourself?"

I wasn't going to argue with the car if he *really* felt more comfortable calling me madam. "Very well. Perhaps we'll go out later."

"Ever at your service."

That was nice to know.

After reclosing and locking the garage door I replayed the scene in my head and considered that I might be on the road to a touch of Obsessive-Compulsive Disorder.

There were perhaps a dozen people in sight, talking on the sidewalk, or on errands. The shop was already open, so I shoved my key ring into my tote that held my purse, two protein bars, and the shoes.

The Hallows was open, but no one was in sight. "Good morning?"

I heard a thump in the back of the store after which Maggie appeared in seconds. "Good mornin', boss."

"Oh. No. Maggie. Please don't call me that. Just Rita will do."

"Suit yerself."

She stood still and quiet, looking my way with expectation. Of what I wasn't sure.

"I thought perhaps, if you have time, you could give me an overview of how the shop works. I mean, um, runs. Operates. Or whatever."

"'Twould be an honor… Rita."

As I started toward the back of the store, on impulse I asked, "Maggie. The Alfa Romeo in the garage?"

"Aye?"

"It's not magical, is it?"

She drew back as if considering whether the Powers That Be had finally screwed up. "Magical, madam?"

"Never mind. It was a silly thought. It's just hard to get used to a car that can drive itself and carry on a conversation like a person."

"Well," she said, "when you put it that way, perhaps my answer should no' come so quick and unconsidered. 'Tis probably human magics. But one of us could check with Lochlan just to be sure. Why do you ask?"

I bit my bottom lip wondering whether or not I should confide something so revealing to a strange fae. I almost laughed out loud at myself for thinking the phrase 'strange fae'.

"Since the car talks like a person, it's hard to think of it as purely inanimate. So, I find myself thinking I should check in on it." Her face and posture softened. "As I did on the way here."

"Well, was the car alright?"

"Yes."

She leaned in close and almost whispered. "Did ye just look or did ye ask?"

I'm sure my responding smile was somewhat sheepish. "I asked."

"And what did the machine say?"

"Excellent, madam. And yourself?"

Maggie nodded. "I can see why 'twould be confusin'. I also see that ye have a kind heart. The best judges would, I think. Can no' decide the fate of others without a measure of understandin'." After adjusting her belt, she continued. "What would ye like to know first?"

I looked around. "Now that my eyes have been opened, so to speak, I'd like you to tell me more about acquisitions. Where the inventory comes from?" I looked down at my tote. "But first, maybe I should just set this down somewhere?"

"O' course. Set it anywhere in the back. Your belongin's are safe as can be."

I gave a courtesy nod as I headed to the back, past the little office, to the kitchen, and noticed a room off the kitchen that was nearly as large as the shop itself. I presumed I hadn't noticed it before because the door had been closed. Perhaps I thought it was a closet.

Having forgotten all about the tote on my shoulder, now being interested only in the adventure of scouting another room, I peeked in. In an instant I knew it to be a restoration workshop.

"Maggie?"

"Aye?"

"What is this?"

I felt her come up behind me.

"Oh. 'Tis where Dolan fixes things up."

"You mean we receive things in need of repair."

"Oh, aye. Quite often. But Dolan is gifted."

"Is Dolan, um…?"

"One of us. I mean magical. Aye. But I've no more to say on the matter. Anythin' else is to be seen."

When she looked down at my footwear pointedly, I got the message.

"Does he have regular hours? Or…?"

"No' exactly. He comes when he wants. But we always have plenty to sell."

"I see."

I stepped into the room, which was a long rectangle with two long waist-high worktables running down the center. Sturdy wooden ceiling-height shelves for smaller items lined one side of the room while the other side was a haphazard storage of larger pieces.

I walked the length of the room, slowly, admiring the beauty and diversity of stock. I stopped to survey a bit of damage to a particular piece.

"If Dolan can make these pieces sellable, he is indeed gifted."

Maggie chuckled. "A miracle worker that one."

A slight bit of shoulder strain reminded me that I had yet to set down my heavy tote. "Let me set this down."

"You do that. I'll start the kettle. I have a couple of thermos-type cups we can use to sip while we talk."

I followed her back to the kitchen and set my tote on

one of the chair seats. "You're sure this is a good place for this? Even if, ah, Dolan comes in?"

"O' course. He's no chancer. Honest as the day is long, he is." She laughed. "And who would have the audacity to steal from the magistrate?" She scoffed. "A body would have to be arseways for that." She set the kettle on the stove and turned on the fire. "Earl Grey with lemon, three sugars, no milk?" she asked.

"You already know the answer. And it's creepy that you do." She chuckled. "I think it's only fair that you tell me what you're havin'."

"Chamomile with a teaspoon of local honey and a spring of fresh wormwort."

"Okay, I'll try to remember."

"As a matter of fact, Dolan's comin' by this mornin' to install a windchime alert."

"What is that?" I asked as I took a seat.

"'Tis a small chime that will sound only when a human enters the store. 'Twas Ivy's idea. Worked the charm herself so you wouldn't *have* to wear the shoes all the time. She likes you."

I smiled. Who doesn't like to be liked?

"So, Dolan is a miracle restorer of antiquities and a handyman? All in one?"

"Sure. He'll take care of anythin' you need at your house as well. Lives just down the hill in the old mill house, he does. The wheel does no' grind grain anymore, mind ye, but he's repairin' it nonetheless. One of these days he'll have it workin'."

"That would be something to see. A bit of history. Do you live close by, Maggie?"

"Oh, I have something small nearby."

The kettle whistled so loudly I almost put my hands to my ears.

"There we are then," Maggie said as she turned the fire off. She poured water directly into our cups that held the teabags and closed the lids for steeping.

I took the cup she offered. "This smells wonderful. So you were going to tell me about the inventory?"

"The pieces arrive during the night. I do no' know how. They are simply here, in the workroom, when I come in."

I took a moment to try to digest that and found it hopeless. "Before dinner last night, I would have laughed and said you're joking, but I suspect you're not."

"'Tis no' a joke. No."

"Where do you think these things come from?"

"I do no' bother with frettin' about it 'cause speculatin' would get me nowhere."

I nodded. "How do you establish value?"

"Well," Maggie said, "I would no' say that I establish value so much as slappin' on a price that I think we can get."

"I suppose that's one approach to valuation. Do you ever negotiate with customers?"

She shook her head. "I do no'. The policy of the shop is this. If you do no' want it, someone else will."

I laughed. "It's not an entirely unique approach to commerce. I'm just as glad. Personally, I hate bargaining." She nodded agreeably. "Would you say that most of the sales go to humans?"

"That brings us to another subject. You see, the Hallows sells things that are pretty or interestin' to humans, and we also sell magical artifacts to people like us."

I looked toward the shop. "How do customers know which is which?"

She grinned. "'Tis easy. The magical wares are cloaked in wards so that they can no' be seen by human eyes."

I took a few steps into the shop and looked around. "There are things here I can't see?"

"Aye."

"If I put on the shoes…?"

She beamed. "Then you'll have the sight of anyone magic born."

I set my cup down on a shelf next to a brass lamp that featured a pair of peacocks with sapphire-colored glass eyes and miniature peacock feathers at full spray. In less than two minutes I returned wearing the shoes and I could see that, indeed, there were marvelous things here and there that I hadn't noticed before.

I considered this. "So, I couldn't sell a magical thing to a human because they wouldn't even know it was here." Maggie nodded. "And if someone magical bought something mundane, it would be deliberate. They'd know what they were doing."

"Aye. Why do you ask?" Her expression cleared. "Oh. You're thinkin' about the statue purchased by Mr. Weir." I nodded. "You can rest assured he knew what he was buyin'."

With a frown I asked, "Should I apologize to him? About insisting he buy something or leave?"

"Ohhhhhhh. O'course no'. 'Tis a great story that'll be circulatin' at the pub for weeks to come."

"I don't want to unknowingly make someone local the butt of a joke."

"My. My. You are sensitive, Magistrate."

"It's not sensitive to want to avoid having a vampire hold a grudge."

"Oh, no worries about that. He's a brooder, but no' a bad sort."

"So…"

The front door burst open and a whirlwind of beautiful male rushed in saying, "Mags! Is the new…?"

He went still and quiet when he saw me and stared in a way that might be considered rude by some. He was about six feet tall with a golden tan, green eyes with prominent gold-orange flecks, and what could best be described as 'surfer streaked' curly hair, worn longish to his collar. His jaw was prominent; defined and square with the slightest hint of cleft, and my thumb itched to reach up and press that spot. His age was enigmatic, but I guessed late thirties, maybe.

At length, after staring his fill, his face broke into a grin that threatened to put the light of the sun to shame.

"Greetings," he said without taking his eyes off me. "I'm Keir. Keir Culain." His accent was definitely English. I didn't yet have an ear to distinguish between classes, but it sounded highborn. His first and last names both began with a k sound. I repeated his name in my head, liking the sound of it. Maybe too much.

He came forward, deeper into the shop where I stood near Maggie, and the closer he got the more self-conscious I felt. I hadn't indulged in sexual fantasies for a long time, but Keir Culain had me cataloguing a list of things I'd never tried.

Seeing me rendered speechless, Maggie stepped in. "This is Rita Hayworth, Keir. She wants to be called Rita, but sometimes I slip and give her the deference of her office. Though she has no' technically accepted yet."

Keir pulled his eyes away from me and looked at Maggie. "Hasn't accepted?"

His eyes came back to me and searched my face for

clues to my soul. "Why in Hades not?" he asked bluntly.

I cleared my throat to be sure I had voice before trying to speak. "Well," I said, "it's a lot to consider."

"Nonsense," he scoffed. "You must say yes."

I couldn't help but smile. "*Must* I?"

"Without a doubt. It's not the kind of offer one turns down."

"So you might say it's an offer I can't refuse?" I teased.

What in Hades was I doing?

Flirting?

Good grief.

I found myself wishing I had traffic-stopping looks like my college roommate had. Believe me. An experience like that is enough to keep an ego in check for a lifetime.

He didn't laugh, but he cocked his head to the side. "Hmmm. You're unexpected."

"Was there somethin' in particular you were wantin', Keir?" Maggie asked.

With a smile I'd remember in my dreams, he said, without taking his eyes away from me, "Just stopped off to get a look at the new judge."

"Well, you've seen her. So, unless you want to buy

somethin'..."

Maggie winked at me and I knew it was in reference to my sale of the statue to John David Weir.

"Have you had a draft of daft, Margaret?" Keir asked her. "I have far too many pieces of junk now. In fact," he turned to me, smile back in place. "I should sell some things to you. Why don't you come over and pick out some things?" he asked me.

"She's no' comin' over to pick or price or anythin' else without a chaperone, Keir."

Chaperone?

I'm sure Maggie heard my silent question loud and clear as it was accompanied by my eyebrows reaching for my hairline.

"Keir thinks of himself as bein' devastatin' to the opposite sex," Maggie confided.

He laughed. To me, he said, "Completely untrue. I think of myself as being reasonably attractive."

That was the understatement of the century. And it was clear he knew it.

"I don't think we're shopping for new inventory. But thank you for the offer," I said.

"Dinner at the pub then. Perhaps I can be instrumental in persuading you to *accept* the position."

Maggie opened her mouth to speak, probably to tell him no, but I found that I didn't like being shepherded. Even if her heart was in the best place.

"Yes. Dinner at the pub. Six thirty?"

"I'll be back," he said.

I snorted so quietly that it was audible only to me.

At the door, he threw a seductive smile back over his shoulder.

I turned to Maggie, who had judgment all over her face. "I was tryin' to tell you he's trouble."

"Yes. I got that. He's human, right?"

Maggie's own brows came together. "Why would ye think it so?"

"I have on the shoes."

She sighed. "So you do. Some of us are two-natured."

"Meaning?"

"He has another side."

"What is it?"

Before she could answer, the door opened.

"Oh, there ye are, Dolan. Come and meet, em, Rita."

Dolan was tall and lanky with dark hair and the suggestion of a goatee. I would've probably thought him attractive if not for his very green, very goat-slit eyes with vertical pupils. It was an odd dichotomy. It was disconcerting and impossible to look away at the same time.

Dolan had walked closer while I was trying to figure out what he was. He held out his hand. "Nice to meet you, Magistrate."

I swallowed and found my voice. "Thank you, Dolan. Call me Rita. I understand that you're responsible for making broken things beautiful again."

He gave me a lopsided smile. "Nice to be needed."

I looked around. "Show me your favorite piece. The thing you love best in the shop."

His eyes glittered like he hadn't expected me to take an interest in his taste then left mine to roam over the shop. He lifted his hand, pointed toward a far corner, and moved in that direction. I followed.

We stopped in front of an object about the same size and shape as a small watermelon. It resembled oxidized hammered copper, but didn't appear to be actual metal except for an elaborately carved plaque in the shape of a large V with Celtic knot patterns and symbols.

"What is it?" I asked.

"Dragon's egg," he answered with unmistakable reverence.

My eyes jerked back to the ovoid. "It's not, um…"

He turned to me and cocked his head as if to say, "Not what?"

"It couldn't hatch. Could it?"

He shrugged and looked at it again. "Don't know. Right circumstances? Maybe."

"Dolan," Maggie called. "We need to get that chime alert in place. Like we talked about. So she does no' *have* to wear the shoes all the time."

He looked down at my shoes, nodded and walked off toward the workshop.

I whispered to Maggie. "What is he?"

"Brounie," she whispered in return. Then leaning in, she said, "He and Molly are seein' each other on the quiet. A right fetchin' couple they make from the looks of it." She nodded as if she'd just passed the juiciest bit of gossip that ever left lips.

I'd never lived in a small town but had heard the

scoop; that everybody always knows everybody else's business. I briefly tried that on for size, wondering how I'd feel about all my comings and goings being 'on the record'. The downside was no privacy. The upside was people who know, and perhaps care, about each others' well-being.

I didn't know what a brounie was, but made a mental note to undertake the study that very day.

"Maggie."

"Aye?"

"I feel like I'm in way over my head. I don't know what a brounie is. I don't know what a wind devil is, but I think I should know before I sit down for a casual lunch with one. Before last night I'd never heard of nurture nymphs and I have a feeling that's a drop in the bucket. There's an entire panorama of things I don't know about. Isn't there?"

She nodded without hesitation. "Aye. 'Tis true. That's what the records are for. By the time you hold the first court at Hallowstide, you'll be up to speed. That I can promise you."

"How can you promise me that?"

She gaped. "Because the Powers That Be are…"

"Never wrong." I finished the sentence with a hint of sarcasm because I believed the old wives' saying, that there's a first time for everything. "Until they are," I said. "I could be the first time."

Maggie laughed. "If this is truly troublin' ye, we need to go see Esmerelda."

"Why? Who is that?"

"She's the weaver from across the way."

"Ye-a-a-h. Who is she *really*?"

"Oh." Maggie made a face like she was thinking. "I guess the best way to put it is that she's the goddess of Boheme, guardian of Gypsies. Something like that. She weaves cloth and dreams, tells fortunes, and plays a mean tambourine."

"Tambourine," I repeated drily.

"Come on. Let's lock up and go have tea with Esme."

"We just had tea." My cup was half full and still warm.

"What has that to do with the proposition? You can no' have too much tea."

I laughed, wondering that a woman her age could speak that sentence seriously. Then I remembered she wasn't coping with a human bladder. She was fae, whatever that meant.

Maggie had grabbed the shop keys and was headed toward the door while I was lost in thought. Again.

"Wait. First, why are we going to see, um, Esme? And, second, if we keep closing the shop during store hours, how do we sell anything?"

"We're goin' to get your fortune sorted out once and for all." She took my sleeve and pulled me out on the sidewalk. As she was pulling the door shut and locking it, she said, "Do not worry yourself about the sales. Everythin' that should belong to a person will end up with that person whether we close for a bit or no'."

It would be a groundbreaking, novel idea for a human shopkeeper, but for all I knew, it wouldn't seem at all strange to a magical merchant.

"By the way, did ye sleep well last night?"

My grin answered for me, but I added words. "The best. The house has what Americans would call a good vibe."

Maggie began walking quickly across the circle.

"I think I should tell you that I don't believe in fortune

tellers."

Maggie halted abruptly, turned to me and laughed. "Rita, you are a delight. You took the news that you enjoyed lunch with an Assyrian wind devil, a creature who's foreign even to me, in stride, but fortune tellin' gives ye pause."

I frowned. "When you put it that way, it makes me sound like I have air between my ears."

"No." She began striding toward the weaver's again. "'Twas no' meant that way. You're goin' through a period of adjustment. Can no' imagine how I would take the idea of learnin' to live among humans." She shuddered for effect. "All things considered, you're doin' just grand."

When we arrived at the weaver's, my eyes again landed lovingly, covetously, on the beautiful shawl before I followed Maggie in.

The shop was warm and had the tantalizing smell of new fibers. Cotton. Hemp. Wool. Silk. Suede. Several pieces were in process in looms that were both horizontal and vertical. It was a clothes horse's paradise.

Hearing me inhale deeply, enjoying the scents, Maggie said, "Good, isn't it? I like it, too." She turned toward the rear and raised her voice. "Esme! The new judge's come for tea."

Esmerelda appeared in seconds, silent but smiling, wearing a long-sleeved, purple Henley, and a Batik wraparound skirt. Her dark hair was arranged in long dreads woven with beads. Her eyes were a pale ice-blue and as arresting as those never-in-nature contacts that extraverts wear. Her skin color was a couple of shades too rich to be British. It was smooth, shiny, and made the pallor of her eyes stand out all the more.

"This is Rita," Maggie said.

Esmerelda's smile never wavered as she said, "Rita," rolling the r, and hitting the t hard, and elongating the a into ahhhhh. It sounded too much like I was what's for dinner.

"Hello," I said.

She studied me, cocking her head the way humans do, and yet, when she did it, it didn't look entirely human. I was on the verge of fidgeting when Maggie said, "Do you have the kettle on?"

Without looking away from me, Esme's smile grew even wider. "I have your favorite, Maggie. I was expecting you."

As if it couldn't get creepier. Maggie seemed unfazed.

"Come on then," Maggie said to me and set off toward the back of the store like she was the host.

I followed, not feeling entirely comfortable with Esmerelda at my back.

Maggie plopped down in one of three chairs at a colorful round table that sat in the rear of the shop. It wasn't that strange considering that the space was more workshop than traditional retail store. I felt like a kid going on a field trip and wanted to ask about the looms and the spindles.

"Do you do all this work yourself?"

Esmerelda offered a grin that revealed extraordinarily white teeth. "Sometimes. Sometimes I have helpers."

I suppressed a shudder and tried not to form images of helpers from fairy tales.

Esmerelda disappeared from view, presumably to fetch tea.

I whispered to Maggie. "I don't think she likes me."

Maggie looked taken aback "What an odd thing to say. O' course she likes you. Why would ye think no'?"

"She doesn't, um, *feel* friendly."

"Ohhhhh, well. You must pay no mind to odd ways."

With a small sigh of resignation, I said, "So you're going to ask her to tell my fortune?"

"Aye. Esme can put your doubts to rest once and for all."

"How can you be so sure of that?" She opened her mouth, but I cut her off. "Don't say the Powers That Be are never wrong." She closed her mouth.

Esmerelda returned with a tray laden with pretty cups and saucers, silver demitasse spoons, raw sugar cubes, and sections of fresh lemon. She set the tray down on a side table and turned to leave just as we heard the distinctive sound of a well-tuned kettle whistle.

Minutes later she returned with three small silver pitchers with lids, each steeping tea in bags.

"Chamomile with wormswort," she said as she set Maggie's pitcher in front of her. When she set my little pitcher down with the announcement, "Earl Grey with extra lavender," I was sold on her psychic gifts. The last pitcher went in front of the empty chair. She smiled. "And orange pekoe for me. Pass the lemon please."

I dropped three sugar cubes in my cup, poured from the steamy pitcher, almost groaned at the heavenly (and much needed soothing) aroma, then began stirring.

"You think you're at a crossroads, Rita." Esmerelda said before taking a sip of her tea. "But it's an illusion. Your course is already decided."

"My course? Decided?" I didn't like the sound of that. "By whom?"

Esmerelda didn't react to the wariness that had crept into my tone.

She shrugged one shoulder. "It's fate. Some things you decide. Some things are decided for us. You were born to be in this place at this time to be peacekeeper."

That was the first time I'd heard anyone use the term 'peacekeeper'. Up to that point my part in the community had been described as judge or magistrate. I liked the idea of 'peacekeeper', but it also conjured images of the Earp brothers at the OK Corral.

"Is there a chance that your desire to fill the position could bias your conclusions?" I said in a soft voice to try to disguise the underlying belligerence.

"No," she said simply. "I'm not human."

I wasn't sure why she thought that was an argument clincher, but it seemed clear she thought that had put an end to exploring her reliability as a soothsayer.

"You'll be happy here," she went on. "And find love."

At that, I laughed out loud. Isn't that what all psychics told people who were feeling desperate for love?

"You don't believe me?"

She seemed to be having trouble with the concept that she might not be believed.

"I don't want to give offense, but I'm here because Maggie more or less dragged me without asking if I was open to being…"

"Read."

"Yes. Read."

"I see," Esme said. "What would it take to convince you of my… authenticity?"

"That's a great question," I said as my own words switched on the lightbulb in my head. "It's also a great answer. Are you open to questions?"

To my surprise, she grinned and waved at the room slowly. "I have time."

I took a slurp of tea, which was too good to merely be

called 'tea', as I thought about the limits of what could be learned from the internet. Things that would be impossible to turn up even if the best investigators in the world were hired.

"How did I meet the first best friend I ever had?"

With an arrogant air and without hesitation, Esme said, "It was your first day of school. Another little girl was crying for her mother. You gave her comfort."

Okay. Seemed really unlikely that would be available on the internet. And I'd never told anybody that story.

"What was her name?"

"Marty."

"Okay. So, you're really, really good."

Esmerelda laughed silently and said, "Thank you."

"One more. What irritated me the most about the man I'm divorcing?"

She replied without hesitation. "The fact that he always followed a yawn with, 'Ho. Ho. Ho'."

I stared. I'd been thinking of something else. But golly gee damn. She was right. That *did* irritate me more than anything else. It was mildly alarming that this stranger knew me better than I knew myself! I didn't want to contemplate what else she knew that I didn't.

Slumping in the chair a little, fight gone out of me, I said, "Okay. I'm listening."

"Everything about you has been evaluated, Rita. You've been vetted. The unique combination of your genetics, your experiences, your psychology, and your personality renders you the ideal candidate to be magistrate. You can't disbelieve that you're the best person for the post because that would be silly." I blinked. "You must understand that you acting as our magistrate is not just the best thing for us. It's the best thing for you as well. You'll be challenged in the most satisfying way to you. Fulfilled in ways that are unlikely in the mundane world. In short, you'll be happy." She smiled. "And in love."

"Now see? You had me at happy. Then you had to go and ruin it. I'm not looking for love, but if I was, my understanding is that there are no humans around unless you count day visitors during tourist season."

Esme cocked her head. "I didn't say the lucky male was human, did I?"

I took a deep breath, took a swallow of heavenly tea, and said, "We need to get back to the Hallows. Maggie is supposed to be showing me the details of the business. Thank you for taking the time to give me a, um, read."

When I rose, my companions stood as well.

"You're welcome," Esme said. "I'll show you out."

She went first and when she neared the front door, she said, "Just a minute."

I watched as she pulled my hearts-desire shawl out of the front window. When she draped it over my shoulders I thought I might faint with delight. I loved the feel of it. I loved the look of it. I loved the smell of it.

"This is indescribably beautiful, but I'm sure I can't afford it."

"No," Esmerelda said. "You misunderstand. It's a gift. No conditions. I want you to have it even if you don't stay."

"Now, Esme," Maggie interceded, "you know perfectly well the magistrate can't accept bribes. Shame on ye for tryin' to take advantage."

Bribes? Suddenly I recalled the warnings about Thomasin Cobb and Lochlan's insistence that I must pay for a dog.

Maggie reached for the price tag then said, "She'll take

it. Put this on the Hallows bill."

"Are you sure I have the, um, resources for something like this?" I asked Maggie.

"Darlin' girl, you have the resources for whate'er ye want. There's no' a frock made you can no' buy."

In some ways the idea of unlimited funds was even more preposterous than elves, pixies, dwarves, goblins, brounies, nymphs, witches, vampires, whatever Esmerelda was, and, oh yes, the occasional errant wind devil.

"Is that true?" I almost whispered.

"Certainly 'tis true. Lochlan told ye so."

"I understood there would be a stipend, but there's a big leap between that and a no-boundaries budget."

"Well, then, I'm glad we had this chat."

"It kind of is an offer I can't refuse."

"Well, nobody ever has before."

I pulled the shawl closer in a symbolic gesture of 'mine'.

To Esme I said, "It really is the prettiest thing I ever saw. How do I care for it?"

Esme's smile turned to a look of confusion. "Care for it?"

"How do I wash it?"

"Oh. No. It will care for itself," she replied.

These people had a way of rendering me speechless at least every quarter hour.

ON THE WAY back to the Hallows, I said, "There's a rule against accepting gifts?"

"Aye. But does no' mean you'll no' be tempted. Plenty of scoundrels in the magical world."

"This is to insure that I'm not partial to a gift giver in the event they'd be a party in a dispute? Sometime in the future?"

"Just so."

"I think I need to hear the entire list of rules. Since this wasn't presented in my, um, orientation. I could've already broken a rule. Innocently."

"Aye. I see what ye mean. It was an error of omission. There are no' any other rules I can think of off the top of my head, except that you have to show up for Court Meet."

"What if I'm sick?"

"Sick?" She laughed. "You'll no' be sick."

"How are you going to guarantee that?"

As we reached the Hallows door, she pulled the key out of her pocket and put it in the lock. "We have charmed elixirs to be certain you'll be at your best for the rest of your days."

"You mean you have something I could take that would keep me from ever being sick again?"

"That. Aye. And feelin' good, too."

As I ran my hand over the shawl that begged to be stroked, I realized the list in the plus column was growing.

As we stepped into the shop, I said, "I need someone to spell out the downside and not leave anything out." Maggie stopped, but said nothing. "Can I trust you to do that?"

"You can trust me. 'Tis my memory that's in question. It's been so long since we've welcomed a new magistrate I found myself admonishin' Lochlan for no' makin' a gift of a dog, havin' forgot that you can no' accept gifts."

I nodded. "There must be a list somewhere."

"I suppose. You could wander over to Lochlan's office. Second story above the bank. He'd either be there, or walkin' the dogs in the hills, probably imaginin' we're in the Highlands and he's off to herd sheep or some such."

"Well, I suppose getting to know more about shop operations could wait a bit."

"Sure. Go on with ye. I'll be here."

Hearing light steps on the ancient wood floor, we both turned.

"Chime's in," said Dolan. I followed the flick of his gaze upward to see that a windchime either oxidized blue or painted that way hung near the door. "If you want to test it."

"Let's do that before you're off," Maggie said.

She walked out and closed the door behind her. When she turned and reopened the door, the chime tinkled a pleasant little musical sound that I imagined I'd never get tired of hearing.

"Good," she said. "Now you."

Since she was looking at me, I assumed she meant for me to follow suit. I went out, but when I came back in the chime was still as could be.

"There you have it. Dolan's worth his weight in gold," Maggie proclaimed.

I looked at Dolan in time to see a smile go as quickly

as it came. I made a mental note that Dolan appreciates praise. Or recognition for good work. But don't we all?

"Now," I said, "I just have to remember which is which. The chime sounds when humans arrive and is quiet when magical people come in." It was a little mischievous to tease, but I was curious to test their sense of humor.

Maggie looked worried. Dolan scowled.

"No," she said. "Other way 'round."

When I laughed, her face cleared quickly. "Oh! You were havin' me on. Good one, Rita. You got me for sure."

I smiled, secretly delighted that she turned out to be a good sport. Just in case I decided to stay and would be working with her. Glancing at Dolan, I could see that he may not have gotten the joke.

"I was kidding, Dolan," I said.

He blinked three times, then said, "Oh. It was a joke."

Maggie winked at me. "Takes all kinds to make the Maypole work."

While I was intrigued by that, I decided it was a question for another tea time.

"Okay. See you later."

THE LATER MORNING weather was perfect for the shawl still wrapped around my upper body. Cloudy. Cool. Looked like a possibility of rain. Of course, it looked like possible rain most of the time in England. That was okay with me. I like it green.

I found myself smiling as I walked along, shawl clutched in both hands, realizing that I'd never felt so glamorous. I couldn't help wondering if the shawl was bespelled to make the wearer feel euphoric. And pretty.

The law office door was right next to the bank and was nothing more than an entrance to a flight of stairs that led to the upper story. I climbed to the landing above and knocked on the wood door. The hand lettering read Lochlan Jois, Solicitor.

After knocking a second and third time, I concluded he wasn't in. I had no trouble remembering the way to his house. A person didn't need Romeo to get around in Hallow Hill. It was tiny.

I wasn't greeted by dogs when I reached the gate. They might have been inside, but my intuition told me that was unlikely. I had no idea why I would have supposed that. I wasn't the sort of person who relied on such ambiguities as 'inner voices'.

Before I turned away, I took notice of the grounds. The gardens were spectacular. Shiny green leaves. Blooming flowers. Aromatic trailing vines. And I remembered something, perhaps from childhood, about pixies being good with plants.

On impulse, I turned left and began to climb the worn path that led up the hill. I was still wearing the red shoes. They looked truly awful with my blue-green shawl, but impossible as everything else in Hallow Hill, they were as comfortable as running shoes.

The breeze that blew around me smelled as sweet as air must have before combustion engines. And I breathed deep in appreciation.

Just before I reached the top of the hill, I turned and looked down on the village below. It was every bit as picturesque from that vantage point as I would've imagined, and the beauty of it tugged at my heart a little. I heard a voice in my head say, 'Rita. You landed on your feet.'

When I gained the high-point vista, I was struck by the beauty. The green horizon and view to the bluest of lakes below made me wonder if the shoes came with a filter that made colors richer. It seemed to me the sky had never been quite so blue. The grass was impossibly green. The diffused light on the lake created sparkles that were hypnotic. And I remembered thinking how spectacular were the flowering plants in Lochlan's garden.

I might've enjoyed feeling like queen of the world if not for the abject terror that struck my nervous system and caused my heart to race so that I felt it throbbing in my neck.

Lochlan was nearby, perhaps returning from the lake below.

"Hello!" he shouted with a cheer that sounded like he was genuinely glad as he raised a hand in greeting.

Since I was wearing the shoes, I saw his true elven visage. That, of course, wasn't the part that had me thinking I'd breathed my last. The two canines with him were not the friendly Border Collies I'd fallen in love with. They were gray wolves, easily half again as big as any wolves I'd ever seen.

They came running toward me like two streaks. That instigated a fight or flight fear which, in turn, released an unpleasant rush of adrenaline. While I was trying to remember whether standing still or curling into a ball is the better defense, the wolves had overtaken me and were behaving exactly as they had in Bordie Collie form; turning in circles and whining, verbally asking for the attention of hands on fur.

I relaxed into the moment and laughed out loud, feeling the relief of thinking I'd narrowly escaped a gruesome death and also from seeing the monsters behave like giddy puppies.

"Good morning, Angus," I said, steadying my voice as I tried to pet both wolves at the same time. It wasn't hard to do since their backs were even with my hip bone. "Aisling, how are the puppies?"

By this time, Lochlan had caught up to me and the magical creatures I'd thought were dogs.

He was wearing khaki knickerbockers over tan and gray argyle knee socks, like a golfer from a bygone era. There in the pristine beauty of the countryside, he almost made it work.

When I was close enough, I was relieved to see a broad smile on his handsome face.

"Rita! Good to see you out and about this mid-day. Are you walking alone or looking for company?"

"Looking for you, Lochlan. I like your, um, outfit."

He looked down as if he couldn't recall what he was wearing then chuckled. "I suppose this costume is a bit dated. Would you like to walk a ways with me?"

I smiled. "Yes. It's wonderful up here. A little breezy."

He nodded. "That's why the trees are all leaning that direction."

He pointed and I wondered why I hadn't noticed that before. "Huh." After a brief pause, I said, "So the dogs aren't really dogs."

With a delighted chuckle, he said, "Magnificent, aren't they?

"Well, yes. They are. I may have to rethink the request for a, um, puppy."

"We'll see. Creatures such as these always end up where and with whom they're supposed to be."

"Huh," I said, when my brain failed to locate a properly profound response.

"How can I be of service?"

"Well, this shawl..." I ran my hand lovingly down the

bound hem. "Esmerelda tried to make it a gift when she saw that I loved it. Maggie wouldn't hear of it. That led to a discovery that there are rules. Bribery rules? That didn't come up in our discussion last night or I would've mentioned that I've already broken a rule. Molly tried to comp my lunch. There was a good-natured tussle with Mayor Mistral."

Lochlan barked out a laugh at that and repeated. "Mayor Mistral, is it? Did Maggie tell you some nonsense about him being unelected mayor?"

"She did." I nodded. "Yes." I hoped I hadn't spoken out of turn.

"Well, I guess it does no harm to call him that."

"Anyway, he ended up paying for my lunch."

"Technically I suppose it didn't count. Since you haven't officially declared acceptance of the position. You didn't know better at the time, but those scallywags did. I should issue a warning."

I stopped. "A warning? So, there are laws that are enforced? By you?"

"No. There are rules that are enforced by *you*!"

That had my curiosity charging to the forefront, moving my other questions aside.

"How does that work?"

"Well, in addition to hearing and deciding on disputes, you may assess fines, or other punishment, of rulebreakers."

I frowned. "Who keeps track of who's breaking rules?"

With a sidelong look, he said, "That would be myself. I issue citations which must be answered during Court Meet."

"You sort of work for the Court?"

"Yes. You might think of me as your clerk. Of course, it will be your privilege to choose another if you prefer someone else."

There was no question in my mind that Lochlan would be crushed if I decided to replace him with somebody else.

"That means you'd work for me?"

He grinned. "I would."

"The reason why I'm out here is because I asked Maggie if there's like a list of rules and she said you'd know."

He threw his head back in an, "Aha," gesture before nodding once.

"A list of rules, is it? Well, let's see. There's the one you mentioned regarding currying favor with gifts. You're obligated to show up for Court and render decisions. Yes. I think that covers it."

"Who decides what cases are going to be…?"

"Heard?"

"Yes."

"You. Three weeks before Court Meet, you'll be presented with a list of complaints. Briefs you might call them. You can decide to rule on all of them or you can decline some if it's your measured judgment that they have no merit."

"Wow. That sounds like a lot of power."

"You could see it that way. We're preserved because of the power of the Court to sort our differences objectively. We tend to be a quarrelsome lot, often divorced from reason. I think that's been mentioned."

"Not the part about being divorced from reason. You mean crazy?"

Lochlan laughed out loud. "Sometimes it might seem so. It will be up to you to sort it out and keep us… civilized."

"Civilized," I repeated. I liked the sound of that. "I suppose what I want to know is, do I have all the information I need? If I accept, am I going to find out that there was something withheld that might have influenced my decision?"

"Ah. A catch."

"Yes. Exactly."

"I trust that I've presented the whole picture, but if you're still undecided, the aforementioned journals could be beneficial. So far as filling in details."

"That sounds like a sound plan. Where are they?"

"In a safe in your residence. Olivia will show you where it is. She doesn't know the combination, of course. That's for you and me alone to know. Normally I wouldn't be making it available until after the new magistrate is committed, but I'm making an exception in this case."

"Because you think I'm going to accept."

He laughed. "I do, in fact, believe you will accept." He had me repeat the combination three times to be sure I'd remember.

"Who's Olivia?"

"You've not met her?" I shook my head. "Another

oversight. It seems we're becoming lax in our duties." He sighed. "Olivia is the residence caretaker. Your housekeeper, gardener, cook. Whatever you need. She's Dolan's sister."

"I didn't know that a caretaker comes with the deal."

"Yes."

"No wonder you're so sure I'm going to accept. I've never had domestic help, or yard help, or any kind of help. But I guess you know that." He confirmed my guess with his silence as we walked. I chuckled softly, trying to imagine having somebody do everyday chores. "That's a nice perk to add to the package." The list in my plus column was growing by the hour. "So, if she's Dolan's sister, she must be a, um…"

"Brounie."

"And she has a key to the house?"

He stopped. "Yes. I hope that's agreeable. She's honest as the day is long."

I laughed softly. "That's exactly what Maggie said about Dolan."

"And it's true. Olivia is also bound by oath to protect your privacy. Of course, if you find that you don't like her, we'll locate a suitable replacement."

"If she's going to do stuff for me that I hate doing, I'm sure I'm going to *love* her. That brings me to another question. Is there a reliable source where I could learn about magical people? Those I might encounter if I take the job? You know, not fiction and fanciful. The real deal?"

He smiled and slanted his eyes toward me as we walked. "It's a question most likely posed by every new magistrate dating back to the beginning. There's usually some truth in the fictions, but a lot is misguided as well. You'll find a book in the safe with the journals. And on that topic, journaling is optional, but it's good to keep records of what's gone before."

"I get that." We walked on for a few minutes without conversation before I said, "So how many magistrates have you broken in?"

"You're the fifth."

"Lochlan. Etiquette may be different in your culture, which is probably something else I should figure out, but would it be rude to ask how old you are?"

"Five hundred and thirty-two years old," he said.

"Wow. No phone. No lights. No motorcar. Not a single luxury."

"What's that?"

"Nothing. Just a lyric associated with an old TV series."

"I like TV."

"Well, who doesn't?"

"Oh!" He chuckled. "'Gilligan's Island'. I take your point. Your wit and way of looking at things will be a welcome change around here. Yes. I've lived long enough to see some big changes."

"And yet you're still wearing short pants."

He laughed. "Some habits are harder to set aside."

"It seems that you can choose how you appear to humans? So why did you decide to initially present yourself as an old man?"

His answering smile was broad and I was treated to a mischievous twinkle in his too-blue eyes. "Because it was what you expected to see. Whether you knew it or not."

"Huh."

I WALKED ALONG with Lochlan and his wolves for a bit

longer before heading down the hill with study in mind. But by the time I returned it was lunch time, and I was thinking about the list of scrumptious things I had yet to try at the pub.

Instead of going straight back to the Hallows, I detoured for a thick soup.

"Rita!" Molly said. "You're back."

I grinned. "If I stay, you'll get used to seeing me. I could pretty much be happy with choosing from your menu for… well, forever, I guess."

She laughed. "Music to my ears. If you're alone, come and sit here at the bar and chat me up while I work."

"Okay. But I'm an older and wiser woman since my last visit."

"Oh?"

"Yes. I know I'm not supposed to accept free meals."

"Oh that."

"You don't sound sorry."

"Why should I be? It never hurts to be on the right side of the Court."

"Hmmm. That may make it difficult to trust friendships. If people treat me well as an insurance policy."

"You could look at it that way. But you seem nice enough. People can like you *and* have a care for your good side. Both at the same time."

"I suppose, but it could be hard to tell the difference. I don't want to be Tony Soprano; have everybody around me feel like they have to laugh at my jokes even when they're not funny."

"If you want to know whether or not you're genuinely liked, just use your intuition."

I chuckled. "The obvious reply, the one that comes to mind first is, what intuition?"

She cocked her head. "All creatures have intuition. Yours may be blocked or underdeveloped, but even in humans it's more reliable than the weatherman."

I laughed. "There's a low bar."

"Your inner voice is there. You've just forgotten how to find it. Perhaps I could help with that."

In an attempt to be playful, I said, "Is that a bribe?"

"No," she said, her expression serious, "it's friendship."

"Oh. Well, thank you. Uh. Maybe."

With a smile, she slid a menu in front of me. "Know

what you're having?"

I looked at the chalkboard. "I will try the winter white soup."

"Your cheeks are rosy like you've been out on the moors this windy day. My soup should be just the thing."

I didn't say that in fact I had been out on the 'moors', but I agreed the soup sounded better than the fare that I imagined might be offered at any Relais & Châteaux restaurant.

The soup came with an individual-sized loaf of coarse artisan bread and a tiny pot of softened butter. I tried to keep my yummy sounds inaudible to others, but I was sure I would remember that lunch as one of my top five meals of all time.

Molly reappeared in front of me when there was a break in the action and smirked when she saw the result. "No one will object if you want to lick the bowl."'

I gave her a frown and deadpanned, "I don't know what you mean. I didn't like it at all." I took pity and didn't leave her looking confused and trying to decide what to say for long. I laughed. "Just joking. I plan to move into the kitchen and live here."

She returned my laugh and was clearly relieved. "Would you like bread pudding?"

"Oh no. Maybe tonight though. I'll be back for dinner."

"We'll be honored to have you. Since you've made a point of saying you prefer to pay, here's the bill." When she slid the small slip of paper toward me, my face fell. I must've looked worried because she said, "Something wrong?"

"Um. Well. After all that, I left the shop without my, um, purse."

She chuckled, shaking her head. "Geoffrey!" she called.

A lanky, aproned young man appeared almost instantly from the rear, throwing a long towel over his shoulder as he neared. He cast a brief glance my way before saying, "Yes, Miss?"

"This customer is trying to slide on her bill."

He looked at me as if he knew who I was and blanched. "Uhhhhh," he said.

Molly laughed. "No. I'm having you on." Gotta love a woman with a great sense of humor. "Run down to the Hallows and tell Maggie MacHenry that we have a wayward magistrate here with a bill to pay and no purse."

Geoffrey inhaled with relief. "Yes, Miss."

He hung the towel on a hook on the back bar and hurried out still wearing the apron.

"That's so much better than calling the authorities on me."

She laughed again. "That would be hard to do, wouldn't it? Since *you're* the 'authorities'."

I watched Molly manage the growing lunch trade, many of whom stared at me with open curiosity, but not for long. Since I was wearing the shoes, I was treated to a menagerie of strange sights and, certainly, there was no lingering doubt that Lochlan, Maggie, and Ivy were telling the truth about who and what they were. At least a quarter of the people who filed in looked fully human to me, even with shoes, just like Maggie, Molly, Geoffrey, and Keir. I planned to ask Maggie to expound on 'two-natured', but it didn't make the top five of my growing to-do list.

In less time than I would've thought possible, Geoffrey rushed back in. He stood on my right and handed a bill over the bar to Molly. "She said to tell you, 'Here's a tenner. If the bill is less than that, you can keep the change.

If it's more than that, you should be ashamed of yourself."

Molly laughed as she took the ten-pound note then looked at me with a smile that formed laugh lines around her eyes, lines that enhanced her attraction factor, in my opinion. But I did wonder why someone as lighthearted as Molly was dating someone as serious as Dolan.

"You're free to go," Molly said.

I nodded as I slid off my stool. "See you later."

"Don't forget the coin. Supper's not free, you know," she teased.

With a smirk I left, thinking Molly must be one of the magical community's best ambassadors.

I RUSHED THROUGH the Hallows front door, confirmed that there were no customers, and called out, "Maggie!"

She appeared immediately. "Right here."

"Change of plans. I can learn about store operations later." I remembered to add, "If I stay," but that amendment was sounding more diluted and less true every time I said it. "Where would I find Olivia?"

"Have ye met Olivia?"

"No. Lochlan told me about her."

"High time to correct that oversight then. She may be at the house. If no', I can send someone to fetch her." Maggie started to unlock the inner door that led to the residence kitchen, but stopped. "I should no' go bargin' uninvited into your new home, Magistrate. Come to think of it, I should have Dolan change the locks so that only you and Olivia have keys. Would ye prefer to access your house this way or 'round front?"

I smiled. "It's thoughtful of you to ask. I may feel differently after a while."

It was Maggie's turn to finish a sentence for me. "If you stay." She smiled like it was both joke and conspiracy.

"Yes." I took a little pleasure in the easy familiarity of her teasing. "If I stay. But for right now, I like going through the front door." I lifted my tote from the chair where I'd left it and looped the strap over my shoulder.

"Front door 'tis!" Maggie turned on her heel and marched toward the front of the shop. "Dolan! Watch the store!" she said loudly enough to raise the dead.

I turned the key thinking the only thing that stood between me and calling the house mine was a simple, "Yes." I glanced over my shoulder at the garage across the lane and, in spite of feeling foolish, wondered if Romeo was okay.

When I opened the door, I felt like I was stepping into aromatic paradise. Apparently, Olivia used cleaners or polishes that left behind the scent of jasmine. Or was it tea tree? Or lavender? It was impossible to nail it down, but suffice to say I liked it a lot. The living area was empty, but there was no doubt she'd been there.

I walked over to the kitchen and leaned in.

A heavy glass pedestal bowl that held a variety of fresh fruit sat in the center of the small table. And the biggest yellow dendrobium I'd even seen sat on the garden windowsill above the sink. It was continually disconcerting that these people knew details about me down to my favorite orchid. It was oddly nice at the same time. The thought also flickered across my mind that this fabulous plant would thrive in that location, just the right amount of filtered light, easy to water once a week.

On the kitchen counter was a handwritten note on heavy linen cardstock the size and shape of a dinner party place card. It read, 'Welcome home,' in an impressive calligraphy script that looked like it had been written with an actual ink pen. An art that was all but lost in modern times.

"Call her," Maggie encouraged.

I glanced at Maggie, retraced my steps to the living room and raised my voice. "Olivia?"

I heard a soft thump and within seconds a female version of Dolan was gliding down the stairs. She was wearing a black shirtwaist dress, a black apron, and black riding boots. An odd combination, and yet it could pass for 'domestic chic', especially with her tall, lean model's body.

"Yes, madam," she said as she descended. "I haven't finished the bath, but you have fresh sheets, fresh towels, I've laid the fires here," she gestured toward the living room fireplace as she reached the bottom of the stairs, "and upstairs." I knew she meant the fireplace in the bedroom. "I've put your things away, mended a tear in one of your scarves, and stocked the kitchen with your favorite things. I would require perhaps half an hour to finish? Or I could come back later?"

I supposed I'd never met a person who took their job so seriously. I was a little gobsmacked by the idea of a person being that dedicated to my service. Life hadn't just taken a turn. It had done an about-face.

I smiled and held out my hand. "Olivia, I'm Rita."

"Yes, Magistrate."

She shook my hand softly, and I could tell she was struggling to suppress a curtsey. Perhaps Molly was right. My intuition might be attempting a debut. I let the 'Magistrate' go. If for some reason she felt more comfortable with formality, who was I to impose my customs on her?

"That was a really comprehensive list," I said. "Thank you for taking care of that." Turning to Maggie, I said, "Thanks, Maggie. I've got this."

"Oh! Aye! Very well, I'll be off then."

After hearing the door close, I said, "Lochlan says you can tell me where to find the safe."

Olivia nodded. "It's upstairs." There was no conspicuous clue that it was a question, but there was definitely a question written on her face.

"Will you show me?"

"Of course," she said, already climbing the stairs as she spoke.

She went straight to the bank of four triple armoires

that occupied most of one wall and stopped at the second from the end. It looked no different from the other three impressive pieces until Olivia opened the door and took hold of a brass pull. The entire section pulled away from the unit and rolled toward me with impressively quiet and well-disguised wheels.

I looked at the floor to see if repeated rolling had left a telltale track, but the armoires sat partially on an extremely low pile, tightly woven Persian rug; the value of which would surely exceed my net worth. The rug was fine enough to withstand hundreds, if not thousands, of trips to the safe without giving up evidence.

The wall behind the now-vacant section of armoire revealed an embedded safe a little taller than I am.

Without looking at Olivia, I said, "That's incredibly clever."

"Yes, madam." She nodded.

I turned to her. "So. Do you live around here?"

"In the mill house. With my brother."

Her eyes were just as arresting as Dolan's. Curious to see what she looked like without the red shoes, I stepped out of them. She looked the same except for human-shaped pupils and it was amazing what a difference that one detail made.

"Do you like it here?"

I could see that she was dumbfounded by the question and my approach to social interactions, which was American-casual. After a couple of beats, her face broke into a grin. The sort of smile I was sure Dolan was incapable of.

"Yes, madam. I like it here."

"Do you like doing this kind of work?"

"Oh, yes. Very much. It doesn't take long to do daily upkeep. I'll always be available for whatever you need. I'm good at cooking. If you want lunches at home, just leave me a note the day before. Same for dinner. My brother is good with all kinds of repairs. Even electronics."

"I don't know what more I could ask for." That sentence echoed in my head a few times. So why was I delaying a decision? Oh yeah. Due diligence. "This is a big surprise for me. A wonderful surprise. But until an hour ago I had no idea that you work here."

"For you," she corrected.

"Pardon?"

"I work for you. If you decided to live someplace else, I would take care of that place instead."

"I see. But I haven't definitely decided to stay."

"You haven't?" she said as if that was incomprehensible.

"I'm close, but I want to review some journals of past magistrates. That's the only way I can see to get a real feel for the job. That's why I'm here." I looked at the safe.

Her eyes drifted that direction. "The bath?"

"Yes. Go ahead and finish up. Oh. And about cooking. I had thought that, if I stay, I'd eat two meals a day at the pub. The food there is…"

I noticed Olivia was smirking. "Adequate."

I was going to say delicious, scrumptious, marvelous, out-of-this-world or something of that sort. I was definitely not going to say 'adequate'. I wondered if there was some rivalry with Molly because of occupying Dolan's time and attention, but that thought came too close to the ear markings of a small-town gossip hole. So, I gave myself an internal slap.

"If your cooking is better than the pub, then it truly is remarkable."

She stood a little straighter and raised her chin. "Anything you can name, I can make for you."

"That is quite a claim."

I could see by the responding gleam in her eye that she'd enjoy being challenged. My newfound intuition was telling me that Olivia got personal satisfaction from her work.

With a plan to start easy and graduate the difficulty depending on performance, I said, "Seafood gumbo with shrimp." She smiled and nodded as if she made that for lunch every day. "Do you think you can figure out hushpuppies?"

"Yes," she said, simply.

"I like a little bit of onion in the batter."

"Yes, madam."

"Okay. You're on. Twelve o'clock tomorrow. Make enough for four. Maggie, Dolan, you, and I will have lunch in the kitchen."

Her face fell. And things had been going so well.

Since she seemed not to be able to talk, I said, "Olivia, did I say something to make you speechless?"

"I…"

"Look. If I do decide to stay, we're going to have to make a pact. I need you to speak freely around me and I need you to overlook my faux pas."

"Well, I've never thought of myself at a station to sit at the magistrate's table. I feel certain Dolan would think the same."

I stared for a couple of beats and then laughed out loud. "Well, indulge me. As you might guess, I don't know a lot of people here and I don't want to have lunch alone. By the way, can I get ginger ale here? The good kind? Canada Dry?"

She grinned. "Stocked in your icebox."

"You know a lot more about me than I know about you. We'll have to remedy that."

Again, she looked uncomfortable. But if I stayed, I would wear her down with my coarse and classless American ways.

"I'll tell Maggie and Dolan we're having Cajun lunch tomorrow."

"Yes, Magistrate."

I sighed. "I prefer Rita. If it's too much of a stretch to call me that, just say okay. Yes, Magistrate, makes me feel like I'm a character in a B movie." I could see that I'd made her feel uncertain again. "Don't worry. If I stay, you'll get used to me." She opened her mouth and looked unsure. So I helped her out. "It's easy. Just say, ok-a-a-a-ay."

"Okay," she repeated.

"See? That didn't hurt at all." I think I saw a little smile. "I'll put the armoire back when I'm through."

"Yes… Okay."

THE SAFE HAD an electronic touchpad with backlights so the darkness in the armoire was of no consequence. I typed in the combination and heard a series of beeps, which I took to mean, "You're in!"

When I spun the wheel and pulled the heavy door open, I wasn't looking at a compartment the size of a refrigerator's interior, which is what I expected. I was looking at a well-lit room, longer than it was wide, with leather bound journals on shelves organized by year. I'd thought there might be a few journals that would provide some bedtime reading. Maybe educate. Maybe entertain. Maybe both. But this was more like what the library at

Alexandria probably looked like before it was burned.

I took a deep breath. Where to begin? The earliest record or most recent?

I finally decided on most recent, partly so there wouldn't be stumbling blocks to expression since language is always evolving. I took the journal on the top of the stack and turned to go. My eyes landed on a tome sitting alone on a shelf. It was covered in midnight blue velvet. Three different shaped mirrors were embedded on the front cover; a circle, a triangle, and a crescent moon, On the right side was a large brass clasp with a keyhole, although I didn't see a key.

My guess was that it was the definitive work on magical people that Lochlan had suggested might be found in the safe. I reached for the clasp, which slid in my hand like it had been made for me to open. The pages were parchment with descriptions written by hand, accompanied by colorfully illuminated illustrations and ink drawings. My first thought was that it was a treasure to rival the Book of Kells.

I took the blue velvet book, which probably weighed ten pounds, sat down in the huge "nap chair" by the fireplace and opened the book on the matching ottoman.

Within minutes Olivia had finished her work and asked if I'd like to have her phone number in case I needed anything at any time of day or night. This was going to take some getting used to.

As she left the room I said, "Looking forward to our lunch tomorrow."

When she hesitated at the door, I could tell her shoulders had stiffened. I smiled. I was going to take some getting used to as well.

"Okay," she said before continuing down the stairs. Among other wonderful things, Olivia was a fast learner.

After that I was, apparently, sucked into a virtual vortex of magic and surreality. Fairy tales and adventure. History and fantasy. It seemed that humans had virtually forever been sharing the world, side by side, with magic and its expression in animate form. It seemed impossible that the two could occupy the same physical space with such a thin veil of separation. On the other hand, it was clear to me that, at various times, the magical world had punctured humans' fragile grasp on denial.

When I heard my phone buzz, I looked at the time

and realized I'd been sitting there for hours.

"Hello?"

"Sorry to disturb you, Magistrate." It was Maggie. "But there's a rascal come to call for you. Somethin' about supper at the pub."

"Oh, gee. I got caught up. Please tell him I'm sorry and I'll be there in five."

"You're on speaker. He heard."

After hurrying to replace the book in the safe and leave the armoire in disguise mode, I eyed my tan leather ankle boots, because I thought I could use a little normalcy, but I knew the best choice was to slip back into the red shoes. I grunted out loud at the idiocy of thinking 'normal' would ever be normal again. If I stayed, extranormal, supernormal, paranormal… Strike the prefixes. Those things would be my normal.

I pulled on *the* shawl. It was all I needed to make me feel presentable. I was sure it was just a shawl, but it made me feel pretty enough to almost think it cast a glamour. As I dashed to the bathroom mirror to check lipstick, I reminded myself that it was not a date. It was outrageously silly for me to feel jittery like a cute boy passed a note in eighth grade.

I ran out the front door chastising myself for making too much of a casual dinner. Perhaps something in Esmerelda's tea caused me to remember Keir Culain's looks as being gorgeous enough to make a woman salivate. Since that was very unlikely, I scoffed out loud as I rushed around the corner and almost ran into him. He was waiting on the sidewalk in front of the shop.

And OMG.

My memory was fine, all cylinders firing. He was every inch a fantasy.

"Hello!" He laughed, as he (thankfully) caught me before I slammed into him. I had a feeling that would have left him unfazed, but me the worse for wear.

My responding laugh was pure nerves and embarrassment. "I'm so sorry I'm late. I'm *never* late. It's almost like a religion with me. But I got caught up in this book about magical people and completely lost track of the time."

He wore a deep khaki-colored sweater that made the green in his eyes even more intense.

"Slow down. All is well. I'm not on a schedule tonight." He said this with a 'fuck me' smile that had me staring at his lips while appreciating the English soft c pronunciation of the word 'schedule'. When my eyes came back up to meet his, he said, "You look beautiful in this." He reached out and rubbed a section of the shawl between his fingers. "Matches your eyes. Is it from Esmerelda's?"

"Um, yeah," I said sounding stupid in comparison to his very smart-sounding British accent. "She tried to give it to me. Next thing I knew Maggie was talking about bribery." Keir laughed. "I guess I bought it. Maggie said something to Esmerelda about putting it on the tab. No plastic was used. No currency was exchanged. But I'm the proud owner of this piece of art and I guess that's what counts. Right?"

On the inside I grimaced at the way I was babbling and hoped that it didn't show on the outside.

"Right." He smiled. "Hungry?"

I nodded as I started walking toward the pub. "The thought of Molly's menu may always make me hungry."

He looked surprised. "You've decided to stay."

"No. I didn't say that."

"You didn't. I thought it sounded like. Well, never

mind."

As we walked, I said, "Yeah. If you think you're hearing inner conflict, it's because my decision-maker is ping-ponging on a five second loop."

"I suppose it's up to me to close the deal over dinner." He slanted his smile toward me. "Feeling the pressure, as you Americans say."

I laughed. "No pressure. I mean what do you really care? If I don't take the job, some other person who is sure to be more qualified will be over the moon to get it. The compensation package is better than a lottery win. The village is a dream. The people are nice. At least those I've met. And the position comes with the kind of respect few people ever get to experience."

"Well, then. Sounds like my job is done." He clapped his hands. "I knew I was good, but even I had no idea my powers of persuasion are so advanced that no persuading is necessary."

With a chuckle, I said, "I guess it does sound like I'm doing a sales job on myself. But there's no denying the perks." I decided to shift the conversation away from myself, even if just for a while. "So, you don't live in the town."

"No. Towns scare me."

I barked out a laugh. "*This* town scares you?!? That's impossible." He shrugged. "Okay. So, it is the noise? The smog? The rush hour traffic? The muggings?"

He smiled. "The herpes." When my mouth fell open, he laughed. "A joke, love. Herpes is a human thing."

"Of course, it is. So, you live in the country all by yourself?"

"If you're inquiring as to my 'social status'? I'm single. Yes. I live by myself." He pulled open the pub door. "You know one of the very best things about Hallow Hill?"

"What?"

"This is one of the last pubs in the whole of Britain that does not have tellies playing football matches all the day and night. It doesn't even have to be a live match. They'll play endless reruns, most places. Bugger if I get it. The whole point of a pub is conversation. Right?"

"Right." I nodded, liking him more every minute. It was easy to be amiable on that point because I happened to agree. Wholeheartedly. Not being familiar with any other place in Britain I didn't know the charm of Molly's pub had become unique. Now that my consciousness had been raised, it was another item in the plus column, which in a way made no sense. If I went back home the question of tellied pubs and non-tellied pubs wasn't on the radar.

Keir caught Molly's eye behind the bar and pointed to a table off to the far side next to the cold, but still ambient fireplace. He let me choose where to sit. I took the chair with my back to the room so that I'd be spared the curious stares and could just enjoy dinner.

When Keir had settled into his chair, Geoffrey stepped over. I looked up and was greeted by a nod and a smile.

"Magistrate," he said simply.

I cocked my head. "I know what you're thinking, Geoffrey. And, yes. I did bring money."

He grinned and looked at Keir, who said, "Dark pint. What's the catch?"

"North Sea haddock."

"I'll have that broiled with lemon on the side," Keir said.

They both looked at me.

"Um. I'll have a Mike's Hard Cranberry Lemonade." I said it knowing that they definitely wouldn't have it, just to see if I could throw Geoffrey off guard.

But he surprised me responding, "Bottle or glass?"

I gaped. "You're not saying you have Mike's Hard Cranberry Lemonade."

Geoffrey was clearly enjoying this. "I am saying that. Yes."

"Ah. Well, bottle. Definitely." When he stood patiently, continuing to smile, I realized he was waiting for me to tell him what I wanted to eat. "Oh. I'll have what he's having." I then glanced at Keir as if Geoffrey might not know who was being referenced. Which was beyond silly. "I don't suppose you have, um, tartar sauce?"

With hands clasped behind his back, Geoffrey rocked on his toes and nodded. "Molly made some fresh for you."

"Okay. So does everybody in Hallow Hill know everything there is to know about me?" It may have come out sounding more challenging than I intended.

Geoffrey's smile fell and he looked like he'd love nothing more than to run, but props for standing his ground. "No madam. I don't think so. I believe Lochlan let your preferences be known here so that your favorites would always be available."

"Oh," I said, calming down a little. I narrowed my eyes. "How could she know I'd want fish?"

"Maybe it was a guess? It's really popular."

I inhaled deeply. "Alright. It sounds less creepy when you explain it like that." Keir barked out a laugh. I looked over at him then back at Geoffrey. "Thank you. I didn't mean to sound…"

"Intimidating?" Keir supplied.

After giving my dinner companion a withering look, I said, "I was going to say harsh."

Keir just chuckled and leaned back in his chair.

"Yes madam." Geoffrey's hurried exit seemed more like a retreat than a departure and I was genuinely sorry I'd unloaded on him.

With arms crossed over his middle, smiling like the Cheshire cat, Keir said, "Creepy, eh? Is that what you think of us?"

"That's an overstatement. But I will say this. Having so many people know so much about me is…"

"Creepy?"

"I'm trying to find a synonym. But yeah. For twenty years I was married to a man who probably couldn't tell you for sure whether or not I like tartar sauce with fish. But Molly, and Geoffrey, people whose last names I don't know, for that matter I don't even know if they *have* last names… These people know I like Mike's Hard Cranberry Lemonade and tartar sauce with my fish."

Keir's eyes were still sparkling and his mouth was lifted at one corner, but he nodded agreeably and said, "I can understand how that could be off-putting for someone used to her privacy." He paused for a drink of black something. "So your husband was a tosser?"

I looked justifiably confused. "I'm trying to imagine what that means and all I'm getting is an image of a game called horseshoes." I could see he'd never heard of it. "You toss horseshoes at a stake in the ground."

He chuckled. "Magistrate. You're like a fresh breeze of delight. I can see why the Powers That Be chose you."

"You can? Why?"

"When did you arrive? Yesterday morning?"

"Um-hmm."

"Your world's been turned on its ear and, from where I sit, you appear to be taking it well. Extraordinarily so, wouldn't you say? I don't think most humans would stick around after the initial..." he leaned forward, mischief in his eyes, and said, "introduction."

"You mean my dinner at Lochlan's house? Last night?"

"Is that how they did it? Fed you Beef Wellington and showed you their true forms?"

"It was pot roast, but what's your point?"

He held up his hands. "No criticism. That's as good an approach as any. There's no easy way to tell a human that the world isn't what they think it is. For most, it would be just as hard to accept as no solid ground, no gravity, no planetary revolution."

"You're not going to tell me that, are you?"

He laughed. "And that's the other thing that makes you precious. Levity."

"These things are only funny to you because you're English and I'm not." After a brief pause, I said, "Was that an assumption? You are English, right?"

"I'm not big on geographical boundaries. I'm at home anywhere on the British Isles. I can speak Irish and Welsh, and I can understand the Scots, which is probably harder than learning another language. And I suspect you're funny no matter where you are."

"I hate to disappoint you, but you should leave the psychic stuff to Esmerelda. If people who know me well were asked to list my better qualities, comedy wouldn't even come up."

He laughed silently. "I don't see how that's possible. But whatever you say. Did Esmerelda tell your fortune?"

"She tried."

"What did she say?"

"That I'd be happy here."

"Is that all?"

"Yes," I lied.

A beautiful bottle of Mike's was set in front of me before I'd even realized Geoffrey had returned. He set a glass mug of Guinness in front of Keir. I'd barely gotten in a, "thank you," before he left without a word.

"Do I need to do some damage control where Geoffrey's concerned?"

"I don't know." Keir was sitting back with his chin tucked. He looked at me through his lashes. "Are you staying?"

"I'm taking that to mean the answer is yes. If I stay, I

need to smooth things over with Geoffrey."

The multicolored locks moved beguilingly when Keir shook his head. "Just playing with you, Magistrate. Geoffrey's fine. Nothing you've done requires forgiveness."

"What is he?"

"What?" Keir asked.

I narrowed my eyes. "Don't play dumb. You know what I mean."

He turned the mug around and around on the table, seemingly deciding what to say. "Some of us are two-natured. I am. He is."

"Maggie said that about herself. She said she's fae."

"Yes. She's fae and two-natured."

"You don't want to tell me what you are, do you?" His face spread into a gorgeous, boyish smile just before he shook his head. "Okay. It's a mystery. This could be fun. So, question? Would I find you in the book?"

"The book?" He cocked his head.

"Yeah, there's a book. A wonderful book. As a matter of fact, it's the reason why I was running late for dinner tonight. It's like an encyclopedic catalog. A compendium of magical people and, um, creatures. Lochlan told me it's the final word on everything I want to know and am afraid to ask."

"Lochlan said that?"

"No. That was paraphrasing. But it's true. So would I find you in the book?"

He thought about that for a couple of beats and said, "I've never seen the book, but you shouldn't shy away from a bet that my kind are represented therein."

"Geoffrey, too?"

"Geoffrey, too."

"But you don't want to tell me."

The smile returned. "If you stay, I vow that I will show you the other side of my nature. When you come to my house for tea."

"Strawberries and clotted cream?"

"Let's not lose sight of priorities."

"Okay. Then I'll add that to the items in my plus column."

He looked interested in that and sat up straighter. "What are the other things in your plus column?"

Before I could start through the list, Geoffrey returned

with two large oval-shaped plates and a cutting board with fresh baked bread, soft butter, and a small pewter container of tartar sauce. The fish was accompanied by mashed potatoes, peas, and carrots.

"This looks perfect," I said to Geoffrey, who didn't respond. "Geoffrey." He looked up when I used his name. "I'm sorry if I was too abrupt earlier. Please don't hold it against me."

His eyes widened. "No, Magistrate. I was afraid I'd given offense."

"Not in the least. I've spent my life doing things for other people and having people try to anticipate what will please me is very new. It's the best kind of privilege, but it takes some getting used to. Thank you."

He flushed like he was embarrassed, glanced at Keir, smiled, nodded, and hurried off.

"Would people who know you well list kindness as one of your well-known qualities?"

"I don't know."

"Yes, you do." I slathered some tartar sauce on the fish, squeezed some lemon on top of that, took a bite, and groaned out loud. "And I understand you're newly single.

We have that in common."

"You're newly single?"

He grinned. "I meant the single part. Not the new part."

"Well, yes. I'm newly dumped. Single part is a legal status I look forward to."

"Dumped," he repeated. "It's hard to imagine a man giving you up voluntarily."

I smiled, took another bite, chewed, swallowed, and said, "Exactly the kind of thing a player would say. You don't have to flatter me to persuade me to stay, Keir."

"I'd tell you that it's not flattery, but I strongly suspect you wouldn't believe me. So, let's get back to the plus column. I want to hear what's on the list."

"Well, it's surprisingly long."

He brightened. "All the better."

"Alright. Let's see. This is not in any particular order. If I stay, I'm set for life financially. I like the house. I like the store and, um, what's in it. I like Maggie. I like Lochlan. And Ivy, I think." He raised an eyebrow at that. "It's not a judgment. I just don't know her as well," I added. "I like Molly. I like Fie."

"Fie?"

"You don't know him?"

"I do know him."

"Well, he and I had lunch here yesterday. He paid, but that was before I knew about the bribery rule." Keir looked unhappy about that development. "Is something wrong? Do you not like Fie?"

"I suppose he's a decent sort."

"Not exactly a stellar endorsement."

He shrugged and looked unlikely to say more on the subject. So I continued.

"The village is almost like time travel to a nicer time. I like walking Lochlan's, um, 'dogs'." Keir grinned when I put that in air quotes. "He said that if I stay I could buy one of Aisling's puppies that would grow up to be a nice, lovable medium-sized dog. I was all in for that when I thought we were talking puppies. Then I saw them with my shoes on. I can't lie and say that having domestic help isn't an offer almost too good to refuse." Looking around, I said, "I like the food. Oh. I like the car."

"The car?"

"Yes. He was given to me at the airport."

"He?"

Being caught at having assigned gender to an inanimate object made me blush. "Yeah. Romeo. It sounds crazy, but it's a self-driving car with a male voice and it can carry on a conversation."

"And you named it Romeo."

"Well, I didn't name it. Exactly. It's an Alfa Romeo."

He whistled. "That tells you they must want you very badly. Like a signing bonus."

"Did I mention the magical garden?"

"No."

"In the middle of the little courtyard there's a tree. Only it's not the same tree. It changes. Yesterday it was a blood orange tree. Today it's a pink tulip tree."

He smiled like a person who didn't find such wonders extraordinary.

"I met the vampire, but didn't know about the magical nature of the population. Molly was in the back. He was standing in the middle of the store not moving and not talking."

Keir chuckled. "That sounds like him." Keir lifted the pint to take a big swig.

"So I told him to buy something or get out."

He almost spit out the beer that had been on the way down. The near-strangulation was followed by red-faced laughter. "I would have loved to see that. What did he do?"

"He bought the most expensive piece in the shop."

"You see, Rita? This is exactly why we need you. The place needs a little shaking up. A new perspective."

"I'm completely unqualified to be a judge, Keir. That's the bottom line that everybody seems intent on overlooking."

"You weren't selected by committee." He wagged his head back and forth. "Well, I guess you were, but the committee that picked you is infallible. Because the Powers That Be…"

"Are never wrong."

"Guess you heard that before."

"What gave you that idea?"

"What's in the negative column?"

That brought me up short. What was in the negative column? I blinked a few times trying to remember what I'd mentally deposited on the downside.

"Um, I don't know what a tosser is."

Keir looked askance. "Seriously?"

"You know what I mean. That's an example of language differences. Then there's culture. No telling what kind of norms and customs I'll stumble all over. I could leave a trail of offense that'll be written about for centuries to come."

Keir snorted into his mug. "You're as dramatic as the Irish. You'll fit right in."

"Where are the kids?"

"Kids?"

"You heard me."

He looked around, nodded toward someone behind me, then said, "We're long-lived and aren't compelled to reproduce. Like humans."

"So, it really is an adults-only kind of community." He had nothing to say to that. "I'm not saying that's a dealbreaker."

"There aren't any families with young who live here in Hallow Hill, but families come to Court Week."

"Oh? Why?"

"Well, sometimes parents are involved in disputes. Mostly it's because of the festival. A gathering of the clans you might say."

"I see."

"I was prepared to do a hard sell, but it seems you've already done the work for me. Your plus column is a long list of excellent reasons to accept the post. Your minus column doesn't have anything on it."

"I was told my daughter would not be welcome to move here."

"You have an adult daughter?"

"The surprise that accompanies that question is a very player kind of line. Just so you know that I know. My daughter is in college. Whether or not she could be called an adult depends on one's point of view."

He chuckled. "Does she want to move here?"

"No."

"Is she likely to want to move here?"

"No."

"Is this a moot point and you know it?"

"Yes.

"What else?" I pressed my lips together trying to decide whether or not I liked being called out on my bull honky. "What's *really* holding you back?"

“The big unknown.”

“And what is that?”

“Precisely. There’s no way to know what the big unknown is until you’re into a thing. There’s always something they don’t tell you about surgery until it’s too late.”

“I admit to not knowing about that.”

“Well, yeah, but there’s going to be that something. The big unknown. The thing that makes you ask yourself why you did blank, blank, blank. You know what I mean?”

“Honestly? No. But here’s the thing. I’ve never heard of a magistrate having regrets about accepting the position. I don’t think you’ve begun to understand how important you are.”

“Tell me this. Why do you care? I mean what does it mean to you personally? Why take time to try to convince me?”

He looked away again. It seemed to be something he did when he thought the next words from his mouth were important and he wanted to get them right. While he was thinking Geoffrey came to collect plates.

“Dessert?” Geoffrey asked.

"What do you have tonight?" Keir asked.

"Crème brulee and sticky pudding."

Keir looked at me.

"Do you like both?" I asked.

"I do," Keir said.

"Then let's get both so I can try a little of each."

"A sound plan," Keir said.

"And coffee," I told Geoffrey.

When he was gone, Keir said, "First, things feel unsettled when there's no magistrate. To everybody in the magical world including me. It's like a disturbance in the Force."

I couldn't help but laugh. "Magical people use *Star Wars* references?"

"I don't think there are any generalities that apply to every one of us, but I love the movies."

"Me, too. What's second?"

"I'm interested in you."

"You're interested in me?" He nodded. Knowing that he couldn't possibly mean 'interested' in a romantic way, I asked for clarification. "Interested in me in what way?"

He blinked several times while looking dumbfounded.

"Rita, if you have a daughter, I feel sure you understand what it means when a male indicates interest."

I felt my lips part while unwanted images of writhing in tangled sheets played across my mind.

"Well, let's see. Molly and Fie offered me meals. Esmerelda offered me this shawl. Now you're offering to give…"

He was shaking his head and smiling. "I don't want to be unnecessarily vulgar, but I'm very much hoping to *take* as much as I give."

When I realized my mouth was making the shape of an, "Oh," while I struggled to overcome speechlessness, I wanted to slap myself. Again. What was that expression? There's no fool like an old fool?

After relocating both my brain and speech, I said, "I'm sure that has to be against the rules."

"It's not," he said smoothly.

"Well, maybe it should be. And besides, legally, I'm a married woman."

He laughed. "Say yes to the offer and there will be plenty of time to explore our, em, compatibility. When you're free in every sense of the word."

The idea of being free in every sense of the word again brought a parade of images that heightened my color.

"Rita. Are you blushing?"

He was far too pleased with himself. I opened my mouth to tell him so, but realized someone who was not Geoffrey had stopped at the table. I looked up at Fie's smiling face.

"Good evening, Magistrate." He nodded at Keir polite-ly.

Keir, I noticed, glared in return. I wondered what sort of issue was between them and hoped it wouldn't show up in my court.

Had I just thought *show up in my court*?

"Hello," I said. "Have you eaten? The haddock was amazing."

"Not yet," Fie said. "Perhaps I'll try it. I just stopped by to see if you're settled in."

"What you really want to know is if I've decided to stay," I countered.

He grinned. "Exactly right. So have you?"

I wanted to keep my gaze locked on Fie as I answered, but I couldn't help a glance at Keir. Fie noticed it, too.

"Right after dessert, I'm going home and diving into journals. I plan to decide by tomorrow afternoon. Right after lunch."

"Very good. You're having lunch here?"

"No. I'm playing a game with Olivia. She claimed to be able to cook anything I could name. So I asked for a Cajun meal for lunch tomorrow and invited Maggie and Dolan to join us."

"That sounds like a gambling event. I'll get odds started on whether or not you'll like lunch," he said.

"Please tell me that's a joke."

He looked serious. "Do you want it to be a joke?"

"Yes. You could even say that I insist it be a joke."

"Very well." He smiled. "We'll look forward to your acceptance tomorrow after lunch."

"My acceptance or regrets that I must decline."

"Is that a joke?" he teased. I laughed. Keir remained silent. "Alright. I'll let you have your dessert in peace."

When he left, I said, "Okay. Now you have to tell me about your beef with Fie."

"My *beef*?"

"Problem. Issue. Is it a grudge? Is it a rivalry? An ongoing argument? What?"

"If you must know, I don't trust him."

"Why not?"

"He's an air elemental."

"I don't know what that means. Should I look it up? In the book?"

He was nodding. "I would."

"Okay. Done. It's so weird that all this is going on without, um, us knowing about it. I'm still struggling with how that's even possible."

He shrugged. "The magical are not as dense as Mundies. Human eyes see the world through a thickish filter because their vibration is different. It allows their brains to process the mundane world and nothing else. Magic kind are less fragile and more ethereal. I know that sounds like a paradox, but it's true nonetheless. We don't have that filter. Seeing both magical and mundane worlds, or either, is optional for us. You're one of a few dozen humans whose vibration has been charmed so that you can see what we see. At least you will when the magic has settled in." He smiled as he pushed the cup of crème brûlée toward me in a silent invitation to have the last of it. When

I shook my head, he scooped up the last. "I noticed you wore the shoes tonight."

"I thought about leaving them behind. I thought maybe I'd reached my daily max for things that shouldn't exist and wanted to step back into Mundiedom for the evening."

"Mundiedom? Rita. You are a treasure."

Keir's seductive smile and suggestive ways reminded me of every lecture I'd ever given my daughter about running the other way when you encounter such a man. On the other hand, as a woman in midlife in the process of being divorced by a man whose fantasy is two twenty-two-year-olds, what do I know?

"I don't know how long it will take, but the magic will adhere itself to you like a second skin. There will be a time, certainly before Hallows, when you'll not be able to retreat to Mundiedom. Your magical eyes will be permanently open. In all but genetics you'll be one of us."

"And there it is. An item for my minus column."

"Nonsense. Here's another movie reference for you. You've been offered a choice between the blue pill and the red pill. Know which one you're going to choose?"

"No."

"Liar."

I sighed. "The red pill," I whispered, knowing it was true.

Keir nodded. "One of the reasons why the Powers That Be are never wrong is because they know better than to choose blue pill people. Blue pill people wouldn't be sitting here calmly discussing a world they didn't know existed before yesterday. They'd be running for the hills."

Geoffrey slid into my peripheral vision and set the check down. Keir leaned out from his chairback to reach for his wallet.

"Jeff," I said. "I'm sorry about this, but I have to have my own separate check. The rules, you know."

Geoffrey blinked. "Jeff?"

"Oh gee, I don't know where that came from. It just slipped out. I mean Geoffrey."

A gradual smile claimed his face. "No. I like it. You shall call me Jeff."

"Good. You seem like a Jeff."

"I'll return with two checks," he said and almost jogged away.

Keir had clearly enjoyed the exchange and was quietly chuckling, which showed off his very white teeth and the captivating twinkle in his eyes. "You see? Geoffrey has been around for a very long time and no one has ever dubbed him with a..."

"Nickname?"

"Just so. He was so proud to be given a name by the magistrate that his buttons almost popped off."

I couldn't help but smile at that image. "Well, I'm glad he liked it. I honestly don't know what made me say it. I don't make a habit of going around renaming people." I scoffed. "Matter of fact, I've always kind of thought it's an obnoxious thing to do."

"There's only one explanation. Your intuition is sprouting."

I narrowed my eyes. "Did Molly mention our conversation? About intuition?"

"No," he said without hesitation and with a tone so sincere I would struggle with skepticism. "But most modern humans have been so thoroughly brainwashed to believe they have five senses and not six, that it's become functionally true."

I nodded thoughtfully. "Perhaps you're right. So

you're predicting that, if I stay, I'll no longer be able to see the world from the perspective of a human by Hallows and that my intuition will grow."

"True as Styx. And add one more to that."

"What?"

He grinned and winked. "I predict you're staying. Here." He reached out his hand." Give me your phone and let me add my number. Call me anytime for any reason. Questions. Errands. Sexual urges."

I almost choked on the little after-dinner chocolate mint I'd just put in my mouth as if sampling two desserts wasn't enough. It had been so long since I'd fielded flirty banter that I didn't have a sense of how to distinguish teasing from real intent.

"I have someone who does errands. Apparently at any time day or night. I might have questions though. So thank you."

One side of his mouth lifted. "I don't suppose you want to reciprocate?"

I blinked. "Reciprocate?" He took out his phone and handed it to me. "Oh. You want my number." *Gods.* How the world had changed. "Sure."

I entered my contact information as simply Rita.

Chapter Five

Jump Jive and Then You Wail Away

KEIR INSISTED ON walking me back to 'my' house while saying it was a mere courtesy of the gentlemanly sort, though not necessary because I was the safest person on earth. Since thousands of magical people would defend me with their lives and none would dare harm me. While it felt like there was a subtext of darkness embedded in that reassurance, I did feel safer in Hallow Hill than ever before.

From a purely emotional standpoint, that item appeared at the top of the plus column.

I said good night and closed the door behind me, but my newborn compulsion niggled at me saying what would be the harm in stepping over and checking on Romeo. I told myself there's nothing wrong with bonding with cars.

Men do it all the time.

The night was so quiet it felt like I could be the only person in the world. The garage door responded immediately to the opener that hung from my keychain. The roller engaged on its track and the lights came on.

Romeo looked just as showroom shiny and fresh as the last time I'd performed this ritual the day before.

"Romeo?"

A muffled, "Yes, madam?"

I found that I was becoming accustomed to being called madam, Magistrate, Judge, and the like.

"Are you okay?"

"Yes, madam."

And then in what was clearly the most irrational moment since I'd arrived in England, I said, "We'll go for a drive tomorrow afternoon, okay?" It wasn't a lie. I would either be headed back to the airport or I'd be going on a little outing to check out the environs, give a little perspective to 'home'.

"I will be here."

"Good to know."

The garage door came down behind me as I turned

back to my front door, but something caused me to stop in my tracks. I'd heard something, but couldn't discern what it was until after the door lift ceased its grinding noise. When the door met the concrete with a little scrape, all was quiet again.

Except for a sound that could only be called wailing. It was coming from down the hill in the direction of the river below. On impulse I started down the cobblestone lane, almost wishing that Keir Culain hadn't gone already.

With every step the wailing became louder, and so mournful that it elicited a visceral reaction. The sorrow in that voice made tears prick even though I didn't know who it was or why they were so sad.

Four houses down the hill, I reached the peak of crescendo but couldn't find the source. The tone was too pure to be originating indoors. I looked around, turned in a circle then looked up and there, above the rooftops a figure hovered like a ghost. Or a nightmare.

When it turned toward me, I'd like to say the reason why I didn't move was because I didn't want to run. But the truth was that I was so frightened I was frozen in place.

The specter began to slowly move in my direction.

It had the characteristics usually associated with a phantom in that it appeared filmy. Yet I couldn't see through it as would be expected of a form that isn't solid. It appeared to be a young, tall, lithe female wearing a long gown of diaphanous green with skirts and sleeves that fluttered even though the breeze had quieted at sunset and there was no wind.

I'd been too frightened to notice that the wailing had stopped. The creature had trained a hundred percent of its focus on me and was drifting slowly down in my direction while maintaining an upright posture, as if standing on something solid.

As she grew closer, I thought my heart would stop beating from fright, but I remained quite alive, quite conscious, and quite unable to move.

When she was just a few yards overhead, the necklace she was wearing caught the light of the streetlamp and projected a prism of colors like a rainbow. *The aquamarine.* My eyes jerked to the face of the spirit. Heart-shaped, like Maggie's probably was when she was young. *Or in the true form of her second nature.* Even if those things were wild speculation, the eyes were unmistakable.

She came to rest on the street a few yards away, said nothing, and made no move to engage. I stared at her. She stared at me. She was elegant, graceful, and ethereal. In some ways the opposite of the Maggie I was coming to know. She lifted her head as if she'd heard my thought and then she was gone in a flash, like a creature who could move almost faster than the eye could see.

My shoulders slumped as I looked up and down the street of a village so quiet I might've been completely alone. I was going to look up "two-natured". Right away.

I hurried into 'my' house, locked the door, and slumped with my back against it. I must have been holding my breath because my lungs gasped involuntarily and dragged in a new supply of oxygen. Being inside and breathing went a long way toward making me feel better, in the most relative sense.

It seemed the mild-mannered Maggie MacHenry had a raging case of multiple personality disorder. Chalk that up to an item in the "big unknown" category. I found myself suddenly wishing for a pair of gigantic gray wolves instead of one totally lovable Border Collie. But I doubted even two magical creatures such as those would be a defense against that thing outside.

The idea of going to bed with wailing creatures hovering over my rooftop was out of the question. So much for feeling safer than I ever had.

On the other hand, that thing that might be Maggie MacHenry's 'other nature' hadn't been threatening aside from the horror show novelty. The worst it did was give me a long, sorrowful look.

After double checking the lock I sank to the floor. When my mind began to clear I was looking at the shoes on my feet. I kicked them away like they were toxic, but it didn't make me feel either less afraid or less alone. Remembering Keir's offer, I pulled my phone from my bag.

He answered on the first ring. "Rita. That was fast. Should I turn around?"

"No. Well." I hesitated, wanting to say yes. "Um, no."

"What's wrong?"

"I saw something."

"Something in your house?"

"No. Something outside."

"You had another date after I left? Was it Fie?"

"No! In order to have *another* date, I would've had to

have had a first date. *And* I'm not interested in Fie."

"Does that mean you're interested in me?"

Frustrated with Keir's singular focus and short attention span, I said, "NO!" louder than I intended. "I, um, went across the way to see about Romeo."

"The car?"

"Yes."

After the slightest pause, probably evaluating me for psychosis, he said, "Alright. I'm up to speed. Then what happened?"

I described the event as succinctly as possible and voiced my suspicions that the creature had something to do with Maggie.

He cleared his throat. "Well, normally I would say that a person's magical form is their news to tell, but you sound…"

"Freaked out."

"Yes. That. So under the circumstances I'm sure I'll be forgiven for revealing that your suspicions are true. Maggie is bean sidhe."

"Banshee? She told me she was fae."

"Yes. Sidhe means fae in Irish. It's a large and diverse

tribe. The troublesome thing is not that you saw her magical visage, but that seeing her wail means someone in the town is going to die. Soon."

"Oh. Who?"

"Where did you see her?"

"Three of four houses down toward the river."

Keir sighed deeply. "That would be Bradesferd."

"The silversmith? Oh no. He's nice. Took my bags upstairs when I arrived." I was having second thoughts about not giving him a tip.

"Indeed, he is nice, but perhaps even more important, he's master of his craft. No one has a command of metals like that anymore."

"That's terrible." I was still holding my keychain in my hand. I lifted it and looked at the chain that had been a sort of welcome gift. "I have something of his. A keychain. It's beautiful."

"Do you want company?"

"No. No, I, um… I'm sorry to bother you."

"It's no bother, Rita. You've nothing to fear. You're one of only a few dozen humans who've ever seen a bean sidhe at work. Even though she was compelled to fulfill a task, she clearly was concerned about being seen and sought to reassure you."

"That's why she came so close?"

"Perhaps she thought you might recognize her."

"I did."

"I know. The offer of company is genuine. It would be my pleasure. A second cup of coffee maybe?"

"Thank you, Keir. I'm a big girl even if I don't always act like it. Tell me this, why is it her job to, um, do that?"

"It's a kindness to know when the end is near. Preparations can be made. Projects can be completed. Goodbyes can be said. Arrangements can be made for legacies when that's a consideration."

"That's more than a kindness. It's a marvelous gift. So, Brad knows."

"Yes. Tell me something before you go. How did hearing that sound make you feel?"

"Sad. Profoundly so. I had to work at not crying."

"So far as I know, all human accounts agree on that. I think Maggie has to actually feel that, death grief, every time."

"Oh," I whispered, trying to imagine that.

"Alright. If you're sure you can sleep."

"Yes."

"If you can't, I can think of other things to do at night in bed."

"So can I. And all of them involve reading magistrate journals or ancient books on magical people."

He laughed. "Well, for now, I'll be satisfied with friendship. And, as the good friend I hope to be to you, my phone will be close by, and I'm only fifteen minutes away."

REGARDLESS OF THE extraordinarily unusual experience I'd had on the way back from checking on Romeo, I felt safe in the house. I grabbed a ginger ale from the refrigerator and headed upstairs, believing I might have two hours of reading in me.

After pulling on my light flannel sleep set, I took the large book out and rifled through until I found the banshee. Some of the handwriting was hard to read and some of the words didn't make sense, but all in all, it was just as Keir Culain had described.

Banshees, all female, are an uncategorized form of fae, born seldom and randomly. A fae couple who has never had a banshee born in their line, may give birth to one. Although it isn't recognized until adulthood, when the nocturnal change and the compulsion to wail possess the young female. They're revered by the fae to such an extent that they might be considered minor deities.

"And they have no choice," I said to the walls. They serve because they must. *Poor Maggie.*

I turned to the first journal I'd picked up and opened it. I knew that most of the journals were written in cursive. So that's what I'd expected. But the one I picked up, off the top of the end stack, was apparently typed and then later bound into a leather journal that matched the rest.

There was no doubt that an old timey typewriter had been used, as opposed to computer word processing paired with a printer. There were a couple of letters that were ever so slightly higher than others, a few handwritten corrections, and an occasional ink smear.

The date read, *Imbolc, 1902.*

Britain is the strongest power in the world economically and militarily. Yet the people closest to magic kind often do not prosper. Magic kind are continu-

ally more distressed about their inability to help in this modern age. That distress is often demonstrated in conflict with their own kind and, ironically, sometimes the plight of the people they feel most affinity with becomes worse as a result. But that is my opinion and not to be taken as part of the official record.

The author continued with commentary for a couple of paragraphs before beginning the record of cases. Knowing that it was true and not fiction made it the most fascinating reading imaginable.

A highlander boy was stolen by a Fae girl to be her boy toy because she'd watched him every day, unseen, and fallen in love with him. RULING: The girl was directed to return the human and her family had to pay a fine.

A sorcerer from a tiny island in the Outer Hebrides had let his dragon get loose, again, and since dragons aren't able to cast a glamour to hide their true forms, the northern Scots who saw him were terrorized. They also suffered the humiliation of being checked for a psychotic episode in the form of mass hallucination. Since sanity is hard to prove, getting the victims of the sightings released had been difficult for their families. RULING: In light of the fact that this was his third warning in just two hundred and fifty years, the sorcerer had to either submit a guaranteed plan to keep the dragon under control at all times, which meant to disguise him when let out for flight, or surrender him to the fae, who would undoubtedly be more responsible. And a fine was assessed.

A dryad was enraged when her forest was cut down by humans. She gave them food poisoning so severe that two of the 'victims' died. RULING: Magic kind are not allowed to murder humans, accidentally or otherwise, for destruction of property in a shared world. The dryad was ordered to accept relocation assistance from the fae. And pay a fine.

One case involved fae brothers who were fighting over inheritance of a small lake with a herd of swans. Apparently, ownership by lineage was unclear and each of them had become determined to inherit by being the last one standing. RULING: One would get the lake and the swans. One of the queens would agree to create an identical lake and herd of swans for the other. And both would pay a fine.

Upon hearing the ruling, the brothers fell to arguing over which would keep ownership of the *original* lake and swans. In less than a minute they'd lunged at each other and were in a full-blown brawl, causing such a disturbance that the sephalian was forced to engage.

As I read on into the night, the pattern of assessing fines became clear. I had no clue where all that money went, but I was afraid it went to buy Alfa Romeos and magic shawls for magistrates. That struck me as far more corrupt than attempting to bribe a magistrate with lunch. A person calling in a favor to the judge might expect a sentence, probably a fine, to be reduced. Considerably.

Lochlan's name came up again and again. As did occasional references to the sephalian, whatever that was. I made a note to track it down in the velvet book. Right after a well-deserved night's sleep.

At times I roused enough to know I was dreaming about fantastical creatures that were so much more vivid in life than in stories. Nevertheless, I woke surprisingly refreshed, thinking I could smell coffee.

On opening the bedroom door, I heard kitchen noises and confirmed that, yes, indeed, coffee had been brewed. Good coffee from the smell of it. I pulled on a robe and padded downstairs to find a variety of fresh citrus segmented and deseeded, my favorite yogurt, my favorite granola, and my favorite topping – fresh berries.

"Olivia?" I called, but there was no answer.

She'd come and prepared breakfast then left. Since I was a person who was partial to some 'alone time', I thought that was amazingly considerate of her.

I took my breakfast to sit and look at the little garden, which featured a blooming mimosa tree, to think things over. I'd promised to reach a decision by mid-day and I would.

As had been suggested, the reading of journals was clarifying. The author of the journal I'd read had, at one time, been a human like myself, oblivious to the fact that we share a world with magic kind and creatures. He, like the other magistrates, had made a transition such that the impossible became the everyday.

I imagined myself 'hearing' every case I read about and thought over how I might've 'ruled' had the outcome been up to me. In a strange twist of psyche, I was able to form a vision of being that person. And, I could see why magic kind would think it an honor to be the recipient of that position.

After dashing off an email to my daughter with assurances that I was having the time of my life, I showered and got dressed hurriedly. I was strangely eager to begin what would, no doubt, be another day of firsts. I'd never thought of myself as a thrill seeker. Just the opposite. Yet I found myself wondering what wonders would present themselves before I returned to the bedroom that night.

Since I'd slept late, it was time for shops to open. I stepped out my front door, looked at the garage across the way, and remembered the promise I'd made to take Romeo for a spin. Or was it the other way around?

Without stopping at the Hallows, I went straight across the circle to The Silver Braid. The OPEN sign behind the half-glass door had been turned facing outward.

No one was in sight when I went in, but that gave me a minute to look around. I'd never been what might be called a 'jewelry person', but each of Brad's pieces was a work of art. Most were complicated Celtic knot designs.

Some were wide, flat chains. Some were heavy chunk rings with diamonds embedded in crevices. Some featured large medallions with dragons or snakes circling to take hold of their own tails.

I was particularly drawn to the medallion that featured a large, diamond-eyed, wolf's head superimposed over a patchwork of Celtic designs.

"Brad?" I called out.

I heard a small thump in the rear seconds before he appeared.

"Magistrate," he said simply. He didn't smile, but did convey steady good-naturedness.

"I just came by to say hello and see your shop." I waved. "Your work is stunning."

"You're very kind."

"Not at all. Truth was never truer. And I came to look for something special."

Brad cocked his head ever so slightly and appeared to be studying me in depth. "You heard the cry."

I was learning that there's no point in hedging with magic kind. I nodded. "Yes."

"And you're here to offer condolences?"

"Not so much as to say I'm sorry I didn't have a chance to get to know you better. For all I know, you're the best silversmith in the world."

He smiled. "Let me put your mind at ease. I am."

Returning his smile, I said, "I have no trouble accepting that."

"It would be my honor to give you something."

"I can't…"

"In this case, you can. It's not possible for a body who's crossed over to collect on favors."

"Hmmm," I said. "I see what you mean."

"It would also be good for business. My nephew, Braden, is coming to take over the shop. Arrangements have already been made. He's not quite at my level of mastery, but I think he may be someday. He's getting married. Going to start a family."

"Children? Where will they go to school? Who will they play with?" He smiled. "I retract that. Those things are none of my business."

"It's good you care about such things. You'll make a fine magistrate. If my nephew is blessed with little ones, it will work out." He looked around. "I have just the thing."

He walked straight to the case that held the wolf's head medallion. I suppose I should've been getting used to the fact that magic kind seem to just know stuff, but it was a surprise.

"I was admiring that. How did you know?"

He shrugged. "I've been a shopkeeper for a long time," he said with the gentlest sort of kindness, but both of us knew that was not the reason. After reaching for the medallion, he said, "Quite often, I hear, half of meeting a challenge is looking the part. If this," he gestured with the medallion, "was paired with a chain of office…"

I didn't know what a chain of office was until he removed it from a display and held it up. It was immediately recognizable from costuming I'd seen in movies. The chain links were about one and a half inches in diameter. When he joined the medallion to the chain, the pairing looked like each piece had been made for the other.

"Try it on. There's a mirror over there." He gestured.

I removed the shawl. What I'd worn underneath was a plain, scarlet, long sleeved knit shirt.

"Fitting," Brad said. "Since the magistrate robes are that same color."

He handed me the necklace. I took it, walked to the full-length mirror, and looped it over my head. When the chain was adjusted to drape over my shoulders rather than hang from my neck, the wolf's head sat squarely atop my cleavage, in the center of my chest. Seeing myself in such a statement piece, made me think for the first time that I might be a decent magistrate.

After all, the Powers That Be are never wrong.

"If you will wear it to Court Meet, it will be good promotion for my nephew. And this shop."

I turned to look at him. "I will. I want it, but I think I should pay for it. And do not give me a discount."

He stared for a few beats before finally saying. "Very well. It's four thousand five hundred and sixty-two pounds. Tell Maggie to settle up with me."

Quickly doing a general conversion of pounds to dollars in my head, I almost choked. "I don't know if I can afford that."

Brad snickered. "Indeed, Magistrate. You could buy the entire store and never miss the expenditure."

I couldn't help but wonder if that was because of all the 'fines'.

"Are you okay with…?"

Brad sighed. "My kind are particularly predisposed to longevity, even for magic folk, and that's both good and bad. It was a good life when my wife was alive. It's been lonely since and my spirit is ready for the next adventure. I feel more grateful than sad." He looked around. "Although I am glad I have someone who wants to continue my work. There's satisfaction in that."

With a nod, I said, "I will send customers Braden's way when I can. I hope he and I will be friends."

Brad chuckled. "Of course you'll be friends. He's a jolly sort. Gets along with everyone."

I grinned, looked down at the medallion, and ran my fingers over it. "I'll remember you, Brad."

"Who could ask for more?" He smiled.

I went straight to the florist a few doors down, walked in and introduced myself to Lily, the proprietor.

"Of course, I know who you are, Magistrate. I'm so pleased you stopped in. You must tell me your favorite flowers so that I can keep them stocked."

I held up my hand. "I'm not here for myself today. You know Brad, right?"

She blinked and looked in the direction of The Silver Braid. "The dwarf, Brad? Yes. I know him."

"I want a suggestion for a bouquet for Brad. Something huge and fabulous. What do you think he'd like?"

I could see the wheels turning. "Stems of yellow orchids." She gestured toward a large bucket in the glass-front cooler. "Trailing green moss. Tree fern. Variegated ivy."

"Sounds very unusual. And very pretty. How long will it take you to put that together?"

"Ten minutes?"

"Excellent. Can I watch?"

"I'd love to have you watch. I don't often get an audience and I might be a bit of a performer at heart. There's a stool if you'd like to sit."

My eyes followed the gesture she'd made with her head and spied an old wooden stool painted with flowers and vines on a blue background. I dragged it over where I could sit and watch her work her magic, so to speak, at the long table that was her workspace.

"Your shop is lovely, Lily."

"Thank you," she said as she was gathering things. She

pointed to large vases. Green glass and clear glass. "Preference?"

"I don't know. What do you think?"

"Flowers for a male dwarf? Is it for the shop?"

"I'm going to take it to the shop, but he can do what he wants with it afterward."

"I'd bet he'll keep them at the shop. The clear glass will go with the overall feel of the place."

"Agree. Let's do that." She went straight to work. "So. Lily. How long have you been a Hallow Hill florist?"

"Not long. About thirty-five years. By local standards I'm a newcomer."

"Do you like it here?"

"Oh certainly. It's just the right mix of quiet and festival."

"Festival?"

"You know. Court Weeks. The village fills up with magic kind. And, even though the trials are serious, there's a lot of celebrating, too."

"I see. Please don't be offended, but you look human."

She laughed. "I do in this form, but I'm pixie. Ivy and I are sisters."

"Really!"

"Hm-hmm." She nodded.

There was a strong family resemblance. I don't know why I didn't see it before.

"This morning I was walking by Ivy's house and couldn't help noticing that the garden is gorgeous. You must both have an affinity for plants and, um, flowers."

Lily brightened with a sunshiny smile that was Tinkerbellish. "Oh. We do. It's a pixie thing."

She worked quickly to create an arrangement that surely would have won a blue ribbon at any competition. It was out of this world.

"Lily," I said, "I don't know how much you're going to charge me for this, but I suspect it's not enough. This is the prettiest thing I've ever seen."

She beamed like I'd given her the coordinates to the end of the rainbow.

"I'll get Maggie to settle up," she said.

Settling into my role as a person who has things done for her, I decided I wouldn't even ask the price. I felt confident that Maggie was uber-capable of protecting my financial interests.

There was a little stand of folded cards for all occasions to be attached to a plastic trident amid the greenery. I chose one that was blank and plucked one of the pens out of the cupholder. I wrote, *Flowers for the living. – Rita.* Then handed the card to Lily so that she could place it artfully.

When it was ready to go, I put both arms around the vase and shifted it toward my left, just enough so that I could see around it to walk.

“Um, can you get the door?”

She laughed. “Let me walk with you and get the Braid door, as well.”

When we were on the sidewalk, I said, “Lily. Do you have plans for lunch? Can you close the shop for a little bit at noon?”

“No. And yes. Why? What are we doing?”

“I gave Olivia a cooking challenge and told her I’m bringing Maggie and Dolan for lunch today. In my kitchen.” It was the first time I used a possessive pronoun and didn’t have an urge to qualify with ‘if I stay’. “Come join us.”

She put her hands together and jumped a little like a

schoolgirl. "That sounds like a wonderful way to mid-day. I'll be there."

"Okay. Just don't tease Olivia if it's not good."

Lily laughed out loud. "Not good? That's impossible."

I smiled, hoping she was right, as we reached 'The Braid'. She opened the door and held it until I was inside, then rushed back to her own shop.

Brad was rearranging a display. The surprise on his face when he looked up and saw me come in with the arrangement was priceless and left me feeling like I'd been given the best gift. I set the vase at the end of a display case near the door, smiled at Brad, and left without a word.

Two minutes later I was breezing into the Hallows like I owned the place, which I guess I did. Since I'd apparently decided to stay and all.

The alleged vampire was standing in the same spot where I'd 'met' him two days before.

"John David Weir. Hello," I said.

His black eyes went straight to the medallion revealed as I peeled back the shawl and lingered there.

"I just got it," I said. "What do you think?"

His eyes drifted back up to mine slowly. "Very nice.

Are you going to make me buy something?"

"I'm new here, but I assume the shop can always use patronage. Do you want to shop?"

"No."

I wondered why Maggie was nowhere to be seen whenever he showed up.

"Well, what can I do for you then?"

"Nothing."

I shook my head. "You're gonna have to help me out. I'm new here and I just don't know how to respond to that."

Perhaps it was a trick of the light, but I thought I might have seen a corner of his mouth twitch. That was followed by a blank expression and no more words forthcoming.

"Okay. So. What do you want me to call you? John David?" He nodded slowly. "Good. We're getting somewhere. So. John David. Do you eat? I mean food?"

He looked first offended and then a little angry. "Of course I eat. What kind of cockamamie question is that?"

"A mistake, I guess. But I have a reason for asking. I'm having a little impromptu lunch in my kitchen at noon. If you're still around, you're invited."

"Invited?" He said the word like he couldn't imagine anything more outrageous.

"Yes. Would you like to come? I've asked Olivia to experiment with gumbo and hush puppies. Lily's coming. And Dolan. And Maggie, of course."

After looking at me like I was certifiable for a full thirty seconds, which can feel longer than you might think when a vampire is staring at you, he said, "I accept your invitation."

"Oh good. Come around at noon. Or if you'd rather stand in the shop and do nothing, that's okay, too. To each his own. Now that I know you're not a creeper, I'm okay with you hanging around."

"Creeper?" He looked sincerely horrified.

I waved that off. "Sorry. It's probably an American term. It's not something you'd want to be, but I used a negative qualifier. *Not* a creeper is what I said. Anyhow, I need to find Maggie. Don't steal anything." I smiled as I walked away, strongly suspecting the suggestion that he might steal something would scandalize him to the very soul that he might or might not have. I hadn't reached that detailed level of study yet.

When I set foot on the threshold that led to the back of the shop, I called Maggie's name.

"Here," she called from the workroom. I turned left and found her with Dolan. She looked up when she saw me and said, "Tryin' to decide what to do with this. I think we should paint it red. Dolan has other ideas."

I walked around the end of the table so I could see the chair from another angle. Certainly, it was unique, a combination of German carving and antlers. It had, at one time, been painted black and the spotty finish didn't help the first impression it made.

"What do you think?" Maggie asked.

"I think it's a monstrosity, but somebody will want it anyway. Dolan, what did you have in mind?"

"Dark stain. Gloss finish," he said with an admirable economy of words I could only aspire to.

Given what he had to work with, that was definitely the best choice.

"He's right, Maggie. If this thing can be even partially redeemed, dark stain with a gloss finish is the only thing I can see doing it." I looked between them. "Annnnnnd,

I'm having both of you for lunch in my kitchen."

"You are?" Maggie glanced at Dolan.

"Yes. Olivia is doing a cooking challenge. The four of us are going to eat together." I remembered the conversation on the sidewalk in front of the Braid. "Oh. And Lily's coming, too." Maggie looked at Dolan who shrugged. "Almost forgot. Jugular John is standing in the shop doing nothing and unable to explain it. So I invited him, too." Maggie looked at Dolan a second time. Dolan shrugged again. "So, I guess we'll be six for lunch. I'll open the secret passage at twelve. Don't be late. We don't want to offend the cook."

I pulled out my keys to try and figure out which one fit the lock to the door that led past my little larder on the right and my little laundry on the left to my big, beautiful, state-of-the-art kitchen.

"And I'm staying," I announced in the most anticlimactic way possible.

I opened the passthrough for the first time to mark the occasion of my decision and was overcome by the heady aroma of Cajun cooking. The scents were so delicious I could almost taste the air.

"Olivia," I sang out to let her know I was coming and not startle her.

"Yes… Okay."

The kitchen looked like a chef was in residence and the table was beautifully set for four.

"I know this is short notice." I looked around at all the preparation. She'd made everything from scratch. "But we're having six instead of four."

"Six?" She turned her deer-in-headlights reaction from me to the food in front of her. "But…"

"I know. My bad. If we were married, you'd have to make me sleep on the sofa. Which wouldn't be a bad thing in this case because I can tell that my sofas are incredibly comfortable. But that wouldn't come up because I have a guest room."

I realized I was babbling because I was embarrassed about being thoughtful with everyone except Olivia. I hoped she didn't leave my employ because of this.

"Okay. Look. First, I don't need much. Just a taste and I can snack later. Second," I came around to her side of the island, "I have a trick to make everything go farther." I grinned on the inside when I saw that she was interested.

"It's easy to make gumbo stretch. Just serve it as a topping on bowls of rice."

The tension left her shoulders as she visibly relaxed.

"I'll add two places to the table. You make a pot of rice."

LUNCH WAS A half and half affair. Dolan, Olivia, and John David ate quietly and may or may not have even been listening to the conversation. Maggie, Lily, and I made up for that. When we were all seated, I announced that it was a celebration of my decision to stay. At Maggie's suggestion, we clinked water glasses all around.

"Olivia," I said. "You cook like you were born on the bayou." She looked uncertain, like she didn't know what that meant. I clarified. "This is the real deal. Maybe even the best I've ever had." I narrowed my eyes. "Have you cooked Cajun before?" She smiled shyly and shook her head. "Well, you know what this means." Everybody looked up, waiting for the punch line. "It means I'm going to give you something even harder for tomorrow."

Olivia didn't look worried.

Maggie laughed.

Dolan reached for two more hushpuppies.

"That's a beautiful thing you're wearin'," Maggie said with eyes on the wolf medallion.

"Thank you. I got it this morning at The Silver Braid."

Lily agreed and then said, "Is that why you were taking flowers to Brad? To thank him for this?"

Maggie looked at me with renewed interest.

I nodded uncommittedly and looked to Maggie. "He said he'd settle up with you."

"'Course," Maggie said.

"Same here," Lily added. "For the flowers."

"Send the bill 'round," Maggie told her.

THE REST OF the meal was spent with Maggie and Lily treating me to stories of past magistrates, most of them comical anecdotes. She even got a few chuckles out of the quiet diners. I couldn't help but wonder what would happen if I added wine to the mix.

When everyone had gone but Olivia and me, I said, "I really am sorry about springing extra people on you. But lunch was a big hit. We should do it more often."

She smiled in a way that indicated she agreed.

"By the way, thank you for breakfast. What a nice surprise that was."

She looked surprised. "Surprise?"

"Yes. I wasn't expecting that."

She frowned. "Oh. The former magistrate..." That sentence went unfinished.

"Should we revisit the job description?" I offered. "I'm not saying I don't love coming down to breakfast. I do. But I'd like to hear your understanding of your duties and compare that to my requirements."

I felt silly saying that. As a person solidly born to middle class, I had no 'requirements', with the possible exception of tire changing, should the need arise.

We sat at the kitchen table. Olivia recited her job description. There wasn't a thing I would change and I left feeling like a very lucky magistrate.

Next I went to the shop, found Maggie, and had a similar conversation with her.

"So, you basically run the shop."

"I know the ins and outs," she said. "You're the boss in theory or practice. My level of management is entirely up to you. And I'll be happy with your choice."

I nodded thoughtfully. "I think we should leave things as they are for now. I think it's more important that I spend time studying the journals and learning about the, um, population. I did enjoy helping to make the decision on renovating that chair. I have an art history education."

"Well, then," she said. "Easy enough. You and Dolan will confer on pieces needin' restoration."

"I'm going to let Lochlan know my decision and go for a drive."

"Sure. Sure." Maggie looked at me like she was waiting for me to say something else. When I didn't, at length she said, "You were out and about last night." I nodded. She cleared her throat and looked discomfited. "I hope my work clothes didn't give you too much a fright."

I sat back down and put my hands in my lap. "Should I be honest?"

"Aye. Always."

"It was a little harrowing, but I called Keir Culain." Her gaze jerked to mine. "He explained things."

"Oh. Did he now?"

"Yes. I hope you don't mind. I wouldn't have been able to sleep."

"I do no' look *that* bad when I'm heraldin'."

"Just the opposite. Your work visage is lovely and, I mean, who wouldn't be down with flying? Or looking twenty-five. I just needed to know what I was seeing. You must understand how, um, alien all this is."

"Aye. I do. To be sure you're managin' better than most. But then the Powers would know that, would they no'?" She paused. "I look twenty-five?"

"Do you not know how you appear as your, um, other nature?" She shook her head. "Beautiful, Maggie. Quite beautiful."

She soaked that in and was beaming as I rose to leave. "Just so you know, I can also take the form of a blackbird. Or a weasel, but I rarely seen the point of that."

After taking a minute to process that, I said, "I guess I can see the appeal of being a blackbird. But I'm trying to imagine when it would be advantageous to be a weasel."

Maggie shrugged. "Exactly why 'tis no' a typical choice. But the Powers That Be are ne'er wrong."

"Right. By the way, do you have a phone?"

"No' personally, but we have one in the office. I pick it up if it rings but leave it here when I go."

I got the office number. It was something.

"You're welcome to come to lunch tomorrow. You and Dolan. If he's here. We're having tapas."

She lit up. "Do no' know what that is but sounds grand."

"Would I be more likely to find Lochlan at home or at the office at this time of day?"

"I'd try his house if I were you."

My intention was to walk through the shop and exit the front door, but as I entered a young woman came in. I turned on my heel and walked straight back to Maggie.

"The windchime isn't working."

"And why would we be thinkin' that?"

"Come and have a look." Maggie followed me to the rear display counter where I pretended to be busy as I shuffled things around. "Look."

Maggie leaned around me in a fashion that was less surreptitious than I would have liked, scanned the shop, then said, "What am I lookin' at?"

I gaped. "The customer with blue hair and orange skin."

"Oh." She leaned over again and pronounced, "Human."

I slowly turned for another look, smiled at the customer, and raised my voice. "Please feel free to look around." The patron nodded, but her attention was already elsewhere, eyes leisurely wandering over the odd, but captivating wares. Turning back to Maggie with lowered voice, "Okay. I grant that people can make their hair look like Ostara eggs, but what about the orange skin?"

"Sunburn."

"Sunburn?" I glanced in the girl's direction. "Isn't it too late in the year for that?"

Maggie fanned her hand in front of her face and tried to talk without moving her lips, like a ventriloquist. "No' if you're under enough *influence*." She stressed the word, influence, to be certain I'd catch the innuendo. "Young ones from the city." She shook her head. "She probably had a weekend in Spain, laid on a riverbank next to a rented Caravan, English skin untouched by sun since her last holiday, wearin' barely enough cloth to cover the naughty bits." I was marveling at the length of that sentence when she decided to add, "Foolishness always has a price it does. 'Tis no' a jiggery-pokery. The lass is simply gormless."

"I don't know if I wish I understood what you just said or not. I think maybe I got the thing about covering naughty bits. How old are you?"

"In human years?"

"Yes. That's how I keep time."

"Well, let me think." She glanced around. "There's a converter online. Let me sign in and I'll…"

"There's an online program to convert magical years?" She nodded. "When people see it, do they think it's a joke?"

"By people, you mean Mundies?" I nodded. "They do no' see it."

"How is that possible?"

She shrugged. "Same reason Miss Colorful can no' see the magical artifacts in the store."

I glanced at the customer again. "Right. Is it a problem that I can't tell the difference without the windchime?"

"Stop faffin' around. Anyone could have made that mistake."

I was beginning to think I'd need a pocket translator

for ongoing communication with Maggie. "Alright. I got that last part. And to that I say this. It could *not* happen to *anybody*. Other people haven't been *'gifted'* with the ability to see magical stuff. They don't have to wonder is-she-or-isn't-she?"

"Well, then. Lucky you."

I looked skyward for a couple of beats before gathering my smile and my best pretend proprietor demeanor, then walked toward the brightly colored person with casual purpose. "Can I help you find something in particular or would you rather browse on your own?"

"American," the woman said without turning away from her shopping.

I smiled exactly as I would've if she'd been looking at me. "That's right."

"Hmmm."

The mother of all conversation stoppers. Okay then. Hmmm you.

"Very good. Someone will be close by should you have a question or wish to make a purchase."

When I returned to the counter, Maggie said, "You know, the shoes never lie. You can always rely on them."

"While that's probably true, there's a problem with it. I'm a shoe person. I love those red shoes, but not enough to wear them exclusively for the rest of my life. And sometimes it may be too cold. Or rainy. Or muddy if I'm walking with Lochlan and his, um," I glanced at the customer, "dogs."

"Ye may have a point about a means of detection when you don other footwear. We'll give it some thought." Her eyes wandered the room. "We might even have somethin' here that would do. O' course you'll be payin' for it same as anybody else."

"I have to buy my own inventory? I thought I *own* this place."

Maggie chuckled. "You own everythin' Mundies can see and touch. Everythin' else comes with a price, even for you."

I shifted my weight to one leg and put on my invisible negotiator hat, one of my least favorites. "If it's my firstborn, I'll have to do without. If you'd caught me before she turned twenty, I might've said yes. But now I like her more."

"'Tis no' your firstborn. Where do ye get such ideas?"

My jaw almost hit the floor. "You think that idea is more outlandish than vampires, pixies, wind devils, and whatever Keir Culain is? Not to mention BANSHEES!"

The customer stopped when I raised my voice at the end of my rant, looked over, and smiled. Apparently, she liked that she was in a curious goods and antiques store where the management was discussing folkloric species. Perhaps it added authenticity to the experience.

"You do no' truly need another device. In fact, it might be a crutch. You need to develop your own awareness." I stared, wondering if Maggie fancied herself to be a magical version of a life coach. "Do no' pretend ye have none. I've seen it."

"You've seen it," I said drily.

"I have. You knew by instinct that Dolan and Olivia are standoffish and could use a little push to be more social."

"That's not a magical skill, Maggie."

"Sure 'tis."

"Speaking of Keir. What is he?"

Maggie chuckled. "Nice try. He'll tell you when he's ready."

I felt my face form a wicked smile as I sing-songed, "He told me about *you*."

"Twas because you'd seen me at my night job and had a fright. The circumstances were different and ye know it," she scolded.

I did know it. She had me dead to rights. So, I slumped in resignation and ended the dialogue with, "See you at lunch."

I ATE UP the short distance to Lochlan's house in my red shoes, said hello to the wolves as they ran to the gate to perform their greeting ritual, then clacked the big Green-man doorknocker three times. In a very short time, I heard the latch move from within.

"Well, Magistrate," Lochlan said as he opened the door. "Come in. Come in."

"No need, Lochlan. And, um, you can call me Rita. I just came by to say I'm staying. You'd mentioned needing some transfer signatures?"

"The papers are at my office. Would you like to take care of that now?"

"No. I'm going out for a drive. Tomorrow morning?"

"Yes. That will do fine."

"Do I need a lawyer?"

Lochlan's face transformed into a mixture surprise, confusion, offense, and temper. "*I'm* your lawyer!"

"You are?"

"Of course."

"Do you have a phone?"

"I do. It's a little old-fashioned. Hangs on the wall. I'd need to be home to hear it."

I sighed. "Well. Maybe I should get the number?"

I typed the number he dictated into my phone and was wondering if Keir Culain was the only other person with mobile communications. I was certainly old enough to remember life without being attached to a phone, but it had been a while.

"I'm going to do a deep dive into the journals. Is there anything else you think I need to do to prepare for the next, um, Court Meet?"

"When you're ready, but no later than the first of October, you'll need to review the cases submitted and establish a docket."

"Okay."

"Come around in the morning? About ten?" I smiled and nodded. "Then, if you like, afterward, we can walk the dogs and talk over what you've read."

I grinned. "I love that plan. See you at ten." I turned to go, but looked back for his verbal postscript.

"I can't get in the habit of calling you by your first name."

After retracing my steps to his door, I said, "Why not?"

"Because I am your solicitor, but I'm also the court clerk. And your advisor if you should see fit. I'm expected to set, uphold, and enforce the decorum of the court. It wouldn't be proper to call you Rita in court. And, if I did so most of the time… Hard as it might be to grasp, I'm not perfect."

"I see what you mean. So okay. I'll make an exception for you." I said it half-teasing, but being honest with myself, I was becoming more comfortable with being addressed by my new title every day. "Hey. By the way. If you're not busy, come for lunch tomorrow. Ivy, too. We're having tapas."

His mouth twitched as the elf twinkle lit his eyes. "The

missus is otherwise occupied most noons, but it would be delightful to try, em, tapas."

I waved as I left, gave the wolves a final rub behind the ears, and headed straight for 'my' garage. I wondered how long it would be before I'd get used to using possessives to describe Hallow Hill things. I wondered when I would get up the nerve to tell my daughter I wasn't coming back to the U.S. Maybe ever.

The garage door lifted as smoothly as any, which meant it did the job, but not quietly.

"Romeo. How art thou?"

I heard the locks click to disengage.

"Very well, madam. Yourself?"

"Excellent. Thank you for asking." After going around the left side of the car to get in and finding no steering wheel there, I rolled my eyes at myself and walked around. As I slid beneath the leather-covered steering wheel with the luxurious emblem, I said, "Let's go for a spin and see the neighborhood."

The engine started and Romeo backed himself out. "Could we be more specific, madam?"

I didn't know what to think about Romeo's choice of

pronouns, but I supposed he was programmed to soften questions.

"Let's put it this way. I want to see the countryside around Hallow Hill, but I don't want to be gone for more than two hours. If you know of a stretch of road with light traffic, I'd like to try driving myself."

"Very good, madam."

In two minutes we were headed south to Ambleside, which might be thought of as a charming small town, but compared to Hallow Hill, it was a metropolis. On the way I enjoyed vistas fit for a TV screen timeout. Every variation of green formed hills and valleys. I saw white sheep with black legs and faces. I saw black sheep with white legs and faces.

We, and by that I mean Romeo and I, traversed Lake Windermere on the east from north to south and started back on the west side. We stopped in a village for an ice cream cone and stopped at one of the Lake District's stone circles. Because it was a Wednesday out of tourist season, I was able to walk around by myself.

When I returned to the car, I said, "What do you think these were, Romeo? The stone circles, I mean."

I didn't expect an answer, but got one anyway.

"Places where thc old ones gathered for sacred purposes. Magic is drawn to this area." I could believe what was being said, but not that the car had been programmed to say it. "There's very little traffic here if you'd like to take over."

Feeling as nervous and excited as I had when I'd learned to drive, I said, "Yes. But if I'm going to crash, you take over."

"Yes, madam."

IT'S HARD TO compare beautiful places. I'd been on a lot of road trips and seen a lot of things, but I'd be challenged to name anything anywhere more beautiful. I'd enjoyed every second of passing scenery and the pleasure of being alone in an enclosed capsule. Well, as alone as one can be with a car that doubles as chauffeur and companion.

Now and then my mind came back to what I'd tell Evie, my daughter. At some point, the focus became a point of perfect clarity.

On the return trip I discovered that the danger of left side driving is getting comfortable with it. Once the initial anxiety wore off, autopilot tried to take control and inch me toward the right side. Romeo had an array of warnings that ranged from, "Uh oh", to "Left. Left. Left. Left." But all in all, the afternoon was wonderful. Restful. Informative. Head-clearing.

I gave him control when we neared Hallow Hill.

"Let me out here," I said when we were in front of my house. "I assume you can put yourself away."

"I can. Yes."

"Romeo."

"Yes, madam?"

"Do you have feelings?" Silence. "Do you have preferences?" Silence. "Does it matter to you whether you're in the garage or out for a drive?"

"Drives are nice," was the reply.

I nodded to myself. "I thought so. See you soon."

"Yes, madam."

When I opened the car door, I almost shut it again. Sometime between my walk in the field with the stone circle and arriving back in Hallow Hill a cold snap had come in, accompanied by a stiff breeze that made the moist air feel even colder.

I'd planned to go straight to the pub for dinner, but was wondering if I should stop off for some heavyier outerwear. I hesitated at my front door then decided that England was my new climate and I'd better start getting used to it. I put my keys back in my bag and decided to distract myself from being cold with considering what new menu item I'd choose at Molly's before getting into flannels for an evening with journals.

When I turned the corner, the wind was blocked. Apparently my lane, that ran downhill to the river, functioned as a wind tunnel.

Keir Culain was leaning against the building. Waiting.

"Keir," I said.

"Rita," he said with a smile that would strip a girl of every inhibition. "On the way to the pub?"

"As a matter of fact, I am."

"What do you know? I'm on my way there. How about some company?"

"You were on your way there," I repeated in a heavy monotone so there'd be no question that I didn't believe his story.

The light in his eyes danced when he laughed. "The

magical world is full of coincidences." I gave him a dubious look as we started walking toward the pub. "What have you been up to today?"

"I had the most marvelous day," I said, realizing that it was good to have someone to tell about it, someone who seemed genuinely interested. "Most people would call it a self-drive tour, but since Romeo did most of the driving, I can't make that claim."

On the walk I told him all about my drive through the Lake District. "I see why they call it the Eden of England."

"What was your favorite thing?"

I didn't have to give it much thought. "The stone circles."

"Ah," he said. "You're one of us. Drawn to the magic."

"That's what my car said."

His brows pinched together. "Your car said that?"

"Well, not precisely. I asked if he knew what the circles were for. He said the old ones used them for sacred events. I remember thinking at the time that it was odd that someone had programmed a car with that answer."

"Hmmm." Keir opened the door. "Where would you like to sit?"

"You're sitting with me?"

"Unless you insist not."

I smiled. It was beyond flattering to have a movie-star beautiful, younger man give me that sort of attention. Since all notion that I might be attractive had been systematically driven out of me by my soon-to-be ex, I wasn't ready to accept that he might be interested because I was a catch. So, I assumed it had something to do with my station.

"Are you trying to curry favor with the magistrate?" I asked straight up. No games.

I was pleased that his initial reaction was surprise. Keir and I shared at least one thing; the curse of a supremely readable face.

"To what end might I try to curry favor with the magistrate?"

"Well, at some point in the future there might be a dispute that arises between you and another, um... someone else subject to the court."

"No. I can't come before the court as a party to a suit."

"You can't?"

"No."

"Why not?"

"Because I work for the court."

I was not expecting that. "As?"

His gaze drifted over the room. "How about over there?"

I agreed, but my short attention span wasn't short enough to forget the question left hanging.

He guided me to a snug on the opposite side from where we'd sat the night before. It was cozy, made even more so by the fact that the fire had been lit. Again, he allowed me to choose which side. I decided to see and be seen instead of turning my back to the other locals who frequented the pub.

Geoffrey was beside us before I'd finished pulling my shawl away.

"Jeff!" I said. "How are you?"

His face glowed with pleasure at being called Jeff. "Well, Magistrate. You?"

"Likewise." I smiled. "How about a ginger ale?"

He looked at Keir. "Your usual?" Keir nodded.

"Is that new?" Keir had been examining the wolf medallion during my brief dialogue with Jeff.

"Yes. I bought it today."

I knew that he knew I'd gone to see Brad because of my experience with the banshee's wail.

"From Brad?"

"Yes." After a brief pause, I said, "If you must know, I took him flowers, too."

"That was kind of you, Rita."

"It was kind of you to take my call last night and keep me sorted."

"It was an honor. Did you sleep well after?"

"I did." I smiled. "So?"

"So?" Keir repeated.

"What do you do for the court?"

He took in a deep breath, looking disappointed that I hadn't forgotten. "I'm the enforcer."

My mind raced, exploring all the possibilities of what that might mean. "You couldn't possibly think you can skate by with that answer. Give me more."

His eyes came to mine and briefly locked with an intensity I hadn't seen before. Then just as quickly, his face softened into a beguiling smile. "A bargain. Come to my house tomorrow for tea. I'll show you around. It's where

Court Meet is held."

"Really? It's not here in Hallow Hill?"

"No."

"Well, naturally I'm curious. Your house must be big."

He grinned. "Yes and no. The castle is thirteenth century. Most of it is a ruin. I live in what you'd probably call a gatehouse. I have electricity, running water, a roof that doesn't leak."

"So, you're like a caretaker?"

He nodded. "You could say that. Sure."

Molly showed up at the table. "Look here, Magistrate," she said. "Are you making a play for my business?"

"What? No!" I saw the corners of her mouth twitch. "Oh. You mean my lunch guests."

"Yes. That's what I mean."

"I didn't mean to step on toes."

"I'm just playing. I think it's cute that you're having people in to share Olivia's cooking. I'd love to be able to poach her for the pub kitchen."

"Nothin' doin'. She's mine," I said.

"No negotiating then?" I shook my head. "Can't say I blame you." She looked Keir's way, then said, "Enjoy your supper," and left without waiting for a response.

"What's that about?" he asked.

"Olivia is a great cook as it turns out. So today and tomorrow I put together small lunch parties and gave her cooking challenges. Today was Cajun. Tomorrow is tapas."

"Rita, you may be the best thing that's ever happened to Hallow Hill."

"Thank you, Keir. So then. Tell me this. Who do you work for? And what does it mean to be Enforcer?"

"I work for you. As to what Enforcer means, I promise that, if you come to tea, I'll tell you everything and, if you want, I'll show you what the other side of my nature looks like."

"Is it more or less scary than, um, what I saw last night?"

He appeared to be thinking about that. "Fairly certain the answer is less, but eye of the beholder."

"Let's try again. In this story, am I Little Red Riding Hood?"

He laughed. "You will never in your life be safer than when you're with me. I'm bound to protect the Court and whoever is serving as magistrate."

"So that's why you're having dinner with me. Two nights in a row."

Growing suddenly serious, he shook his head slowly. "No, Rita. Why am I having trouble conveying that you're desirable? As a woman?"

"Is that what you're trying to convey?"

He dropped his chin and looked at me through his lashes. "Yes."

I took a deep breath that was ragged enough to betray my damaged self-esteem. I was filled with the doubt of someone with decimated belief in her romantic mojo.

"Are you monopolizing the magistrate, Keir?" Fie had come to stand at the table's edge.

"That's my plan." Keir's smile was more predatory than welcoming.

Fie looked at me. "What do I need to do to get invited to one of your lunch parties?"

"Gosh. Word gets around, huh?"

"Small town." Fie smiled.

"And I'm the new kid in town."

"If I understand your meaning correctly, then yes.

There's natural curiosity."

"I'd love to have you come tomorrow, but you'll make six and that's as many as we can seat in my kitchen. Twelve o'clock. And don't spread it around. I think I'm on the verge of being in trouble with Molly."

"Aww. Don't worry about Molly. She makes enough during Court Weeks so that she could close down the rest of the year. Of course, I don't know what we'd do if that happened. Have to figure out how to feed ourselves I suppose."

"Was there something else you need?" Keir challenged. "Mayor?"

On Keir's lips the term mayor sounded like a pejorative.

Fie's eyes slid to Keir slowly. "Well, I'm getting the feeling I'm not wanted."

"Imagine that," Keir replied.

Fie smirked and turned to me. "See you tomorrow."

I gave him my best smile, hopefully to make up for Keir's bad behavior.

When Fie had moved off, I said, "That was unforgivably rude."

Keir didn't look the least daunted. "Why do you think I want forgiveness?"

"Because you should! Why did you do that?"

"My relationship with Fie was established before you arrived. He's not my favorite person. In time, if we become close, perhaps I'll tell you why."

I sat back and relaxed a little. I couldn't know Keir's heart and mind or his history with Mayor Mistral. For all I knew, he could have good reason for acting that way.

A tiny laugh bubbled up from my solar plexus.

"What's funny?" Keir said.

"I was just thinking, 'Who am I to judge?', and the question struck me as laughable."

Jeff returned with drinks and took our orders for food. Mine was Shepherd's Pie. His was thick chowder and a ploughman's sandwich.

A change of subject was in order. "Tell me how you're managing to be the only person in Britain with a tan like that."

He grinned. "Sunlamp."

I knew he was lying, but let it go.

We chatted more about some of the sights that stood

out on my little tour. I sampled his chowder and added it to the yes list. I told him about one of the more interesting cases I'd read the night before that was comical.

He laughed softly. "I remember that."

"How old are you, Keir?"

"Lost count."

"Roughly."

"Not a whole millennium."

After a lengthy pause in which I tried, unsuccessfully to digest that, I said, "You're nine hundred years old?" His silence was confirmation. I stared at my empty ramekin and said, "Have you been doing this enforcing thing a long time then?"

"In a sense I was created for it. But Rita, understand this. In some ways we are not that far apart in age, you and I."

"I don't claim to be a math whiz, but I believe that's a difference of eight hundred fifty-seven years."

"I know it sounds like a lot." I snorted. "Hear me out. The world stayed pretty much the same until your grand-parents' generation. Technology sped things up in ways that made us dizzy. Information. Communication. Modes of travel. Nuclear power. Satellite surveillance?" He shook his head. "Next year and the one after that there will be astounding changes that you and I will experience for the first time."

"So, you're saying that you're a lot older, but not that much more experienced than I am."

"More or less."

"I give you credit for creativity in attempting to make a case for equality." I looked away in time to catch several faces I didn't know turn away quickly. "Are people staring because I'm new in town or because I'm having supper with you?"

Keir grinned. "I think it's because you're the new magistrate, which, you may not yet fully grasp, is a very big deal."

I sighed. "Maybe I should start having Olivia leave me something and eat at home."

"*That* is the last thing you should do. It would just prolong the fascination of newness. The sooner everyone has seen you and looked their fill, the sooner you'll be ignored like the rest of us."

"So much for being a very big deal."

He chuckled. "Come tomorrow. At four."

I realized I was nodding before I'd decided to say yes. "Okay. Give me the address."

"I put it into your contacts when I added my phone. Dessert?"

"I think I'll skip. You stay and have some though. I'm going to call my daughter and let her know I'm alive and well and enjoying jolly old England. She thinks I'm on a self-consoling vacation."

He cocked his head. "What's her name?"

"Evie. She's finishing undergrad studies and wants to go for a PhD."

"It must be nice to have… somebody."

I couldn't miss the undertone of sadness in that. "No family?"

"Siblings. No exes. No offspring."

"You've been alive for over nine centuries and you've never been formally attached?"

He shrugged, then winked. "Guess the right girl hasn't come along."

I laughed. "You really are a movie buff. Because nobody says that stuff anymore." At least I didn't think so.

"Guilty."

ON THE WALK go my house, he said, "Warmer air is coming in tomorrow."

"Oh? How do you know?"

He laughed. "Weather radar. See you at four."

"Okay. Would you like me to have Olivia put something together? For tea?"

"Wouldn't hear of it. I can't miss the chance to show you I'm good in the kitchen."

IT WAS SURPRISING that I was able to sleep well after reading cases that involved magical beings of all kinds; beautiful creatures of fantasy, monstrous creatures from fairy tales and argonaut myths.

And yet I did.

When I woke, the bedside light was still on. The journal I'd been reading was open on the bed beside me. And the smell of coffee was powerful enough to have wafted upstairs and slipped under the door. I smiled and realized that I probably hadn't awakened to a smile since I was ten and anticipating a visit to the carnival at the state fair.

It was nice.

I looked at the time. Nine o'clock. I was going to have to start setting an alarm.

I showered, had breakfast that somebody else made and would clean up, and put on my running shoes. I could walk with Lochlan in the red shoes, and they'd be comfortable, but it would look ridiculous. I'm no slave to fashion, but I do have standards.

AT TEN I was waiting outside Lochlan's office. His light, quick surefooted steps on the stairs would belie his old-man visage even without the shoes.

He smiled when he saw me. "Rita! A good day it is."

Yes. I agreed with that. "Concur, counselor."

He laughed.

It took forty-five minutes to sign the papers, only because I thought it would be prudent to at least scan and pretend to understand the legalese. British legalese, which is even more impossible to understand than American legalese, replete with trickery because, in contracts, some words don't mean what an ordinary person thinks they mean. I never asked Maggie what jiggery-pokery means, but it sounds like a description of what lawyers do.

Eventually I reasoned that I had enough money from my pre-Hallows life to get a ticket back to the U.S. The worst that could happen is that I wouldn't be any worse off than I was before I'd received the mysterious envelope at the residence motel.

That done, Lochlan and I walked past his house. When he whistled, the two Border Collies cleared the fence effortlessly and ran ahead of us.

"I can't wait to ask about some of the cases I've been reading, but first I want to ask again about established law? It seems like the magistrates are just sort of making it up as they go. Is that right or am I missing something?"

"It's right. The Powers That Be are careful to choose someone fair."

"Is it usually a man?"

"Hmmm. Perhaps more than half the time. It's always someone born in the first three weeks of October. This is the first time we've had an American."

"Why's that? October, I mean."

"Astrology. There's nature. There's nurture. But those things are the building blocks on traits established by the stars."

My thoughts wandered to my previous world in which such things would be called superstition and nothing more.

"Interpreting the law is one thing. Establishing new law with every case seems like a very big responsibility."

"It is. But not too much for you."

"Because the powers are never wrong."

"Precisely." He smiled.

"When do you think Aisling will whelp?"

"I'm thinking another week or so. Are you truly interested in a pup?"

"I'm not sure I can figure out how to make it work. Keeping a wolf in a townhouse."

"Oh. Well. That could be easily remedied."

"What do you mean?"

He came to a dead stop. "I've been remiss. And I hope you'll forgive me. It's a dollop of an overlook to be sure." He glanced at me. "The residence is yours to do with as you wish. You can change anything about it."

"You mean like move the furniture around? Repaint the shutters?"

"No," he said carefully. "I mean you can reshape it into *anything* you wish."

I was shaking my head while marveling at the beauty of the lake country. "Lochlan. I don't understand what you're saying. Spell it out like I'm a Mundie because that is what I am."

He inhaled deeply. "Sorry. Of course that was shorthand." He chuckled. "You're probably too young to know what shorthand is." I said nothing. He glanced over at me then made some hand gesture that brought the dogs nearer. "Your house has windows to a little garden."

"Yeah. I think of it as a courtyard, but that's not accurate since there's no entrance or exit."

"Right. But if it doesn't suit you to a T, your courtyard could be anything you want. If you'd like a larger house complete with acreage, stables and horses, or a tennis court, or a labyrinth… It can all be rearranged according to your preference."

I laughed. "Okay. You really are joking now."

"About what?"

"About finding any tennis players in Hallow Hill."

He scowled. "You have a point."

"I was kidding. I meant you have to be joking about redesigning reality to suit my whims."

"Not a bit. We can prevail upon one of the creatives to make your environment what you please. It's the least fae can do in exchange for your service as magistrate."

What was being said was still too far outside my ability to comprehend. I was having a hard time processing reorganizing reality. But it may've been even harder to absorb all the respect and appreciation being directed my way.

"So you're saying that, instead of looking out my kitchen window to a little courtyard with a tree that changes identities every day, I could be looking out at a piece of property large enough for a, um…" I looked over at the Border Collies. "Dog."

"Or two!"

"Two!"

"Well, a pair is nice because they keep each other occupied."

Rats. He'd planted a thought.

"With a dog door so that she could come and go when she needed to?"

"She?" he queried.

"I want one of the girl puppies."

"I see. Well, yes. We could arrange for an entrance that appears only when your pets approach."

"Don't think I didn't notice the plural, Lochlan. Are you thinking you'll have trouble finding homes for the puppies?"

"Oh, not at all," he scoffed. "Far from it. They're a prize by any measure."

"Are they…? Do they live a long time?"

"They do." He took note of my ensuing silence and added, "Are you afraid they might outlive you?"

"Crossed my mind."

"Well. None of us knows the whims of fate. But I can tell you this. Creatures such as these will always be in high demand by folk who'll treat them like the treasure they are. Have you had dogs before?"

"Not since I was growing up. My husband…" I didn't finish that sentence because it drew me up short, how many things I'd sacrificed for nothing.

"With this particular breed all that's required is love and sustenance. Little training is required since they can sense your emotions and have an incomparable desire to please."

I smiled, feeling a tingle of excitement rush through me like this was really happening. "But I still don't understand how my house can become something so different. I mean there are houses behind my house."

"Let's come at this from another direction. If you were to imagine your dream house and place it somewhere around here." He swept his arm in the direction of Hallow Hill below. "What would it look like and where would it be?"

I thought about that for a few minutes.

"I love the way your house looks. On the outside. I might make a few interior changes. But it's like a fairytale cottage with a beautiful garden. And..." I changed my mind about finishing that thought.

"And what?"

"I, um, thought better of what I was about to say. I mean nothing could be worse than a person who's been given everything and finds fault. I don't want to be her."

"There's no one here but you, me, and the dogs. And, since I'm your solicitor, everything you tell me is confidential."

I chuckled. "Good to know. Well, if you're pressing and really want to know my deepest thoughts about housing, I don't like the door that connects the Hallows and the house. It doesn't feel right."

Lochlan nodded. "Go on. I can tell there's something else."

"Well, there was this TV show once where a private eye sort of lived with his car. I mean there was an overhead door that opened to his living room? With space for the car? And if I was designing from scratch, I'd do something like that."

With a smile, Lochlan said, "A fairytale cottage with a car in the living room. Sounds perfect for you."

"Stop it!" I laughed. "When you put it like that, it makes me sound like a ninny."

"You're entitled to your druthers, Rita. As we all are. Now here's what I want you to do. Think through exactly what you'd like. I'll make a call to someone who can make that happen."

I stopped abruptly. "Just like that?" He nodded. "Wow."

"We own a lot of property around Hallow Hill. Where would you like your house to be?"

"On this side of the town."

He smiled. "Like where Ivy and I live."

I returned his smile with the appropriate sheepishness. "Well it is a good location. I don't want to be close enough to crowd you. But it is a great location. From your front gate you can see most of the village and all the way down the lane to the river. It's charming."

"I'm flattered you like it. As you know, there's nothing across the way from us but field. Do you think you'd be happy there?"

"I would, but like I said I…"

"You would not be crowding us. It would be a pleasure to have you as a neighbor. And I'm sure the dogs would love having their pups close by."

I laughed. "Back to that, are we?"

LOCHLAN AND FIE joined Maggie, Dolan, Olivia, and I for lunch. It was a fascinating study in group dynamics to see how changing the composition of the group changed the atmosphere and conversation.

"Olivia," I said. "I'm starting to think you really could cook anything I name." I took another bite of tapa with spicy chicken in perfect pastry.

Everyone around the table complimented Olivia in turn. She blushed, but perhaps slightly less than the day before.

After lunch I picked up reading where I'd left off, but had some trouble focusing. My mind kept wandering to my upcoming tea at Keir's house and what I was going to see.

The organization that Olivia had made of my clothes was magazine worthy. But that didn't stop me from plowing through drawers and hangers to try to find the right thing. When I found the perfect thing for a gate-house tea, a ruin exploration, and a creature unveiling, it didn't fit. Of course.

My jeggings, that should be flatteringly sexy, pushed my womanliness up so that it spilled over the waistband. Ugh. Pub food. And wine.

With regret I set them aside and dubbed them 'goal' jeggings. I pulled on thick cotton tights with plenty of give in fabric and seams, topped that with a long sea-blue knit tunic, and grabbed my vintage knockoff bomber jacket. I tried on the red shoes, but they looked so outrageous that I decided to wear my ankle boots that could sub as hikers and carry the magic pumps in a tote.

I GAVE ROMEO the address.

"Very good, madam."

"How long until we're there?"

"Five minutes."

"Oh. It's really close."

"Yes, madam."

"Well, carry on." What can I say? It was becoming one of my favorite expressions.

While Romeo drove, I texted Keir.

ME: *Five minutes.*

KEIR: *Waiting.*

By the time we were halfway there I could see the castle ruins at the top of a hill.

"Is that where we're going?" I asked Romeo knowing he could not see where I was pointing.

Still, he said, "Yes, madam," as if he could.

It was glorious. It was majestic. It was romantic. Perhaps more so than when it was new and in a fine state of repair. When we neared the entrance, I saw Keir waving.

"Drive toward the man who's waving," I instructed.

When the car stopped, Keir opened my door and whistled. "Nice car, Magistrate."

I looked back like I'd forgotten what it looked like. "I didn't pick it, but I have a feeling that, if I'd been given a choice of all the cars in the world, I probably would've picked this one."

"A perfect match," he said. "How was the trip?"

As we began walking toward the castle, I said, "I didn't know it's walking distance."

"It is, but it's just as well you brought the car because it will be dark on the way back and your eyes are…"

"Not magical?"

"Well…"

"Keir. You don't have to pussyfoot around the truth. I'm a Mundie."

"Hmmm. You are and you aren't. Soon you'll have the sight." He bent his head slightly toward me. "Without the shoes. You'll have perfect health and a very long life. Your background will be what it is, of course, but your constitution is changing."

"I'm not entirely sure how I feel about that."

"You want bad health?"

I laughed. "Of course not."

"So welcome to Tregeagle. I live over here." He pointed to an outbuilding with pinkish-rust colored stone that matched the castle and other buildings. "Would you like to see the place first or have tea?"

"Tour before tea."

"This way."

"This is my first ruin."

"There's not much to know other than to watch your step."

"You're vying for worst tour guide ever."

With a chuckle, he said, "Oh. You want a dash of history." He gestured toward a nearby plateau. "These stones came from a Roman fort that sat right over there. The materials were here already and just needed to be moved. It was built by one of King John's barons then slowly fell apart when it wasn't properly maintained. About three hundred years ago one of the fae queens fell in love with it.

Liked the look and feel and the fact that it occupies a strategical location, from a magical point of view."

"What kind of strategy?"

"She recognized that it had all the makings of a powerful faerie mound with the perfect disguise above."

"Um. This is probably going to sound woefully ignorant, but I don't know what a faerie mound is."

He dropped his chin to his chest and smiled. "Seems I have my work cut out for me then. The fae have the ability to create entire worlds underground and undetected, generating their own light and climate, independent of the sun. Magic kind aren't subject to the restraints of physics as understood by humans."

"You're saying that there are people, um, fae living here? Beneath this ground?"

He nodded. "Indeed. There are worlds unknown to humans, undetectable by the human magic of technology."

"Do you think there may be a mind-blowing point at which my head will actually explode?"

He laughed. "Rita. If you weren't supremely adaptable, the Powers wouldn't have chosen you. Your head will not explode. Every time you learn something new, you just shift your concept of reality a tad and keep moving forward."

I felt like giving Keir a fist bump because that's exactly what I'd been doing ever since I received the envelope from Lochlan.

"Was it here before the town was named?"

With a grin, Keir said, "Put that together, did you? Yes. The town was named Hallow Hill because of the location of the mound."

"Can I see it?"

"Sorry. No. Your composition is too dense to enter. That may change over time. When the sight settles on you permanently, you'll gradually become more like us."

"I see."

We both laughed and I was grateful that he 'got' my sense of humor.

We spent an hour looking around the beautiful ruined stacks of stone. Climbing stone staircases with steps so worn they slanted downward at an angle.

"I'll bet this was dark inside when it was still fully enclosed," I said. "There aren't many windows and the few that are here are so narrow they wouldn't let in much light."

"Weather was a concern in old drafty castles with high ceilings. Did you know that's why tapestries came to be popular?"

"No."

"They were originally rugs, but humans started hanging them on the walls in winter to insulate from the cold and help retain the heat generated by fires." He waved toward the building he'd pointed out as his house. "I have some of them."

"Tapestries from the eleventh century? They have to be priceless."

He chuckled. "I suppose they would be. If they were for sale."

"You don't worry about theft?"

He looked at me like I'd lost my mind. "That is utterly impossible, Rita. I assure you."

My first impulse was to ask why theft was impossible, but decided I'd put that 'consciousness shift' off for another time. "Magic kind never have to worry about such things as paying the light bill, do they?"

With a shake of his head and a single barked laugh, he

said, "No."

We'd reached the highest level of the castle and, when we stepped outside, I realized that, aside from defense, there was another reason why that spot had been chosen as the build site. The countryside could be seen for miles around, on all sides. I turned in a circle thinking each new view was more stunning than the last.

"You should come up here with me after dark. The stars seem close enough to touch."

"Stars," I whispered. It had been a long time since I'd been able to enjoy the night sky as it can only be appreciated in darkness. Light pollution had robbed us of a view to the stars. With a small internal shake, I said, "You're far enough away from the big towns to see the night sky?"

He grinned. "A deity owed me a favor. She erected curtains that block human-made light."

"A deity," I repeated. "What did you do for her?"

He just laughed. "Let's go have tea. Then I'll put on what you Yanks call a dog and pony show."

Shrugging in agreement, I took one last look, and said, "Okay."

THE CONVERTED GATEHOUSE was one large square room, half living room, half bedroom, with a galley kitchen in a corner. It looked like Ralph Lauren had personally decorated it for a British bachelor. Deep lush greens. Deep lush reds. Dark polished wood paneling. Old distressed wood floors. Riding boots by the door. And, as mentioned, museum-quality tapestries on the wall. It could easily be the cover of *Architectural Digest*. Or, sans riding boots, the set of *Home Alone*.

It was also as seductive as a nocturnal fantasy. And the fact that the bed was the focal point of the room did nothing to keep my mind above my elastic waistband.

A table for two was set by the fireplace replete with goodies that made my mouth water. I imagined it fit for the queen. The, um, human queen. Beautiful to look at, scrumptious to the taste. It also meant the day of jeggings reckoning receded further into the future. Oh well.

"This is lovely, Keir. Do all the new magistrates get treated to tea?"

"No one other than myself has ever enjoyed tea here. Until today."

"In that case, I'm honored. And, in that case, why

me?"

"I've already declared my interest. Why are you not hearing me?"

That was a good question. One I decided to set aside.

While Keir turned on the fire under the kettle, I said, "Should I be anxious about the dog and pony show?"

"No. You're afraid that I'm gruesome in my altered form? An ogre perhaps? Bent on consuming the flesh of small children?"

"Ew. I hadn't thought of it, but now that image is in my head. If your intention was to assuage my worry, you missed the target. Big time." My eyes returned to the riding boots by the door. "Did Thomasin Cobb make your boots?"

Keir glanced in that direction. "Yes. Did you have an unpleasant encounter with him?"

"You could say that."

He smirked. "It's part of the service. He's like the soup Nazi of goblin cobblers."

I looked at Keir with a new appreciation. "You're a fan of Seinfeld?"

"Of course. Who doesn't like Seinfeld?"

"I don't see a TV."

He picked up a remote and pointed it at a nine-hundred-year-old tapestry, which immediately responded by drawing to one side like a heavy curtain. An immense flatscreen TV was revealed, mounted on the wall behind.

"Wow."

"Nice, huh?" he said. "Humans are not all bad."

"Thank you?" He laughed. "Put it back. My illusion of days gone by was just smashed."

He closed the tapestry over the TV just as the kettle whistled. "Here we are."

"So, he doesn't give you that same treatment, I take it?"

"He wouldn't dare." He looked over at me. "If you want me to adjust his attitude, I'll be happy to do it."

I SET ASIDE any pretense of dieting to enjoy strawberries with heavy clotted cream on shortbread, making yummy noises all the while. The lunch tapas had been marvelous, but that was five hours ago and felt like ten.

"I have a secret. This is my first real tea, but I can't imagine that there's any lovelier or tastier anywhere."

"A gracious compliment. I accept." He smiled. "It's a day of firsts. First ruin. First tea. What else can we add to the list?"

Seeing that his smile had turned sultry, and allowing myself to think he might be flirting with me in earnest, I decided the smart thing would be to find a new topic.

"How many magistrates have you worked for?"

His smiling expression became guarded. "A few."

"And do you like being the, um, enforcer?"

His brow pulled into a frown and I hated that I'd put it there. "Like or dislike is irrelevant. It's what I was created to do."

"That's the second time you've said something of the sort. What do you mean by created?"

As he sat back and drank the last of his tea, I had an opportunity to openly stare at his beauty, the masculine planes of his face, the suggestion of muscle underneath his thin pullover. The direction of my thoughts had me feeling more like a pervert than a guest for tea.

Raising his gaze to meet mine, he said, "I'm not a natural born. The fae created me, and my kind, long ago to save themselves from extinction. They're a passionate race that doesn't shy away from conflict, provoked or otherwise. No. That's an understatement. If left unrestrained, they run toward conflict and revel in it.

"In brief, they were killing each other off. Their numbers were dwindling and even they came to recognize that there are better ways to spend time. Perhaps they could have developed the discipline to curb their primal impulses. But instead one of the queens, who was capable of willing a new species into being, created us to referee. It effectively put a governor on worst instincts."

For a time, I was speechless while sorting through and editing my thoughts. I struck responses again and again before finally saying, "This is all so alien to me. I don't know what to think, much less what to say."

"Well," he said as he replaced the pretty Royal Doulton cup on its saucer, "the fact that you're not running from the building screaming is certainly a credit in your favor."

"To be honest? I did think about it. If you're powerful enough to stop fae wars, you must be a fearsome creature. In your alternate, um, guise."

He stood abruptly. "Come with me. I want to show

you something before it gets dark out."

"What?"

"You'll see, Mistress Magistrate. Be patient."

I put one last bite of shortbread in my mouth for the road and followed him out.

"Oh," he said, looking down. "You're going to need the shoes. The other shoes."

"They're in the car."

He walked downhill with me to where I'd left Romeo. I heard the satisfying sound of doors unlocking as I neared. I smiled at Keir. "That means he likes me."

"Does it now," he said indulgently, more a statement than a question.

I pulled the tote from the rear seat and changed my shoes with my back to Keir and the castle, replaced the tote then turned around to say something about how ridiculous it was to wear red glittery pumps. But what I saw caused me to gasp and step back quickly. I don't know how far I would have traveled backward, but my shocked retreat was abruptly stopped by the very solid side of the car.

What I saw on the hill just above me, in place of the

ruined pile of stones I'd explored earlier, was a castle transformed into what it must have looked like when it was newly built, complete with grounds full of flowering bushes and fruit trees heavily laden with ready-to-pick pears, apples, and oranges.

"What…?" was all I could manage. Every time I thought I had a tenuous handle on the whole the-world-isn't-what-you-think gig, I would be blindsided by something even *more* impossibly impossible.

Keir looked concerned and held out his hands. "Rita. Breathe."

"I am breathing!" I was a little angered by the insinuation that I was a shrinking violet about to faint. "I wouldn't be *talking* if I wasn't *breathing.*"

His face spread into a relieved-looking smile. "Right then. When you're ready, let's take a second tour with your senses tuned to match my kind."

I pushed myself upright and away from the car and was gratified that my knees were holding my weight.

"Off we go then."

I kept pace with Keir as we climbed the gentle ascent.

"Alright. Explain. What am I seeing?"

"Without the shoes you see and experience Tregeagle as a ruin. This is the version magic kind experience." He grinned. "Hiding in plain sight, eh? Every so often the National Trust tries to buy it. That isn't going to happen. Ever."

"What keeps people from driving up here and wandering around on their own?"

"There's a ward around the property that discourages Mundies from wanting to stop."

I gave him a dubious look. "How does that work?"

"Beyond my pay grade as they say. I can't explain how magic works."

I slowed as we walked through the gardens, the crunch of crushed granite underneath our feet. It was paradise.

The general layout of the castle foundation and the type and color of outer stone were the only things that were similar to the ruin. Rather than a few sparse windows, three walls of the great room featured stained glass windows, as many as the famed cathedral at Cologne. I knew this because I'd once dreamed of a trip to Germany.

These windows told stories of mythic creatures, wars, famous lovers, notable monarchs, and many things I wasn't equipped to interpret. The bank of windows at the head of the enormous nave were slightly larger, the one in the middle depicting a figure in a scarlet-colored robe. To his right was an elf writing on a scroll with quill pen. To his left was an enormous, fierce-looking winged lion sitting like a sphinx with one paw raised as if either protecting the magistrate or demonstrating a threatening prowess.

The large dais supported furniture that resembled a modern courtroom judge's bench, but was intricately carved, undoubtedly with more tales or history of magic kind. To the left and right of the dais were raised galleries, carved to match the judge's bench, with rich-looking upholstered seating the same scarlet color as the magistrate robes. The pair of galleries looked like they could function as choir lofts or jury seating.

The floor of both nave and aisles was a mosaic of gardens in full bloom underneath seating that was shaped like long benches, but covered in deep plush velvet upholstery in various shades of green that would be found in gardens.

"Beautiful," I whispered.

"Is. Isn't it?" Keir said from beside me. "The fae

queens are known for their decorating skills."

"I can see why."

"I'm glad you like it because, during Court Week, this is your kingdom."

I jerked my head in his direction. "This is…"

"Your court, Magistrate."

Of all the things I'd expected, holding court in a space as grand and immense as the interior of Tregeagle, wasn't one of them. I'd never been a huge fan of public speaking. Or having a lot of attention drawn to myself.

I hadn't realized that I was shaking my head no until Keir said, "Why are you shaking your head? Is there something about it you don't like?"

I breathed in a muffled laugh. "That's not the problem."

"What is?"

"I'd thought court would be small. A few people at a time."

"Oh." He looked around like he was trying to imagine that. "No. It's a gathering. It won't always be filled to capacity. There will be a lot going on outside. Much like a human carnival. But there will be cases of high interest that draw spectators and, at times, the aisles might be filled with what you call standing room only?"

"What about the fire hazard?" I said lamely.

"Not an issue." He laughed softly. "But I think you were joking. Would you like to see your chambers?"

"Chambers?" At that point I decided I might as well relax into the full Alice-down-the-rabbit-hole experience. After all I'd signed on for the ride. "Sure. Why the hell not?"

We walked the length of the nave, slowly, turned right at the dais and Keir opened a side door at the end of the columned aisle. The magistrate's chambers were like a private apartment with living and dining areas, bedroom, study, and toilet.

"Why is there a bedroom?"

"It's easier for you to stay here in Court Week. It also discourages people from trying to get your attention and influence your decisions."

"Is there security?"

"The only security you need is me. And my reputation. During Court Week I will sleep at the door to your chambers. You'll be as safe as if you were with the gods." I looked his way. Something about the way he said that made me believe it. "Will this do?" He looked around the apartment like he was trying to imagine how it might look through my eyes and I was struck by the sense that he was invested in my reaction.

"Of course, Keir. How could I ask for more?"

I was gratified by the obvious pleasure he took in my answer. "It was very thoughtful of you to arrange this, um, tour. So that I'd know what to expect and not be overwhelmed when..." I trailed off.

"When the next Court Week is in session. At Hallowstide."

"Yes. Hallowstide," I repeated. "Although I expect no amount of preparation and pre-warning will stave off the being overwhelmed."

"You know you're the right person."

"Because the Powers That Be are never wrong?"

He grinned. "Exactly." Looking up at the windows he said, "It's getting dark. Let's go outside."

"Okay." We retraced our steps, the length of the nave. Several times I stopped to admire the mosaic on the floor. Several times I stopped to turn in a circle to take it all in.

"You could make a fortune if you charged admission to see this."

Keir chuckled softly. "Perhaps. But fortunes in the human sense don't mean much when you can have what you want."

"I guess that's true."

When we reached the gardens, Keir steered me toward one of the pathways as wide as the pedestrian trafficway of a mall.

"You ready?" He grinned, but didn't wait for me to answer.

The space he'd occupied became a Keir-shaped mass of shimmering air for a couple of seconds. Then, with a soft pop, what stood in his place was a winged lion so enormous he was at eye level with me. I may have whimpered from the surprise of it, but would never admit it if pressed. The new Rita doesn't run from vampires who go still as the grave in the middle of a shop, or Border Collies that turn into bigger-than-life wolves, or nasty little goblin cobblers, or even banshees. Certainly she would not run from a creature of such mythic magnitude.

I stood my ground, but did inhale deeply. Involuntarily. As if my lungs decided on their own that courage requires more oxygen.

The lion's fur was a golden tan, much the same color as Keir's skin, sleek and shiny. The eyes were the same green with gold and rust flecks. The mane had the slightest suggestion of curl, as did Keir's blonde locks. As if he could read my thoughts, he shook his mane, stretched his neck, and angled his head as if he was inviting me to touch.

I reached out my hand slowly, chanting the assurances I'd been given that I would not be in danger from magic kind. When the lion didn't move, I lightly touched his mane and found it soft as newly conditioned hair.

He angled his body slightly away from me. I didn't know if it was permission to look or touch. I ran my hand along the silky fur of his neck to his back and to his shoulders that supported mighty wings. When my fingers touched the joint where the wing closest to me met his back, the wings lifted in a slight flutter, but did not expand.

The feathers were gold and gray with silver under-down.

When I found my full-throated voice, I said, "Can you fly?"

"Yes," came a deep rumble.

I jerked back because I hadn't expected him to be able to talk in this form. "You can talk."

I supposed the sound that followed was a chuckle, but it was too growly to be sure.

Dusk was spent walking through an enchanted garden beside a creature so fantastic, he defies description. When the last trace of light had faded, the air shimmered and Keir walked toward me smiling.

"Look up," he said.

I did. As he'd promised the pitch-black sky above was resplendent with stars bright and twinkling like diamonds. I laughed out loud. "It was cloudy. How am I seeing this?"

"I told you. A deity owed me a favor."

"This is all…"

Keir stepped in front of me and stood close. Close enough for me to smell wind and musk.

"Tell me what I want to know," he demanded.

"What do you want to know?"

"You know."

"I don't."

With a scoff, he said, "Can you be attracted to someone like me? Now that you know everything?"

There wasn't enough light to read his face but his eyes glimmered even in the dark. "I don't think I know *everything.*"

"Everything you'd be angry about if you found out later."

I hesitated. "I'm not really sure what you're asking."

With an exasperated huff, he pulled me into his body and brushed my lips with his. Testing.

"Kiss me," he said.

"I can't. I'm married."

He released me and stepped back. "Is that the only reason?"

The question begged to be thought through. After all, Maggie had suggested I beware of Keir, the player. And she did it right in front of him.

"If I said that's the only reason, what would you take from my answer?"

"That you're interested in me and will be open to getting to know each other better when you're no longer bound. Technically."

I had to agree that the whole married thing was an excuse to stall while I sorted out my feelings. I'd never thought I'd have the experience of being pursued by someone as desirable as Keir Culain. The fact that he could become a mythic being at will wasn't as strange and difficult to accept as I would've thought just a week ago.

"I like you, Keir. I don't need to tell you that you're ridiculously appealing because you already know that. But if you really work for the magistrate, what you're suggesting would be risky. We could be creating some irrevocable problems just by behaving like we aren't mature." He sighed deeply and looked away. "Let's get to know each other as friends. Explore our compatibility before diving headlong into something that would be awkward to the max if it didn't work out. How does that sound?"

"It's not my first choice." I smiled as I reached up and pulled a lock of his silky hair through my fingers. "We'll have suppers at the pub?"

"I can't promise every night." Truthfully there was no reason why not except that a girl can't be *that* easy.

"When you can."

"Perfect."

"Most nights."

I laughed. "You get points for persistence." I looked in the direction of the car, suddenly wanting my Mundie shoes. "I'd better start back."

"I can make dinner."

"Thank you. I'll grab something at home. Journals to read." That's when it hit me. "You're the sephalian."

"I am."

"I'd never heard it before. Not outside the journals. That's you in the big stained-glass window."

"Humans call me a gryphonic shifter. Sometimes chimera of sorts. Yes. That's me."

There was a question in my throat struggling to get out while I tried to exercise enough self-discipline to suppress it. I failed. I had to ask again. "Why me?"

He lowered his chin and stared into my eyes. "You mean why do I find myself thinking about you throughout the day?"

"Well, I didn't know that, but sure. Let's start with that."

He cocked his head. "The bugger you married must've

been a horror to your self-image if you don't know. Rita, you're everything a male could want. Beautiful. Smart. Funny. Gracious. Kind. I like your voice. And I *love* your laugh. I hear it in my dreams."

Wow.

I was near speechless, again, not because my voice had frozen, but because my brain had frozen. In less than a minute Keir Culain had given me more reason to feel attractive than over two decades combined with my soon-to-be ex. My sensuality was responding by blooming to life. *Stay for 'dinner'. Stay for 'dinner'. Stay for 'dinner'.*

"I can't deny the part of you that will remain human is like a magnet." I wasn't expecting that. "Fae live a long time and can usually have what we want. That's fertile ground for boredom. The self-awareness that you're not here forever, that time is limited, it creates an urgency to everything you do. It's like sparks are shooting off all around you all the time, the sense of urgency, the desire to *really* live while you can."

Keir had a way of rendering me speechless. He made it sound like mortality was the better way to go. So much for all the people who'd died looking for the Fountain of

Youth.

Bringing to bear self control that was extraordinary for me, I said, "Thank you for tea, the tour, and for showing me… everything. It's a day I won't forget."

"If you ever need me, I can change forms and be at your house in seconds."

I turned back. "Seconds?"

He grinned. "I can fly really fast when I want to."

"Oh." I let that sink in as I neared Romeo. "Thank you. That's good to know." I hesitated as I started to get into the car. "Where's your phone?" He pulled it from his pocket and held it up. "Where does your phone go when you change into your, um, other form?"

He smiled and shook his head. "It waits with my clothes until I want it again."

Of course, questions came to mind, but that sounded like an in-depth interview for another time. So, I settled on, "Good night."

AFTER BRAD PASSED on, and I use the human phrase because there's no magic-kind equivalent, his nephew moved into his house and took over the shop. I liked the kid very much and he liked me. He even gave me a 'rapper name', Just Ice.

I said, "Why? You find me cold?"

"No." He smirked. "Don't you get it? Just Ice? Justice?"

Braden became a regular at my luncheons. He was beyond charming. He was entertaining.

The days began to take on a routine. My mornings were occupied with social media including email and walking with Lochlan while discussing cases I'd read the night before. My lunch parties had become such a hit that I was beginning to feel like a salon hostess. Hallow Hill residents vied for invitations. Olivia thrived and bloomed from recognition for her outstanding cooking. It was such a hit that I planned enough space for a round table to comfortably seat six in my cottage-to-be-built.

Afternoons were divided into learning the operations of the shop, including my favorite part, which was viewing the new pieces that had arrived overnight, by mysterious magical methods, and planning my new house.

Because I had a tendency to get enthralled by the journals and read until the wee hours, I frequently took naps. At six I headed to the pub for supper. When Keir realized that I liked using my front door that faced the side lane, he began waiting on the stoop in front of my house. Even in rainy weather. He'd be standing there with an extra-large umbrella that would shelter, or partially shelter, two.

Gradually I began to relax into the possibility of actually being sexually attractive. One day I realized I might fit into the goal jeggings, tried them on, and whooped as I jumped in front of the mirror. Nothing sheds pounds like a romantic interest. So I gave Keir the credit for making me feel 'hot' for the first time since I was old enough to legally drink.

I'd suggested to him that we might revisit the love connection thing if I thought we were compatible and, if I was satisfied that, somehow, it wouldn't interfere with my commitment as magistrate to the magical community. I took it seriously. As I was prone to do with everything that mattered to me.

It seemed that the first condition had been met. So I'd determined to bring up the second at supper that evening.

Chapter Six

Jealousy and All That Jazz

MY LUNCHEONS HAD been an unintended means to get to know the people of Hallow Hill faster than I might have otherwise. They'd also become so popular that I began creating charts to rotate invitations for fear that someone would feel neglected or left out.

This had become clear to me on my return home late one evening after first having supper with Keir, then having coffee with Baileys at Lochlan's and Ivy's house.

I discussed my thoughts on my house and had decided I was ready. Lochlan was quick to assure me that the plan didn't have to be perfect, that details could be changed just as easily as created.

"And you don't need to worry about the garden," Ivy said. "I have sisters who will care for the green things."

"That sounds like borderline bribery to me."

Lochlan gave Ivy a warning look. "I agree," he told her. "The magistrate can afford to pay for gardening, Ivy. Come up with a reasonable barter so that the magistrate isn't indebted."

Ivy slumped like a teenager, saying, "Okaaaay," a word she'd begun using more and more, although the pronunciation was odd sounding more like okai than okay. She grinned at me under her eyelashes like we shared a conspiracy.

"No, Ivy," I said. "I really can't accept help that I don't pay for in full. I'd hate to have to hire humans from a nearby town."

Her eyes flew open in surprise and she sat up straight, looking to Lochlan. "Can she do that?"

Lochlan chuckled and sucked on his pipe that he'd recently taken up again. He'd had Aoumiel spell it so that there was satisfaction but neither smoke nor smell.

"Of course, she can."

Ivy scowled and crossed her arms in front of her. "Alright! Market rate."

"Where did you learn a phrase like 'market rate'?"

Lochlan asked her.

"I overheard Rita say it to Dolan as I was coming to lunch last week. She said there's no such thing as market rate when a piece is one of a kind." She smiled. "We had salad sampler because I was there."

Lochlan looked at me. "That was very thoughtful of you. Do you always tailor the menu to the dietary preferences of your guests?"

"Only if I happen to know about them."

I LEFT LATE, feeling excited about seeing the cottage of my dreams come to life.

As I passed the corner where the Hallows sat, just a few feet from my door, a figure hidden in the shadows stepped into my path. To my credit and personal pride, I didn't scream. Or even squeak. I stilled and waited.

When I realized it was John David Weir, it didn't lighten my concern one bit.

"I wasn't always a vampire, you know," he blurted, sounding defensive.

Though I didn't know how to respond, I did relax a little. It was a far cry from, "I want to drink your blood."

"Honestly, John David," I began, "I don't know much about you at all. When you came to lunch, you never said a word."

"That's what I want to talk about."

"Lunch. Or extreme reticence?"

He stepped further into the lamplight. "Lunch."

"You want to talk about lunch. Okay. I'm listening."

"Why haven't I been invited again? Everyone else has."

"First, some people haven't even been invited a first time."

"Like who?"

"Like Thomasin Cobb."

"He doesn't count."

"He doesn't?"

"That disagreeable little podger. If he didn't make the best bloody boots…" The vampire sounded exasperated, on the verge of getting worked up. "Thomasin Cobb has never been invited anywhere by anyone in the entirety of his singularly drab and bitter history."

"Wow. When you get going, it turns out you know how to use your words."

"Use my words. You mean talk?" I said nothing. "You

are being facetious."

"Guilty."

The vampire moved so fast that I didn't see it. He was standing on the sidewalk then he was directly in front of me. Inches away. Having closed the distance in less time than it takes to blink. It was startling and I'm not ashamed of jumping. Or of being very conscious of the fact that he was very tall.

"So. Are you going to tell me why?" he demanded, looking down at me so that I had to rear back to see his face.

My heart was racing, but I remained where I was and struggled to keep my voice even. I was suddenly acutely aware that the town was utterly deserted at that time of night. "John David, you're scaring me. Do you intend to be scaring me?"

Even in the dim lamplight I could clearly read confusion on his face. He took a step back. "No."

"Tell me now. Should I be afraid of you?"

"No."

Taking him at his word, which sounded sincere, a little of the tension melted away from my neck and shoulders.

"This is a personal question. So, I hope you don't mind me asking. Do you have any friends?"

"Friends?" He looked down and away, appearing to be thinking about it for a few seconds. I couldn't tell if he was trying to decide if he had friends or if he was trying to decide whether to answer the question. "Not anymore," he said softly, the implication being that they'd died while he'd gone on living. Though he didn't expound, I got the distinct impression that wasn't his first choice.

"Would you like to make friends with the people who live here?"

"They're not interested."

"Why not?"

"Because I'm not like them."

"Not like them in what way?"

"Not part of the fae world. Like all of them."

"I don't really understand that distinction."

"Humans see me as I am. I can't just decide to be something else."

"Do you see them the way they see each other?"

"How can I know how others perceive?"

"Are you always so philosophical?"

"If you mean, do I see past the guises of fae, the answer is yes."

"Why didn't you decide to live somewhere with other, um, vampires?"

His laughter, though mirthless, was beautiful to look at and to hear, but I was again startled because it was so unexpected. "We don't get along well with others."

"I see." I sighed. "You feel left out. You're lonely." The lack of denial was confirmation enough. He struck me as the sort who'd be defensive about loneliness if it wasn't true. "Did you… ever have friends?"

He nodded so sorrowfully that I almost felt grief coming from him in wafts of vibration.

"Do you want to tell me about it?" Again, he nodded. On impulse, I said, "John David. Can I call you John David?" He nodded. "Would you like to have tea in my kitchen tomorrow? You could come at four. I have someplace to be at six, but we could visit for a while."

He was genuinely surprised. That was easy to read. But I also saw something else flit across his handsome face. Excitement. "Yes," he said. "Four."

Just when you think life is becoming routine.

When I reached my door, I turned to see if he was still there. Perhaps he was and perhaps not. I didn't see him, but I'd learned that vampires are very good at blending into shadows.

THE NEXT DAY arrived with a buzz that I could feel when I stepped into the Hallows. Perhaps Molly's intuition lessons were doing some good.

Following the voices coming from the workroom, I arrived without removing my jacket or setting my bag down.

"Rita," Maggie said. "We received a shipment."

"Go on," I prompted.

"It contained a… thing," Dolan corrected.

I looked at the piece on the table. The sculpted head of an unusual creature was supported by a thick rod that looked like rebar.

"What is it?" I said.

"It's a hobknobbit. I think they're extinct."

The head was blue and wore a Turkish-style hat with gray and black spots. This representation of a hobknobbit had a short forehead, a nose so large it was a caricature, a small mouth, and eyebrows that seemed to be asking a question. It was hard to place whether the intention of the piece was to convey comedy or evil. It could have gone either way.

I set my bag down and pulled the lapels of my jacket back so that I could free my arms. "Were hobknobbits good or bad?" Maggie and Dolan looked at each other. "Well?" I said. "It's not a hard question."

"Aye. 'Tis harder than ye may believe. We do no' think in those terms."

"No?" She shook her head. "So you're saying that magic kind are amoral?"

"I'm no sayin' anythin' of the sort. I've no idea what amoral is."

I huffed. "Dolan. Why do you think it's a magic thing?"

He passed his palm through air a few inches above the hobknobbit. "I feel it. You could, too."

With a smirk, I said, "Doubt it."

"Try," he challenged.

"This is going to be a waste of time."

Maggie moved aside so that I could come to stand in

front of the thing. I looked at Dolan. He nodded encouragement. So, my hand hovered over the odd-shaped head for a couple of seconds before I jerked back. I believed I'd felt something akin to static electricity.

"You planted that thought in my head," I accused Dolan.

He looked at me with curiosity. "I can do that?"

I grunted. "How would I know?"

"You're the magistrate," he said coolly as if that explained the meaning of the universe.

"So you think that makes me *all-knowing* all of a sudden? I don't think so."

"Well, forgive me for saying so, but when it comes to the new pieces, you act like you're *'all-knowing'*."

"Wow. Dolan. You just called me a know-it-all."

My tone and the hand on my hip must have conveyed that being a know-it-all is not a good thing because he said, "Is that bad?"

I couldn't contain a smile. "Is this the most words you've ever spoken in a two-minute span in your entire life?"

I took it as confirmation when he said nothing, but

slowly smiled.

Good enough.

"What needs to be done about this…?" I turned to Maggie for help, having already forgotten what to call the ugly thing.

"Hobknobbit."

"Yes. I can't imagine that anyone in their right mind would want to collect something so unattractive. Can't we just, um, dispose of it?"

Maggie and Dolan both looked at the sculpture.

"Could be a titch difficult," Maggie said. "Magic artifacts are near impossible to get rid of. Chances are that's how it's ended up here. As our problem."

"You mean like hot potato?"

Maggie looked at Dolan, who simply shrugged, before saying, "We do no' know hot potato."

"Oh. Sorry. People, usually children gather in a circle and begin tossing something small, like a potato, to each other while music is playing. The person holding the potato when the music stops is eliminated."

Maggie's already pink, Irish face pinkened further in horror. "It's a game to eliminate children?" I stared at her trying to imagine what she was seeing in her head. Hand going to her hip, she turned to Dolan. "And Mundies think *we're* a dark and bloodthirsty lot!"

I took a deep breath. "No, Maggie. I didn't mean eliminated as in killed. I mean their participation in the game is over. Not their lives."

"Oh."

"So, there are two possibilities. Someone may have just sent this to us like tossing the hot potato, which for all we know could've been going on for a very long time, or someone may have sent us this with mischief in mind? Or worse?"

"Crossed my mind," Maggie said.

"Who's on for lunch today?"

The question sounded like I was beginning to fit in with Hallow Hill culture by doing such things as abruptly changing subject with no segue. Since that wasn't unusual, Maggie rushed over to the lunch clipboard without missing a beat. It now hung on the kitchenette wall next to the passage to my house.

"You're havin' Geoffrey, Esmerelda, Braden, Ivy, and of course, Olivia."

"Ooh. Esmerelda. After lunch I'll invite Esmerelda to linger for a look and opinion. What do you think?" Dolan and Maggie exchanged a look. Neither looked thrilled about the idea. "Are you worried it's dangerous? Tell me the truth."

"Well, aye," said Maggie. "Does no' mean 'tis. But prudence is the best part of valor."

"I don't think that's how that quote goes, but I take your point. If you're afraid of this thing, we don't want to put anyone else in danger." Pause. "Here's a crazy thought."

"Well?" Maggie said.

"Never mind. I don't know enough about such things to brainstorm."

"'Course you do. You're the magistrate."

"Maybe that's what you see, but on the inside I'm an insurance adjuster."

"Tell us anyhow."

"We could ask Esmerelda if it can be destroyed. If she says no, or she doesn't know, or she doesn't know how, then Plan B is John David Weir. Is he different from the other people who live around here?"

"Oh. Aye. He's a vampire."

"I know he's a vampire, Maggie. What I don't know is how he fits in? Are all the rest of you part of the fae world?"

"Aye," she said.

"So, he can see you in, um, any form like he was part of the fae world, but he's not." She nodded. "That could be useful. Is there a chance that whatever you fear from this thing wouldn't have any effect on him?"

Maggie looked at Dolan who gave his favorite response, a shrug.

"'Tis a possibility. Why?"

"Well, he's coming to my kitchen for tea this afternoon." I caught the look that passed between Dolan and Maggie. "I could ask if he might take it for safekeeping?"

"Bridgid's Balls. You're no' havin' that vampire for tea."

There was no attempt at hiding the judgment in her tone.

I raised my chin slightly in a gesture that is universally understood as standing one's ground. "I am."

With a sigh and a look askance, she said, "Very

well. 'Tis your reputation. So far as safekeepin'?" She looked thoughtful. "He might bury it in a cellar of salt. That might take the potato out of circulation."

I nodded amiably without having enough background on magical matters to know if that was a viable solution. "Right. Good idea." I glanced at my watch and started toward the door walking backwards. "I'm late to meet Lochlan. But Dolan. Give that thing a wide berth until we either conclude it's harmless or decide how to..." I hesitated. "I don't suppose we could return to sender?" They both shook their heads. Of course, that was a dumb idea since nothing ever arrived with sender information. "Yeah. Thought not. Later."

I SHOUTED, "AH!" at the cold wind when I left the cozy warmth of the Hallows. Pulling my scarf tighter and buttoning up, I wished I'd worn another layer.

My morning only got more interesting when Lochlan said the creative who'd been engaged to build my house would be arriving before midnight.

"You mean work is going to begin on my house at midnight?"

"No," he said patiently, but I caught a look of consternation on his face. I took it to mean he was worried that I might be slow.

"Lochlan. Do you think the Powers That Be made a mistake this time? With me?"

"What?" He seemed genuinely shocked by my question. "No! Of course not! I sometimes realize that I'm failing you and I hope you'll forgive me for it. I should be educating you in the ways of the fae, but instead I've mostly left you on your own to fumble about." After a brief pause, he continued. "Sometimes you can know a thing so well that it's easy to forget someone else may not have the same knowledge.

"Fae are divided into seven clans. Each has a monarchy. The queens are empowered with the ability to create in both the magical and mundane worlds. It's a gift that only appears in the feminine sex because that level of creation is akin to birthing. Or something like that."

I nodded, believing wholeheartedly that was true; the part about teaching being hard. I'd tried my hand at training new insurance adjusters. It's not as easy as it sounds.

"Please never fail to speak up if something is unclear," he continued. "It's part of my job to answer."

"Sure. I do have questions. Like when and how will work begin on the house?"

"The queen will stay with Ivy and me so that she has a few hours to get a feel for the underlying magical properties of this place. She can't rearrange matter without first familiarizing herself with the materials at her disposal. Tomorrow morning, instead of walking, you'll meet with her and she'll recreate the essence of what you want. There'll be a walk-through for refining details and, when you approve, I'll make payment from your accounts."

I was dumbstruck. Again.

"You mean the, um, queen is going to create my whole house, like, in one day?"

Lochlan chuckled. "No. Once she has an understanding of what you want, it will be done in the blink of an eye."

I stopped walking. And blinked.

"Is this a joke?" He shook his head. "That kind of thing isn't just magic. It's godlike."

"Potayto. Potahto."

"'Let's Call The Whole Thing off'."

"Why? Was it something I said?"

I briefly wondered how long I would live in Hallow Hill until I understood my neighbors and was understood by my neighbors.

"It was a response to what you said. A song title. Gershwin, I think?"

"Oh, yes." He chuckled. "Gershwin."

The claim of creating a house in a second was outrageous and yet, I'd seen enough to know it'd be foolish to question that such a thing was possible. And, once the door of acceptance was opened a crack, my eagerness to see such a feat fueled the thrill of anticipation.

I grinned. "About the house though. I can't wait."

"You have no choice."

I sighed. It would be a while before communication was glitchless. "It's just an expression that means I'm excited."

"Oh. Of course. You see I have much to learn as well."

I decided Lochlan might get my prize for kindest person I'd ever met, and I was glad he was my solicitor, clerk, teacher, guide, and 'handler'.

"And there's more," he said.

"What?"

"It's time for you to begin your review of cases to determine what will make the Hallowstide docket."

My shoulders sagged because, whereas watching a dream house manifest into creation sounded like fun, docket selection sounded like work.

"You sure I'm qualified for that?"

He slanted his eyes toward me with a mischievous little half-smile. "You know what I'm going to say."

"That the Powers That Be are never wrong."

He chuckled. "There's one case that's especially interesting. I'm lookin' forward to hearing your thoughts on it."

"Are you going to tell me which one?"

He laughed. "No. That might influence your view."

"So, you think it's time to set journal-reading aside and actually go to work?"

"You'll have many years to make your way through the library, should you decide to do so, but whereas there's no time constraint on that, we do have deadlines to meet regarding Court Week. People must know which cases will be heard so they have time to prepare."

"How exactly are cases presented? Does each side have an advocate? Do they speak for themselves? Is there a jury?"

"The parties can choose whether to speak for themselves or put forth a representative. Members of the fae monarchy sit at the front when they please hoping to exert influence over decisions with their presence. They're free to offer opinions on your rulings but can't overturn you. You are the absolute final arbiter."

"Yikes, Lochlan. Sounds like a way to make enemies."

With an amiable shake of his head, he said, "Even the most ambitious and power-hungry of the fae monarchy knows that all magic kind, including themselves, were well on the way to extinction before Merle's system was put in place. They're deferential. And grateful. Theoretically. Most of the time."

I jerked my head toward him. "One too many qualifiers, Lochlan. And when they're not? Deferential and grateful?"

"Well," he smiled, "that's what the sephalian is for. The fae monarchy are consumed by passions and love of power. They had to impose this system on themselves because dwindling numbers forced them to concede their lack of self-control."

"I know what the sephalian is."

Lochlan sighed. "I suppose it's another thing I forgot to mention."

"Keir Culain had me for tea. He showed me the court, which is beautiful in an other-worldly way. He also showed me his, um, alter ego."

With a small laugh, Lochlan repeated my words like I'd made a joke. "Alter ego."

"The elf in the stained glass? The scribe? Is that you?"

"None other," he said. "The magistrate depicted was one of the most famous, thought so because of his gift for both fairness and innovation. Perhaps one day your visage will take his place."

"You sweet talker. How many magistrates have heard that from you?"

He laughed. "Where do you plan to review the cases?"

"How many cases am I reviewing?"

"On this occasion, since Mabon was missed in the transition, there'll be fifty or so."

"And I need to whittle that down to how many for the docket?"

"You and I will need to confer on that. You'll prioritize in order of what you think demonstrates merit. Then we'll establish a court calendar based on the particulars and my estimation as to how much time to allot for each."

"Sounds reasonable. As to where, I was thinking the study I'd planned in my cottage would be a good place to work on magistratey things."

"Well, in that case, we'll wait to deliver the files until tomorrow, when your study is ready to receive." I smiled at the idea of that and found myself eager to see what sorts of things would come before me as magistrate of the Hallowstide Court Meet. "By the way." He waved toward the dogs. "Aisling is about ready to whelp. Have you given more thought to claiming one of the pups?"

"You said one or two."

With a delighted laugh, he said, "Indeed I did. Angus and Aisling will be so pleased to have *two* of their offspring just across the way."

"Not so fast. I didn't say two. Definitely. But I was wondering. Is it possible to have, um, 'dogs' *and* sheep?"

"Oh, yes. Border Collies were bred to be shepherd assistants."

Rolling my eyes like a teenager in the full bloom of snark, I said, "I know. It's not the Border Collie side of their nature that concerns me."

"Your dogs will do as you please, Rita. If you tell them to leave the sheep alone, and give them enough to eat, there'll be no cause for worry."

"How do you keep Angus and Aisling from leaving your property? They could easily jump your little fence."

"Certainly they could, but they wouldn't unless Ivy or I was in danger."

"That's comforting." He nodded. "Would my pups be happy staying inside at night?"

"Your pups will never be happier than when they're close to you. That's the way of it."

"So, you're giving me first pick then?"

"I cannot agree to that."

"You can't *not* agree to that," I said, imagining somebody else walking away carrying the most precious magical puppy. Or puppies. "You work for me. Right?"

"Already wearing *that* hat, are you?"

"The privilege hat? No. I'm teasing." But after another minute I said, "Have you given first choice to someone else?"

"Yes."

"Who?"

"Aisling."

"Aisling?"

"She already knows which pups are yours."

"She does?"

I looked at Aisling, who showed me a comical one ear up, one ear down trick.

I WAS PRACTICALLY whistling when I arrived at the Hallows for lunch. We were having chicken enchiladas with verde sauce and white cheese. I knew I was about to have the pleasure of making Tex-Mex converts of some of the lucky residents of Hallow Hill. That is if Olivia managed her usual prize-winning performance.

I'd asked her earlier to arrange a four o'clock tea for John David Weir and myself in the kitchen with the door to the shop left open. I'd also requested that she hang around the house while he was visiting. Maybe watch TV in my bedroom or whatever.

There was a part of me that supposed he wouldn't try to bite me with Maggie, Dolan, and Olivia within earshot. The other parts of me thought the idea of that was stupid. If he'd wanted to bite me, he could've done so with no muss, fuss, no witnesses the night before.

AS PREDICTED, MY lunch guests gushed and asked if they could come back and have that for lunch every day. Olivia no longer blushed and looked down when people complimented her cooking. She smiled, glanced at faces and, any day now, she was going to bring the house down by opening her mouth and vocalizing a "Thank you."

I asked Esmerelda to stay behind for a few minutes to have a look at our mystery 'thing'. She stopped at the threshold of the workroom door, about ten feet away from where the statue sat on the center table. She seemed disinclined to venture closer.

"I'm taking the fact that you've stopped at the door to mean you agree with Maggie and Dolan. That the thing is up to no good."

"You need to get it out of here. And you need to find

out who sent it."

"The first thing might be easier than the second. I'm going to see if John David will take it and devise a containment. Maggie suggested a cellar of salt?"

Esmerelda nodded enthusiastically. "Excellent plan. Would he do that for us?"

"We'll see. If he does, I hope people will be nicer to him."

Pulling back, Esmerelda said, "Have people been hostile to him?"

"Perhaps not 'hostile'. My understanding is that people have excluded him and made him feel unwelcome." Esmerelda appeared to be giving that thought. "So, as I said, if he agrees to take care of this, maybe you could pass it around that he did a favor for Hallow Hill?" She nodded slowly. "Regarding the second thing. Finding out who sent it? Maggie says we don't know where the stuff comes from. I guess there hasn't been a problem with inventory supply in the past."

"Necessity is the mother of invention." Coming from Esmerelda, it was a quip.

"You're quoting Mundies?" It was hard to believe, given the level of prejudice I'd come to expect.

With a feminine shrug of a shoulder, she said, "What makes you think Mundies are responsible for that expression?"

"Why, Esmerelda. Was that a joke?"

At the end of a sharp look, she said, "Of course not, Rita. You know I don't joke."

I watched her walk to the exit and step out into the wind in a sleeveless sweater, seemingly impervious to the cold that had tried to bite through my clothes.

Turning back to Dolan, I said, "Did this hodge-podgette…?"

"Hobknobbit," he corrected.

"Yes. What did it come in?" He pointed to a small wooden crate lined with heavy foam. "Is that unusual?" He looked at the crate. "I mean is this the way pieces normally arrive? Packed like this?"

"There's not one particular way," he said.

"So, nothing about the packing raised your antennae."

He looked offended to the point of color rising in his complexion. "I don't have antennae."

"Dolan!" I confess that I was beginning to lose patience with people for not sharing my culture, if it can be called that. "It's an expression. When you opened it, was there anything about it that made you think it was unusual?" I was finding it exhilaratingly refreshing to be on the other side of acting like someone was dense.

He looked back at the crate. "No."

"Okay. So, it was after you took it out that you perceived something off kilter."

"Not after. It happened as I was removing it, I..."

"What? Got a creepy feeling?"

"If that means what I think it means, then yes."

"What do you know about hobknobbits?" I felt very proud of myself for getting the term right. I knew I was right about that because no one corrected me.

"Not very much."

"Well, like would this head be life sized?"

He stared at it and nodded. "I think so."

"In general, would you say that people, magic kind, had a favorable view of hobknobbits?" I was feeling at home with this line of questioning, hitting my stride while I pulled on my insurance adjuster experience.

He shook his head as if to say he didn't know, but I

could tell by his expression that he wished he did, that he would've liked to be able to give me what I needed.

"Thanks, Dolan. Will you be here for a while? Until, say, five thirty?"

"Can be."

"If Mr. Weir agrees to take the thing with him, I'll need you to wrap it back up."

He nodded and turned away.

Then I added, "We can wave some white sage around you afterward if you like."

Poor Dolan squinted in confusion. "What?"

"Um, never mind." Having thus exhausted my feeble contribution to magical solutions, I decided to quietly withdraw.

I HEADED UPSTAIRS to the safe to retrieve the blue velvet book. There was sure to be some reference to hobknobbits in there.

It wasn't the sort of book that lent itself to leafing through quickly, but I did the best I could with limited time, catching glimpses of all manner of creatures I had yet to read about. Just past the halfway mark, the book being open almost equally on both sides, was a collection of sketches of hobknobbits. Two wearing hats like the one downstairs and two without. My initial impression was that the hat was an improvement as the thing was even less attractive without a head covering.

The script wasn't easily decipherable. Among other things the letter s looked like *f* and the letter u looking like *v*. But I gathered that the creatures were prevalent in Western Europe and the British Isles during the Middle Ages. They were "city dwellers", not fond of the wild. They preferred areas with larger populations, particularly the fae court. The fae regarded them as inconsequential except for the fact that they liked to get underfoot and trip people. Their diminutive stature of four hands, which I believed to be about twenty inches, made it easy for them to go unnoticed until victims of their mischief were splayed on the ground.

I concluded that they must've thus pranked someone powerful once too often and a decision was made to 'exterminate' the species as one would any pest or varmint. Since neither Maggie nor Nolan was personally familiar with hobknobbits, that could only mean that the consequential process had been successful. It also meant the origin of the piece downstairs was very, very old.

That, in turn, begged the question, why would someone want to attach malevolent magic to a hobknobbit sculpture? And why would they want to send such a thing to the Hallows? Was it connected to the timing of my arrival? It sounded paranoid, but was a question worth asking.

A few minutes before four I descended the stairs.

“Good God,” I said to Olivia. “I know I’m new to tea, but this must be the most beautiful tea ever served.”

I’d gushed enough to make her blush return. She ducked her chin but looked up immediately as the tap of the brass knocker sounded at my front door. I looked at my watch. Four o’clock. John David was punctual.

Gotta like that.

Olivia opened the door to the shop, as we’d discussed earlier, then filled the silver pot with steamy water while I answered the door.

In a nineteenth-century sort of way, John David Weir was dashing in his jodhpurs, riding boots, and tweedy-looking sweater. I looked out to see if he’d tied his horse somewhere nearby.

Following my line of sight, he said, “Am I forgetting something?”

“No.” I smiled reassuringly. “I just noticed you’re wearing riding clothes and wondered where you left your mare.”

“There’s a post on the green,” he said.

“And you’re not worried that someone might tease her? Or steal her?”

His mouth twitched, eyes lighting with amusement, just before he shook his head no.

“I’m sorry to leave you standing there. Come in.”

I closed the door behind him, noticing again how tall he was.

“Olivia has set out a nice tea in the kitchen.” He followed without a word. I gestured for him to sit in the chair closest to the wall and took the chair nearest the door to the shop for myself. “How are you today?”

He turned his face toward me. His expression was akin to euphoric. Like he couldn’t believe someone was asking something as simple as how he was. My heart clenched in sympathy.

"I'm… well," he said, clearly out of practice with the simplest of niceties.

"I've been looking forward to resuming our conversation."

"You have?" He sounded surprised.

"Yes. Last night you hinted at your history and I'm interested. You said you weren't always a vampire. I guess that probably goes without saying, but I'm new to alternative realities."

I opened the rosewood box that contained a variety of teas and motioned for him to choose. He picked a Black Russian and handed it to me.

I smiled, happy to open it for him. He tracked every movement closely as I tore the paper wrapper away and placed the teabag in his cup. As I poured hot water, I said, "As an American, I don't know much about hosting tea. So, if I'm doing this wrong, let me know."

"You're not doing it wrong," he said quietly.

I chose a lavender chamomile for myself and poured the water.

"Please have some of Olivia's pastries. She could be the best cook in all the world for all I know."

He nodded and put a dainty triangular sandwich on his plate.

I studied him while steeping my tea, added a splash of cream, three raw sugars, and stirred until the color was just right. All the while I was aware that he hadn't accepted my conversational invitation to tell me more about himself. When I lifted my cup to take a sip, he watched as closely as if he'd never seen someone drink from a cup.

"Hmmm," I said. "Just right." Setting cup in saucer, I turned my attention to him. "What would you like to talk about?" He looked like he was at a loss for an answer. "How long have you been here? In, or I should say near, Hallow Hill?"

"A hundred and… forty? Years?"

"That's a long time. What brought you here?"

He swallowed and quietly cleared his throat. "I'd done a favor for Prince Edward. Something he considered worthy of a bounty. He rewarded me with an estate that included farms and tenants." His eyes wandered. "Here."

"Go on," I encouraged. I didn't need to pretend to be interested. I was hooked.

"I liked it here but was still young enough to be… restless. So I visited from time to time to check the manager's accounts and make sure he wasn't making off with the candlesticks. At best it was a youthful, halfhearted stab at responsibility.

"I had enough money to indulge in travel and the daughters of society. Eventually I was punished for my misguided ways."

"How?"

"Have you ever been to Venice?"

I shook my head. "No."

"It's a labyrinth of outdoor hallways. Almost impossible to navigate unless you were born there. At least that's how it seems after a few Spritz Venezianos. I was attempting to find my way back to my rooms one night when I crossed paths with a vampire. A female vampire who was the essence of horror; the perfect amalgamation of doom lurking within a hypnotically beautiful form." He sighed deeply and looked away. "I'd like to say I feel fortunate that she didn't kill me, but that would be a lie. I wish she had. I've spent most of my time as a vampire trying to find a way to commit suicide. I haven't given up the quest, but I'm beginning to resign myself to the idea that it can't be done."

I could think of nothing to say. So, I waited quietly.

His eyes glazed over for a time like he was reliving events long passed. When they cleared, he refocused on me and said, "After my encounter with the Venetian vampire, it took time to come to terms with what I'd become. What it means. I decided this was the best place for me. The people here aren't human. They aren't afraid of me. And they leave me alone."

"And therein lies the problem?"

He sighed deeply. "I want to die. But I can't."

I thought that over before responding. "Do you really want to die? Or do you just want a better life?"

He looked at the little sandwich on his plate. "This is nice."

I smiled. "Having tea with someone?"

His gaze came up to meet mine and I was struck by his good looks as I had been the first time I saw him.

"Yes," he said.

"If I have you to lunch again, you could make more of an effort to join the conversation."

His knee bounced up and down, indicating either

nerves or excitement, while he thought about that. After what seemed like an interminably long silence for modern times, he agreed. "I could."

"In that case, I'd be delighted to have you join us next Thursday."

The corners of his mouth threatened to lift. "What's being served?"

"Oh!" I laughed. "So now you're picky about what we're having?"

His grin showed me why he must've been a popular fixture with the in-crowd of his day. He was stunning when he smiled.

"Were you ever married?" He shook his head no. "Tempted?" He grinned again and shook his head no. "Because you were in constant demand?" He ducked his head, but the grin stayed in place. "Maggie told me that you can satisfy your, um, vampire urges in the bigger towns. That there are people willing to…"

He nodded. "You don't need to be afraid of me."

"I'm not." I remembered the 'thing'. "Hey. I wonder if you can help with something. If you can't, it's fine. If you don't want to, that's fine, too. But if you're willing, it might be a way for you to finally break the ice with the locals."

"What?" After telling him everything I knew about the hobknobbit, he said, "You are right about the fact that I'm not vulnerable to the effects of fae magic. But how did you know that?"

"Just a hunch. Molly, at the pub, calls it intuition. I hope it pays off this time because Maggie and Dolan have got me a little freaked out."

"I might be willing to make a trade."

"For what?" Asking that required a little boldness because I couldn't help being afraid of what the answer might be. "You buy back that ridiculous statue and I'll take the hex off your hands."

Both pleased and relieved by that answer, I smiled. "I didn't say it was a hex."

"What else would it be?"

"When it comes to magical vocabulary, I'm in kindergarten. If you dub it a hex, who am I to argue?"

"Do we have a deal?"

"I would've bought back the statue regardless. You may think it's ridiculous, but I kind of like it. I might put it in my new house."

"You have a new house?"

"That's the plan." I almost laughed at the cuteness of my own word humor, but decided against it for two reasons. First, it wasn't worth the explanation that would almost certainly be required. And, second, after going to lengths to explain, he still wouldn't find it funny. I'd have to be satisfied with internally entertaining myself. "By the time you come to lunch next week, it'll be an actual building. At least that's what I'm told. Look for me across the way from Lochlan and Ivy."

"Alright. Show me the 'thing'."

He followed me into the workroom, walked up to the hobknobbit, ran his hand over it, and said. "Yes. I'll take care of it. I can't carry it on horseback. But I'll send a man back to pick it up."

"Today?" I asked hopefully. I glanced at Dolan and noted that he looked just as eager to have it gone.

"If it's urgent."

"It is."

His responding smile made me think the vampire had unthawed in record time. The more he relaxed, the more I saw what a charmer he must've been in his heyday. With a little encouragement from the magistrate, and a little help with scary hobknobbits, he was going to be okay.

"I'll ride home and send him back to get the thing and buy the market out of salt."

"Can't you call?"

"Call?"

"You don't have a phone?"

"I do have a phone." Pause. "At home."

I shook my head. "No. I don't mean a landline. I mean a mobile phone."

"No. I don't have one." I stared until he added, "I can get one."

"Good." I smiled.

He smiled in return, looking more confident and at ease in his skin.

It was a moment.

AT FIVE FORTY-FIVE I rushed out my front door, breathless as a schoolgirl planning to surprise Keir Culain by being there first. For weeks he'd been waiting at the corner, rain or shine. The certainty that he'd be there gave me frequent little moments of pleasure. Knowing he'd want to hear all about my day, the house, the puppies… It was a gift that couldn't be measured.

It was a foundation.

If I wanted it to be.

Mentally I pulled up short having just realized that I liked that relationship. A lot. As expected, I turned the corner, but I wasn't greeted by *that* smile. The one that made me ask myself every day what I was waiting for.

Keir wasn't waiting for me on the corner. He was having a conversation with Aoumeil, two doors down. Even though his body was angled away, the body language had the look of a talk that was both intense and intimate. When Aoumiel glanced my direction and saw me, a smile spread across her face that sent the nastiness meter off the charts. No doubt that smile was the result of recognizing my dismay at seeing the two of them practically in clutches.

I ducked into the store, not wanting Keir to know I'd witnessed that. I supposed I'd bring it up when the time was right. That would be when I wasn't on the verge of a jealous meltdown.

Maggie came out from back carrying a feather duster

and chattering about something to do with Braden and his bride-to-be. She stopped when she saw me.

"Rita, are ye ill?" I shook my head. "Then why the fussy face?"

I debated whether or not to tell the truth, but it was impossible to hide anything from Maggie.

"I just saw Keir with Aoumiel." Her response was a blank look. I pointed toward the sidewalk behind me. "Out there. In front of her shop." Maggie blinked, but clearly didn't see a problem. To my dismay, I was going to have to spell it out. "They looked like they were…" I almost said 'having a moment', then I remembered that was exactly what I'd thought about John David Weir and me. Quickly editing my description, I said, "It looked like they know each other very, *very* well."

When my meaning dawned on Maggie, she practically guffawed. "Saints and sinners, Magistrate. The witch does no' hold a candle to ye. Aoumiel." Maggie practically spit. "'Tis no' even her *real* name. Fancies herself a temptress, she does. Why," Maggie laughed again, "she thinks her love potions actually work! You've nothin' to fret about. Keir's been 'round enough to be too smart for shenanigans from the likes of her."

Her eyes flicked to something behind me and I turned to see that the subject of discussion had arrived on my corner.

Taking a deep breath, I said, "Thanks, Maggie." I meant to give her sincere thanks for her reassurance but didn't believe for a second that there was nothing between Aoumiel, or whatever her name was, and Keir Culain.

He wasn't expecting me to come from the shop and looked surprised. "Well, there you are."

"Here I am." I managed a smile, though undoubtedly tight.

All the way to the pub he tried to make conversation while I answered in grunts or monosyllables. It was passive aggressive, but I wasn't in a mood to be fair.

Finally, he stopped and said, "What's the bother?" I looked away. "The only way we're to get to the bottom of this is for you to speak up and say why you're troubled." When I didn't respond immediately, he added, "Out loud."

I looked him full in the face as we stood steps from the pub's door. "I saw you."

"Saw me?" He looked confused, which was good since that's what I'd intended by being obtuse. Like I said, passive aggressive. I'm not especially proud of acting like a petulant teenager, but I'm only human. At least I was until very recently.

"With Aoumiel or whatever her real name is."

"Oh."

"That's all you have to say?" That made him look all the more confused. "Look. I know we've never talked about exclusivity. We just said we'd try out friendship. So, you're perfectly free to do whatever you want."

He took me by the elbow and guided me around the building where we had a thin illusion of privacy.

"You're not jealous of that witch," he said matter-of-factly.

"Well..." I worried my bottom lip. "Is there a reason why I shouldn't be?"

Tucking his chin so that I could see he was serious, he said, "*Every* reason. If you must know, I was asking her for something special for you. A surprise."

The tension in my expression went slack as sheepishness claimed my face. And it was my turn to say, "Oh." I brightened. "A surprise? What?"

"If I told you then it wouldn't be a surprise." It didn't take much of a disappointed look to get him to spill. "Alright. I'm trying to find a way to invite you for a flight and be a hundred percent sure you're safe."

"A flight?" Inexplicably, the image of a barnstorming biplane was the first thing that came to mind before I realized he was talking about taking me for a ride *as a sephalian*! "Ohhhhh." Pause. "Oh no." It seemed that once I began shaking my head I couldn't stop. "I'm scared to death of heights." He leaned back against the brick of the building and crossed his arms. I smiled. "But I'll stay on the ground and watch you?"

A tiny silent scoff was paired with a lopsided grin in response to the very ridiculous thing I'd just said. Then he grew serious. "I'm over the moon knowing you were jealous, love. But if you want to talk about appearances, that vampire was seen leaving your house today." I opened my mouth to reassure him that it was purely platonic, but before I got that out, he said, "And I feel compelled to point out that I've never been invited to your house."

"You haven't?" I thought back and realized it was true.

Since I had dinner with him every night, I'd never included him in luncheons and, other than 'the vampire', I'd never invited anyone over except for lunch.

"No." Catching me by the shoulders, he moved me so that we'd traded places, my back now against the brick. His body pressed me against the wall in a thought-stealing maneuver. "And I would like to be invited in." The phrase was dripping with innuendo that hung heavy in the air.

"I invited him for tea because he's lonely. Olivia was there and Maggie and Dolan were close enough to hear everything."

"Fair enough. What about an invitation?"

"For tea?" I giggled. "Sure."

"Is that all you've got for me?"

My answer was to initiate the kiss he'd asked for when I'd visited the castle, taking a leap of faith that I remembered how; to kiss, that is. Since he didn't pull away, I took that to mean that it was like riding a bike. He immediately took control of movement and intensity in a way that had me picturing twisted limbs and white linen sheets.

Nobody heckled us, or embarrassed me by calling out, "Get a room," but we'd drawn some triple takes from diners arriving for supper.

I pulled back, almost aroused enough to suggest skipping food. "Let's go in. I'm cold."

He inhaled deeply and smiled. "Let's start over. How was your day?"

I grinned. "I can't wait to tell you about it."

With a nod and the most masculine version of a self-satisfied smile, he said, "That's more like it."

I PROBABLY TALKED too fast, conveying my excitement about the puppies and the house, unsure which took precedence.

"Is there a room for me?" he asked just as Jeff arrived with food. Cheese and Grits Souffle and Prawn Bisque for me. English pork pie for Keir.

Hearing the question, Jeff gave me an interested look. I could tell that he was dying to stay and hear the answer, but to his credit he forced himself to move away, past hearing distance.

"Why would there be a room for you, Keir?" I was interested in hearing the answer to this question, myself. "You already have a place to sleep."

"Not a bedroom, you ninny. I'll be sharing a bed with you. Of course. But every gentleman needs a room for his books and treasures and such."

"And whacking off?" I was ecstatic that I'd caught him so off guard that he almost spit out a mouthful of Guinness. I continued eating calmly while he coughed into his napkin a few times. There was no need for concern since he was practically immortal and all. While he was busy sputtering instead of answering, I continued. "I missed the discussion about sharing my house *or* my bed with you."

When he was fully recovered, he said, "Perhaps details haven't been hammered out in a conspicuous manner."

"Details?" I was a little astonished by this reaction.

Ignoring that, he pressed on. "But certainly the implication hangs in the air."

"Implication?" I pretended ignorance.

"Of living as a couple…" Lowering his chin, he said, "*With all that implies* is tacitly inferred."

"Is it?"

Suddenly the tone was more serious and less banter. "You know perfectly well that we've been moving toward an understanding. At. Your. Pace. With no pressure or complaint from me."

He had a point.

"You might have a point."

"A *very* valid point."

"Hmmm. Well, I already gave you that. But I think we moved things forward just before supper tonight."

His answer was the transformation of his face from stormy scowl to sexy smile as he buried a huge spoonful of porkpie in his beautiful mouth. He appeared to be reveling in a victory that seemed small to me, but was apparently monumental to him.

"Did we just have our first fight?"

"I wouldn't call it a fight."

"Close enough. So. Makeup sex?"

"I might agree to makeup making out."

He nodded thoughtfully. "Are we ready to talk timetables?"

"Timetables for sex?"

He grinned. "I would love to have that talk. Anytime. But I was thinking more about sleepovers?"

"Well…" I wasn't sure what I wanted to say, so I let my eyes glaze over as a parade of all the things that could go wrong with that marched across the screen in my head.

"If you're serious about getting puppies, I should be a regular in the household before then. They'll never think anything of it if I'm around from the beginning."

I wasn't certified in canine psychology and didn't know if it would help with magical beasts even if I was, but what Keir was saying made sense.

"Timetables. I don't know how long they'll need to stay with Aisling. With real, um..." I looked around to make sure that I recognized all those within earshot as non-human, "dogs, it would be at least six weeks. "But I don't know about..." I had to stop and laugh. "I don't even know what to call Angus and Aisling. I wonder if there's a name for magical wolves that look like approachable Border Collies to humans."

"Wolfdogs?"

I shrugged. "I guess that's as good a term as any. So you're a dog person?"

He smiled while chewing. "You were expecting me to be a cat person?"

"Funny. I really hadn't thought about it. I've just been so taken with the idea of getting 'dogs'." I chuckled. "I guess you could say I'm expecting."

"Have you always had dogs?"

"No. My ex didn't like them."

Keir sat back. "So that meant you couldn't have what you wanted?"

"Yep. That's what it meant."

He shook his head like he disapproved of that. Put another score in his plus column.

"I would not describe myself as a dog person. You probably noticed I don't have one. But I am British. There's a cultural mandate to like dogs. If the pups get used to having me around from the beginning, they'll think it's the most natural thing in the world to live with a sephalian." Pause. "But my room is off limits," he teased.

"Right. We both know why and it's not fear of puppy peepee." I wiggled my eyebrows.

KEIR WALKED ME home, as he did every night. Only that night he looked at my door pointedly. The message was silent, but it was also loud and clear.

"I'd ask you in. For a few minutes, but I don't want to create any misunderstanding. I'm not offering a 'sleepover'." Yes. I used air quotes.

"Makeup making out?"

I smirked as I opened the door and held it open for him to follow. Upon turning to close it behind me, I was about to offer coffee when I found my back pressed against my door and Keir pressed against my front, eager to pick up where we'd left off before dinner. Apparently, the embers had continued to smolder during dinner because it took mere seconds for my body to fully rally a primordial sense of mating urgency.

How surprising it was to have those feelings at my age! I supposed that the shared chemistry must be off the charts for me to be combatting wild abandon like somebody newly legal to vote. It was hard to think when my body had taken control, being busy with feverish kisses made more feverish by wandering hands and magic shawls being pulled away. I started to protest when the shawl was tossed aside like a vintage store rag, but remembered Esmerelda saying it would take care of itself. And besides, I had more *pressing* matters.

After what was perhaps history's shortest, most frenzied 'makeout' session ever, I ducked out of the embrace and said, "Maturity checkpoint. That's enough forward momentum for one night."

Keir dropped his hands and turned to me with eyes that glittered in the soft lamplight. "We're adults, Rita. We're also friends with feelings for each other. Friends who want to be lovers. It's time." I opened my mouth to speak, but he put a finger to my lips. "I'm not going to insist tonight." Pausing just long enough to make sure I was paying close attention, he continued, "But soon."

With that he reached behind him, opened the door and was gone. On their own my fingers found their way to touching the puffy lips he'd just teased into ecstasy and left tingling. It was time to come to terms with the stark truth. Aging might mean being more careful, logical, and analytical, but those things couldn't save me from unknowns like adventure. And Keir Culain.

Nobody ever intends to make bad choices.

I recalled the old carnival saying, "*You pay your money and you take your chance.*"

Keir deserved a romance with somebody who wasn't too afraid of hurt and disappointment to take a chance. Surely there was a lesson to be taken from the jealousy that had risen to the surface so quickly when I thought he was interested in someone else. The lesson was that I wanted to pay my money and take my chance.

I thought about calling him to come back, but decided I'd surprise him the next day. With his own room. Lochlan had said I could make changes to the plan while the creatrix was here.

GLAD TO BE in my house, alone, I was looking forward to what the journals would reveal. But first I needed to talk to Evie. I knew it would be mid-afternoon, after classes. I hoped she'd pick up. I made myself an echinacea tea with honey, took a deep breath, and called.

"Mom?"

"None other."

"How are you?"

"Better than you think."

"That's good. I still can't believe Dad's divorcing you. At your age!"

Did she mean 'my age' because I'm so young or 'my age' because I'm at the end of days? It was impossible to tell.

"Um, well, sometimes these things are for the best."

"Yeah. Sure. I like your positive spin."

"No, really. As a matter of fact, I've made a big decision and need to share."

"Okay."

"Well." I took a breath knowing the rip-the-band-aid-off approach worked best with somebody like Evie. "I'm staying. Over here. I'm the proud new owner of an antiques shop in a little village in Cumbria." When she said nothing, I added, "I have a house." When silence persisted, I said. "I have a car."

I decided to wait her out. Eventually she'd get tired of the silence and respond.

"It's not good to make big decisions when you're in the middle of an emotional crisis. *Everybody* knows that."

"I'm not in the beginning, middle, or end of an emotional crisis."

"See. That's the crisis talking. Of course, you are. So, you're trying to run away to Brigadoon."

"First, Brigadoon is fictional. Second, it's in Scotland. And, third, I'm not. Running away that is. Honestly. Your dad and I should probably have gone separate ways twenty years ago."

She gasped. "What? You mean my whole life has been a lie?"

I had to give it to her. My kid always had a full tank of drama.

"No, Evie. *Your* life has been good as gold. *My* adult life has been a set of alternative facts." Before the dialogue devolved into more handwringing, I rushed to say, "And there's good news for you."

"What?"

"Well, I've come into a little bit of money. Enough to pay for grad school and living expenses."

I didn't have to be with her in person to know that her mood had brightened instantly.

"Really?" she said.

"Yeah. You can stay in school for the rest of your life if you want."

"Wow, Mom! That's amazing!" She sounded like she'd won the lottery and, as a born academic, I guess in a sense she had. "So, I *really* don't need to worry about you?"

"You *really* don't need to worry about me," I repeated.

"I want to come and see for myself. Christmas break?"

"We have lots of time to plan." I was proud of that dodge and knew there was a chance she'd have things come up and forget all about it.

"Send pictures?"

"I will. I'm off to bed and reading."

"Kinda early for bed."

"It's a lot later here," I said defensively. "And there's the part about reading."

"Okay. Nighty night."

"Night."

"Mom."

"Yes?"

"Are you really gonna be okay?"

"I'm really gonna be better than ever. Promise and a butterfly kiss."

She giggled like she was eight.

I sent a newsy email to the few other people who would miss me, carefully avoiding naming the town that was my new home, warmed up my tea, and headed upstairs. I didn't have a huge social life because Cole had made a point of using up whatever free time I might've had. He left me lists of things to do for him when I wasn't working. The longer I'm away from that incarnation of myself, the more I wonder why I went along with it.

The fact that I felt excited about reading journals was the best indication I could have that I was in the right place, at the right time, doing the right thing.

As I opened the journal du jour, my mind drifted to a certain green-eyed Adonis with flawless, golden skin and a bio that placed him as already old when the Crusades began.

Chapter Seven

Juggernauts and Jabberwocky

THE NEXT MORNING when I arrived at the proposed site of my new house, I found Keir already there and waiting in the empty field that I'd soon be calling home.

"Hey! What are you doing here?"

"Big day," he said. "I wanted to share it. You don't mind?"

"Of course not. I'm glad you're here."

"I have an ulterior motive."

"That thing about your own room."

"That," he confirmed, "and wanting to see your reactions."

What a heartbreaker he was. "That's nice."

"I love it when you wear that shawl. It makes your eyes

look like…"

"What?"

"Magic."

"Huh."

I saw Lochlan emerge from his house at the same time I saw the dogs jump the fence and come bounding toward us. They wiggled and wagged and turned in circles for me like always, but gave Keir nothing more than a watchful eye.

"Are they afraid of you?"

He nodded slightly. "Very likely."

"I see what you mean about becoming part of the package deal."

"Package deal?" Lochlan said. "What's that?"

I grinned. "We're talking about the puppies."

"Magistrate." I couldn't help but notice that he used my formal title. "This is the contractor." Lochlan gestured toward the fae queen, a blonde so flawlessly beautiful she looked like she'd been airbrushed. No discernible makeup. She was simply perfect without it. Though she gave the impression of someone who'd be completely at home in long, flowing robes, she wore a nubby hemp caftan over jeans and boots. Her hair was set in a complicated do of braids, wisps, and tendrils. As a final touch, she had pale blue eyes that twinkled even in broad daylight. "Maeve."

Ignoring me altogether, she looked at Keir in a way that suggested previous carnal knowledge. I *hated* her.

"Keir Culain," she said. "You're as beautiful as the day I made you."

Made him? I *loved* her.

He smiled and put a claiming arm around me like he was presenting me in the oddest version of a meet-the-parents moment.

"This is Rita Hayworth."

It was clear that she had to drag her attention away from Keir. No doubt he was the cover page of her portfolio. She nodded to me in a formal way that suggested a slight bow. It made me eager to adjust the tone and get off on a more contemporary footing.

"Hi," I said.

There was a flicker of surprise in her reaction. Perhaps she'd never met a human, much less an American human. Perhaps no one had ever addressed her so casually. But she gathered herself and returned my greeting, although stiffly.

"Hi."

"So how do we do this?" I asked.

Maeve first looked surprised then turned toward Lochlan as if an explanation was in order.

"Oh, well," he began. "There's nothing to it. Maeve will have a quick look in your head…"

"MY WHAT?"

"Let me rephrase. You will impart your vision to Maeve, more or less, telepathically."

I looked at her with suspicion. "What's the more? And what's the less?"

"It's perfectly fine, love," Keir said. "Not painful. She's done it thousands of times."

I looked at her warily. "With humans?"

"Maeve, would you please offer reassurance that she won't be harmed?"

"Of course not," she said, but I thought her smile said otherwise. "Just relax and think about what you want."

I looked at Keir for confirmation. He nodded.

No one had suggested I close my eyes, but that's what people do when they're 'imagining' things. Maeve reached up and lightly brushed her fingertips down my temple. My eyes jerked open because of being startled by the unexpected and slightly electric touch.

Looking at Lochlan like she was put out, she was saying, "Surely you jest. It's a mess in there."

"I beg your pardon," I said defensively. She was probably right, but what kind of woman would I be if I wasn't prepared to defend my mind? Messy or not.

Lochlan ignored me and spoke to Maeve on my behalf. "She's not magic kind, but she is our magistrate. You were called because you're the best." The flattery was obvious and Lochlan didn't try to hide it. "I've got great confidence that you can work miracles."

The look on her face said she wasn't above flattery and was probably suffering from Narcissistic Personality Disorder. "Oh, very well." She looked me up and down to make a mean-girl point before saying, "I'm going to touch you." She then spoke to me while looking directly at Keir. "But it will not harm you."

I also looked to Keir, who nodded. My eyes drifted toward Aisling. Her ears stood up and she wagged her tail. Good enough for me. "Okay."

Maeve put the fingertips of both hands on my temples for two or three seconds. This time I didn't close my eyes. The effect of being that close to physical perfection, even for seconds, was to make belief in my attractiveness hopeless. I wished I'd kept my eyes closed.

Moving away, she said to Lochlan, "No warranties."

Facing Lochlan's house, I started to ask what was next, but something made me look over my shoulder. I twisted, stepping back at the same time, so fast I almost stumbled. But Keir was there to grab me with strong hands and a chuckle.

"I hope that means you're surprised in the best way," he said.

And there it stood, the perfect fairy tale cottage complete with picket fence, flowering garden, and thatched roof. It wasn't exactly what I'd had in mind, but it was exactly what I wanted, which meant that Maeve was able to read me on a soul level. While that level of probing might have been disturbing if I thought about it too long, it would be hard to argue with the results.

"A fine house it is," Lochlan proclaimed. "Shall we go have a look inside? Maeve," he said, "if you'd be so kind as to remain until after the walk-through. Just in case changes are required?"

She crossed her arms and adopted a posture that said she wasn't going anywhere.

"This is the house of your heart?" Keir said with a touch of wonder. "It's beautiful."

"It is. Isn't it?" There was nothing to do but agree wholeheartedly.

Lochlan looked overjoyed. "I'm so glad you're pleased, Magistrate."

Unable to look away from the house, I said, "Pleased is an understatement. She blew the lid off the popper."

"Well," Lochlan chuckled. "I'm going to assume that's a good thing."

Stepping inside for the first time was an adventure in the kind of giddy anticipation I hadn't felt since I was a child expecting a trip to the circus to be life-altering. If Maeve, in spite of her distaste for humans (or perhaps just me), could get the inside as right as the outside, I was going to thank fate for making me magistrate.

Indeed, my subconscious mind had been plumbed for discovery of what I *truly* wanted. Like Lochlan's house, it was *much* bigger on the inside than would have seemed possible by visual estimation from without. The front room was cozy, with sofas covered in my dream crewel embroidered fabric, a big burgundy leather nap chair with ottoman, Venetian rugs on dark, distressed floors, and lamps that were works of art. A fireplace big enough for a castle occupied one wall with shelf units bracing either side. A stunning copy of Van Gogh's *The Starry Night* hung above.

"That's my favorite painting," I said. "It's the best recreation I've ever seen."

Standing just outside the open door, Maeve scoffed and adopted her snootiest tone to say, "It's not a copy."

My head swiveled from her to the painting. "It must be. The original is hanging in the Museum of Modern Art in New York."

Maeve looked at her nails as if she was bored. "No. It's not. Now you have the original. They have the copy. The differences are undetectable by humans." Her inflection punctuated how much she despised humans, which frankly, made me uncomfortable. I was glad when she turned and walked back to the gate to wait.

"That painting suits you," Keir said. "It could be our little town on a clear night. It's as close to magical as..."

"Go on. You were going to say as close to magical as humans get. Do you have your, um, Maeve's prejudices? About humans?"

"It's not a prejudice to say we're magical and humans are not. It's just a fact. With the single exception of you. Because you're becoming a form of hybrid. I was trying to say that magic kind couldn't do better than that." He pointed to the painting. "Maybe we never have."

Choosing to accept that carefully worded explanation, I said, "I haven't seen art done by magic kind, unless you count Tregeagle, but I'm looking forward to it."

"Someday you'll be invited into the faerie mound that's closest to Hallow Hill. The one at Tregeagle."

I nodded, then proceeded through the house slowly, hunting for anything I might want tweaked while admiring everything I saw to the last detail. I understood the concept of *speak now or forever hold your peace.* But everything was perfection.

My study was off the living room to the right. It was exactly the kind of place I'd imagined myself pouring over briefs and making decisions that would save the fae from themselves. I noticed some of my favorite books on the shelves along with some of my favorite framed photos.

Lochlan excused himself for a moment. When he returned, he went straight to a section of bookcase, and removed three books at eye level. That revealed an electronic pad.

"The safe, Magistrate," he said and nodded toward me. "It has a new code that only you know."

A code that only I know?

I thought about my most obscure six-digit password, typed it in and nothing. Nineteen tries later, when I was almost out of ideas, I tried the month and year of my first kiss. Glory be, the tumblers rumbled, the locks slid, and the bookcase opened out into the room. Inside was a space somewhat larger than my former safe. All of the journals had been moved and were in place. The dark blue velvet tome sat on a rosewood podium in the center, spotlighted from above. Dramatic flair aside, it was perfect. The study had a large black baroque desk with gold accents, identical to one I'd once seen in an antique store. I'd even gone so far as to close one eye and squint the other while reaching for the dangling price tag. $27,500. I'd sighed as I dropped the tag thinking nothing was more certain in life than that I'd never see that desk again. Yet here it was in all its seventeenth-century French glory. There was also a library table with two lamps and three stacks of folders.

"Lochlan," I said, "are those the briefs? Of the possible cases for Hallowstide?"

"They are," he replied. "Ready for your review."

The master bedroom was to the left. It was completely done in the palest of sage greens, so restful it elicited a sigh. The only thing that broke up the color pattern was the red-stained bed featuring four large square posts intricately carved with vines and flowering plants. As spectacular as that was, the standout focal point was the ornate, white, concrete fireplace sculpted with an Eden-like garden scene and barely clothed people. I tried to not look at Keir, but his stare was so compelling I couldn't help myself. One peek at his smile had me blushing. People shouldn't have to endure having their subconscious thoughts laid bare and made public. I moved on quickly.

While I appreciated the beauty of the armoires in the townhouse, the desire of my heart was a walk-in closet with an island that housed built-in drawers on four sides, a wall of shelves for shoes, upholstered benches to use for lacing shoes or taking off boots. It seemed clear that the interest in art that motivated me to matriculate for that degree was still alive and well. The closet walls were covered in a contiguous hand-painted mural of a garden setting that looked like it had been done by a Dutch master. It was the perfect background for my clothes and shoes. Which were already moved and in place, though lonely looking in the enormous space. Excellent! Lots of room to expand my wardrobe. Velvet hangers begging to be covered by new clothes had been thoughtfully provided. I couldn't help wondering how Romeo would like a trip to London.

It was an even bigger surprise to find *two* such closets, mirror images of each other, across the short hall from one another. Likewise, there were two bathrooms, each with state-of-the-art jacuzzi *and* a walk-in shower.

The only word that came to mind was overwhelmed. If I counted the number of front-facing windows in the living room, study and master bedroom, the total was nine. When compared to the number of front-facing windows when viewing the house from the outside, which was four, there would be a serious math problem. But I was learning to not question the impossibility of magic.

The kitchen was at the back of the house and populated with the appliances I'd come to adore during my stay in Hallow Hill, including a red AGA stove with six compartments. To the left of the kitchen was a wide archway that looked directly into a large, open room with a composite floor. The walls were painted in a gorgeous mural depicting narrow Cumbrian roads, hills, sheep, and manor houses. Romeo sat happily in the middle, basking in small spotlights set at just the right angle flatter the deep red and gleam of his finish.

"Romeo!" I exclaimed.

"Yes, madam?"

"How do you like your new room?"

Romeo rolled down the windows so that I could hear him clearly. "It suits me perfectly, madam."

I looked between Lochlan and Keir with a huge grin. "Well, there you have it."

Keir leaned toward me and said under his breath, "You can be a little on the strange side, Rita." After the briefest pause, he added, “It’s one of the things I love most about you.”

I stopped myself from making too much of that declaration, telling myself that Keir hadn’t just professed his love for me. It was a common expression used to express feelings about everything from dogfood to weather.

“It’s hard to argue with results,” I said. “And you heard for yourself how appreciative he is.”

Keir shook his head with a smile and looked at Lochlan to gauge his reaction. Lochlan’s good nature was unshakeable. He might not outwardly indicate a negative reaction to anything. Ever.

There was no formal dining room in the house, but there was more space allotted in the kitchen for six-person lunches next to a fireplace that looked like it had been taken straight out of a sixteenth-century tavern. Dolan had made me a replica of Arthur’s round table after Fie began calling my luncheons legendary. And it looked like it had been made for the room.

On the other side of the kitchen was a quarter bath, a larder, the laundry, a storage room that was empty except for my two tired suitcases that were overdue for retirement, a largish mud room with a rear exit containing a dog door. And one last room on the other side of that.

"What is this?" I asked Lochlan.

"Let me ask."

While Lochlan was gone I played with the dog door closure, sliding it up and down, imagining my own dogs coming and going to the space outside. The picket fence ran around the house, but it was nothing more than decoration. There would be no stopping my magical wolfdogs from doing what they wanted, other than a desire to please me. I hoped they came with a desire to please me. I was going to need Lochlan to spell out the return policy.

Lochlan returned. "She says it's Keir's room."

Keir laughed out loud, clearly as delighted as a person can be.

After making my way out the back and around the house to the front, I looked at Maeve and said, "It's mind blowing. I wouldn't change a thing."

She shrugged as if to say, "Duh."

"In my room I'd like an entire wall of monitors so that I could watch twelve different sports events at once," Keir told her.

"Seriously?" I said.

"Well, yes. Sometimes you'll be busy with matters of justice. I want to be occupied so that I'm not tempted to constantly disturb your concentration."

"What happened to books and treasures?"

"Monitors are treasures."

I turned to Maeve. "Can you put a child lock on the programming so it doesn't become a porn den?"

"I don't know what that is." She sniffed like she might not know what it is, but there was no doubt in her mind that it was distasteful. In this case she'd be right.

"She was joking," Keir told her before turning his smile to me. "She does that a lot."

I leaned toward him and lowered my voice. "I wasn't joking this time."

With a laugh, he said, "I don't know what I did for fun before you came."

Impatient with Keir's public acknowledgement of affection, Maeve said, "Are we done here?"

"I have a daughter who might visit from time to time. I need a place for her."

Maeve blinked and out of the corner of my eye I saw a smaller building emerge from the mist. It was a miniature of my house, about one quarter the size and cute as could be.

"Living, bed, bath," Maeve said. "When you want it to appear, you can just look in that direction and say, "Evangeline." She waved and the house disappeared. "Do you want to test it?"

There was no point in asking how she knew my daughter's given name. She'd done a walkabout in my head. I looked toward where the house had been and said, "Evangeline."

I must say nothing can make you feel godly like seeing whole buildings manifest with a thought and a word. It was gratifying all the way to the pit of my stomach. But…

"What will happen if I say 'Evangeline' and don't want the guest house to show itself?"

Maeve sighed deeply. "When was the last time you uttered the name, Evangeline?"

"Just a second ago."

With undisguised exasperation, she said, "Before. That."

I thought back. I'd had flighty romantic notions about naming a daughter Evangeline, but she'd become Evie before she could learn to recognize her name. There was a chance that the last time I'd said it out loud was when I told the hospital what to put on her birth certificate.

I smiled. "I take your point. Evangeline was a good choice. How do I get it to go away?"

"Think of a word you're unlikely to use under any other circumstances."

"Abracadabra."

"Done," she said. "Is our business concluded?"

"Almost," I answered. To Lochlan, I said, "I want to borrow Aisling for a minute."

Lochlan turned to the dogs, who were sitting prone on haunches under one of my shade trees. "Aisling. Go with Rita."

Aisling trotted over like she'd understood perfectly.

"Everybody else wait here, please," I instructed.

Aisling followed me into the house then looked to me as if to ask, "Why am I here?"

"Will this be okay for the little ones?"

She looked around, lowered her head and began sniffing. She followed her nose through every part of the house, stopping now and then for something of interest. When she'd thus canvassed every room, she stopped by the dog door and wagged her tail. As soon as I raised the panel that covered the multi-flap opening, she was outside and barking happily, from the sound of it, running to the front of the house.

I replaced the panel, smiling. Life wasn't going to be good in Hallow Hill. It was going to be grand.

The little cluster of magic kind was waiting for me at the gate to my new house.

"Well?" Maeve said in her curt and demanding way.

I smiled. "It's perfection. What about a key?"

She scoffed like I was an idiot. "You don't need a key. It's *your* house. When you leave it will lock. When you return, it will unlock."

"I have a housekeeper." I glanced at Keir surreptitiously. "And I might want to give a friend access."

"The house serves you and will do what you want. Just say out loud, 'House. Give Olivia and Keir access when I want them to have it'."

I thought about suggesting that Keir wasn't the friend

I'd had in mind, but that would be pointless. My secrets were common knowledge.

"I can change that directive at any time?" With a look of exasperation, she didn't bother to answer. She simply vanished. "Okay. I'll take that as a 'yes'."

Keir chuckled. "Old fae who live in the bubble of the upper echelon are frequently pompous, impatient and haughty."

"Not into manners."

He shook his head, chuckled more, and repeated. "Not into manners when it comes to interacting with those they believe inferior."

I turned to Lochlan. "You said no one in the magical community would think me their inferior."

"You said that?" Keir asked Lochlan.

"It's a broad statement, I grant you, but largely true," said Lochlan defensively.

"*Largely true*? You people are very good at qualifiers, you know that?"

With a snicker, Keir said, "Think of Maeve as being the exception to a rule. She was probably bothered by my attentions to you."

"What are you saying? That I have a brand-new enemy who has the power of a god? Because of you?"

Keir said, "No. No. Calm down. Being discourteous doesn't mean she's your enemy. Her bad. Not yours."

As an afterthought, Lochlan added, "You could have her disciplined for it if you want."

"Disciplined?" I didn't believe there would ever be a time when I'd feel comfortable wielding that kind of power over others. "About that. It seems like punishments are always in the form of fines. But what kind of punishment is that for people who have so much money it's meaningless? For all I know, Maeve can *manufacture* money. From thin air!"

Lochlan cocked his head. "Where did you get the idea that the fines are monetary?"

"I, um, assumed." After letting the implication sink in, I said, "How else might fines be exacted?"

"Hmmm. The history of magistrates is long and colorful. Some have been exceptionally creative. For a specified amount of time, the party decided against might be placed in servitude to the injured party. Or be stripped of a principle form of magic. Or be struck mute. Or be sentenced to solitary confinement. Or be taxed a precious object or rare creature, like a phoenix or flying horse."

"How would I…?"

"Everyone who comes before you is required to present a list of assets. So, you know what you have to work with." Lochlan left me with that thought as he called the dogs and strode toward his house.

"Wow." I couldn't think of anything else to say.

Just as Lochlan reached his door, I remembered what I needed to ask. "Wait!" He stopped and turned back as I jogged over. "Does this mean that I own two houses now? This and the one connected to the Hallows?"

"To a point. Yes."

"What point is that?"

"These things belong to you for your lifetime as magistrate. Upon your death they revert to the trust set up for that purpose. Why do you ask?"

"I'd like to give it to Maggie. According to what you're telling me, I could give her the use of it for my lifetime, but promise nothing beyond that."

"You could," he said slowly. "But," he cleared his throat, "Maggie has a night job."

‘Oh. I know. She’s a banshee.”

He looked surprised that I knew. “Well. That means she’s not home much.”

“Still, everybody should have their own place. And if anyone should occupy the house that connects to the shop, it’s Maggie.”

“You’re free to offer it. Of course.”

“Thanks, Lochlan.”

Chapter Eight

The Gist of Justice

When Maeve, Lochlan and the dogs were gone, Keir pulled me into his arms, nuzzled my neck and grinned as he spoke into my ear, "I love my room."

What could I say? Maeve had exposed my true, innermost desire to have him around.

"Hmmm," was the best I could do. "Was she really your creator?"

"Yes."

"She seems super proud of you. And super disapproving of me."

"Well, then she shouldn't have given me free will. Our relationship is not up to her now, is it?"

"Not if I have anything to say about it."

He chuckled. "So. Are you ready for me to move in?"

"Um."

"Why the hesitation?"

"We don't know if we're compatible."

"Yes. We do."

"In *every* way."

He inhaled deeply. "Oh." With a deep and sexy laugh he said, "You want an audition! I'm up for that. How about now?"

"It's not just that. It's *that* plus my concern about what happens if things don't work out? We still have to work together, I gather. For the rest of my life? That could be a decades-long era of awkward."

"Awkward will not be instigated by me. I've lived long enough to know what I want. You're it."

I smiled. "That was as romantic a speech as I've ever heard. I've filed it away for replay whenever I need a reminder that you're wonderful. But aside from the afore mentioned compatibility, I can't know in advance what relationship stressors are lurking, waiting to be discovered. Who knows what it might be? Walking around in socks then wearing them to bed, which means that all the stuff on the floors is now in the bed? Ew. Paying more attention to fantasy football than me? Saying ho ho ho after a big yawn?"

"What?" He scrunched up his face at that one and who could blame him?

"The point is, I need a trial run, but there's a catch. A trial run might lead to nirvana, but it might also lead to…"

"Awkward?"

"Yes! Forever means something different to you, but what remains of my life is of preeminent importance to *me*. 'Cause my time is finite."

"What exactly are you saying?"

"No promises. Let's just see if we light each other up."

"You have a lot going on in that head, Rita. Are we doing this or not?"

"Yes," I heard myself answer without hesitation, which was not like me at all. "But if things get icky, don't say I didn't warn you."

"I've been put on notice and promise to refrain from saying you didn't warn me about icky and awkward."

"Keir."

"Yes."

"Would you like to come for a sleepover tonight?"

Keir's handsome face spread into one of the smiles that never failed to make him even more beguiling. "I would. Does it start now?"

Suddenly anxious, I shook my head. "Um, no. Tonight? After supper?"

"How will I be able to think about anything else between now and then?" He brightened. "I know. Let's do that thing." I looked at him with a question on my face because people do a lot of things. "Take out!"

The evident eagerness radiating from Keir made me confident enough to want to preen. "Is the pub equipped for that?" He gave me a look. "Oh. Never mind. I forget that magic kind are always equipped for everything. But you know what? That would be silly. I'll have Olivia make us something."

"Even better."

"What do you want?"

"Stroganoff. The way they make it at the Russian Tearoom in New York."

"So. Towns like Hallow Hill scare you, but New York doesn't."

He shrugged. "New York scares me a lot less than Hallow Hill. In New York, nobody knows or cares what you're doing. Hallow Hill is full of busybodies."

"The classic response would be to ask what you're afraid of them discovering." He said nothing. "But I won't. There's nothing wrong with wanting a measure of privacy. But having supper with me at the pub, at six every night for weeks, is a fairly big public statement."

"Is it?"

Clearly, he wanted to play dumb.

"Look. I've never been to the Russian Tearoom and I'm pretty sure Olivia hasn't either."

Keir's smile turning seductive ramped both anxiety and excitement up a notch. "I don't really care. I'm not coming for the food."

"I guessed as much. But it's still a work night for me. I made a commitment to begin prioritizing cases to be heard at Hallowstide Court Week."

"Maybe I can help."

I hadn't thought of that. Certainly, Keir Culain had extensive experience. He'd been a 'man on the scene'. His thoughts might be helpful and, over the past weeks, I'd come to appreciate his perspective on things.

"If it's not against any rules?"

He shook his head. "You're in charge of the rules, Magistrate."

The idea of being powerful was going to be even harder to get used to than seeing centerfold-worthy gardeners morph into Tinkerbell.

I WAS CALLING out Maggie's name as I rushed into the shop, noticing the front door was standing open, but not paying too much attention. Until I began to choke on the smoke.

She poked her head around from the back right away. "Right here."

"What in hell, Maggie? Is the place burning down? Do we have a fire department? Call 911 and get everybody out!"

She sniggered at that. "The things you say. I'm burnin' some herbs I got from Esmerelda to make sure that thing didn't leave any bad jubee-wubee behind."

I coughed. "Are you into hoodoo now?"

She shrugged. "Little of this. Little of that. Whate'er works. Do no' tell the witch I get my supplies elsewhere.

No point in needless hard feelin's."

"I'm sure that we have rid ourselves of all remnants of, um…"

"Jubee-wubee."

"Yes. That. So can we get the smoke out of here before it permanently seeps into every aspect of shop and inventory?" Maggie waved her hand, said something in Irish, and every trace of smoke was gone, including the smell.

"That's better. I have news."

"I'm partial to news," she said brightly.

I laughed, grateful to have full use of my lungs again. "You're partial to gossip. It's not the same."

"'Tis," she insisted.

"Not." I held up my hand to stop the retort. "My new house. It's a dream. And I'm already moved in!"

"Well, now. I can see on your face that you're pleased as a body can be."

"So my former residence is officially abandoned."

"Aye. Makes sense."

"And I want you to have it. Lochlan says I can only offer you the use of it for my lifetime because it belongs to a trust or something. But maybe I'll live a long time."

"Well, o'course you'll be livin' a long time. Nary a soul would question it."

It wasn't hard to read the hesitation. "But?"

"But you know I'm no' home much. Most times I'm called upon to travel great distances when I'm no' mindin' the store."

"Lochlan said as much. Not about the travel. About your second, um, job. So you don't want it?"

"'Tis no' that. No. No' at all. Your gift is precious as the Shannon. But I truly could no' get the good out of it as others might." I couldn't help but feel a little dejected. "If you want to see it occupied by someone who'd love and care for it, what about Olivia?"

"Olivia?"

"Perhaps if she had her own place, Dolan'd be free to invite Molly over." She gave me a salacious wink.

"But then Olivia would be alone. Maybe she doesn't want to live alone."

"Or maybe she's been choosin' to keep her brother company all this time so *he*'d no' be alone. He's no' very outgoin' if ye may have noticed. Maybe she'd like to pursue her own interests." Maggie wiggled her brows.

"Do you know something?" She treated me to her best Mona Lisa smile. "What is it?"

"I believe the mayor may have designs on our Olivia. And who wouldn't? There's no' a better cook, well, perhaps no' in all the world. You may have had a hand in that, puttin' 'em together at your lunches. The match-makin' magistrate."

"I had no idea. Well," I shrugged, "if you think that's the best use of it. I really wanted *you* to have it." Suddenly feeling bad for Maggie, I said, "It makes me sad that you go from one job to another. It's like you have no life of your own."

"Far from it. My work is my life and I'm happy. If 'tis sympathy you're feelin', 'tis misplaced. Nature is destiny. You do no' feel sorry for a dog bein' a dog or a bird bein' a bird."

"Well, no."

"Enough about that then. Go on with ye. Let Olivia know that the gods have smiled on her and things are takin' a turn for the better."

I LET MYSELF into the residence through the pass-through. Olivia was in the kitchen getting ready for the day's lunch bunch. I couldn't tell if Olivia was becoming more lovely or if I was simply becoming fonder of her. But she seemed to have a blush on her cheeks that hadn't been there when I'd first arrived. She'd also begun adding touches of color to the monochrome black that was her choice of uniform. Certainly I'd never suggested a dress code.

She was wearing an army green apron that made the swampy color of her eyes pop against her fair skin and jet-black hair. The apron was covered in a design of a beautiful leafless tree that was otherworldly. Somehow, I knew there was significance in the imagery, but the knowledge of what it meant was just on the other side of consciousness and I couldn't place it.

"Olivia!" I sang.

She looked up, smiled, and said, "Okay." It had become our joke. She seemed to revel in the conspiracy of having a private joke between us.

"This will be the last lunch in this house. I'm all moved into the new place, just across from Lochlan and Ivy."

She nodded. "I saw your things were gone."

"So, the rest of the time I'm magistrate, which I guess is the rest of my life, this house will just sit empty." The way she looked around told me all I needed to know. "How long have you been caretaker here?"

"Over a hundred years, human time."

"Well, like I said, it would just sit empty if you don't take it for your own, and that would be a shame. So, I'm granting you the leasehold, free of charge, for the duration of my tenure as magistrate."

Olivia was clearly deer-in-headlights dumbstruck. When she found her voice, she said, "Me?"

"Do as you please with it."

I pulled out my keys and began removing them from the ring. "I'm keeping the key ring that Brad gave me. This one is for the front door. This one is the pass-through to the shop. We could have the door permanently closed if you'd rather."

I looked up to see if she was further along with digesting the announcement. She wasn't. "Do you need help moving?" She shook her head vigorously. I set the keys on the counter. "Well, here you go. Once you're moved in, I think you'll be closer to work than you are now.

"Now I need something special. I have a guest coming for dinner tonight. At the new house. It's been, um, magically programmed so that you have access without needing a key. We'd like to have beef stroganoff over wide noodles with a mixed green salad and vinaigrette, the tangy citrus kind you make." She nodded. "Could you manage to do that by six and leave it warming? I'll do the serving and clean up."

"Yes. I will."

"Okay. Super. I'll be back for lunch. Smells good." Seeing that receiving a gift of that magnitude had left Olivia discombobulated, I decided the kindest thing would be a quick departure so that she could process.

As I reached the shop door, she almost shouted, "Magistrate!" I stopped and turned. "Thank you."

I smiled. "I hope you enjoy it as much as I have these past weeks."

I HURRIED BACK to *my* new house, the house of my heart and dreams and soul, wanting the chance to spend a little time alone there. I opened the gate and began to memorize the pattern of the flagstone walk that led to the red front door. As I approached, I heard a soft click and stood with my mouth open when the front door opened for me just as I was within distance to take hold of the iron latch handle.

Gads. It was the best parts of *Sleeping Beauty* and the Starship Enterprise. My subconscious mind apparently does marvelous mashups.

After admiring my living area, I turned right to my warm and welcoming study and set my bag down. I loved every inch of it from the leather sofa underneath shelves of my favorite books and photos, to the pair of priceless Bouillotte lamps with Tôle shades on the library table, to the small fireplace at the end of the room.

I knew there were four fireplaces in the house but only two chimneys visible from outside. I also knew that those chimneys at either side of the house, which created a wonderfully symmetrical picture, didn't line up with the fireplaces inside. But compared to other things I'd witnessed, that was minor magic I supposed.

I'd thought that I'd just peek at the first file on the stack of possible cases for Hallowstide but was immediately engrossed in the facts of the case. The sound of my phone ringing had become such an odd occurrence that I was immediately alarmed.

The caller ID said it was Olivia.

"Hello?" Before she had a chance to speak, I'd glanced at my watch and realized I was late for lunch. "Oh, geez, Liv. I'm so, so, so sorry. Be right there. Go ahead and start without me."

I hung up without waiting for an answer, didn't even grab my bag because… why would I need it? And jogged over to the Hallows.

For the rest of the afternoon my mind ping-ponged between reviewing cases and the impending 'dinner'. Too much time had passed for me to remember how I'd felt on prom day or my wedding day, but I thought I was far more jumpy about the prospect of Keir's 'audition', as he'd put it, than I had been on either of those benchmark occasions.

When I heard Olivia come in to start dinner, I decided to take a bubble-bath break.

I stopped by the kitchen.

"Hi Olivia." She glanced up from what she'd been doing, going through cabinets and drawers to make sure she had everything she needed, learning where everything was. "If you need to move stuff around, feel free. If you need something you don't see, just let me know and we'll get it."

"Okay."

"Hi Romeo."

"Good day, madam."

"You alright over there?"

"Yes. I like it here."

I wasn't expecting that, but it confirmed that my instinct had been right. Yay me.

I RESTED MY head on a rolled-up towel as I soaked in a hot bubble bath, feeling like I'd truly arrived in heaven, and tried not to overthink what the evening would bring.

After all, what was the big deal? People 'hook up' all the time and think nothing of it.

But you're not one of those people, the little voice in my head chided and chanted.

When the water grew cold, I pulled on loose-fitting linen drawstring pants and topped them with the blue tunic that always got compliments from Keir.

Once resettled at the library table, I was again quickly

caught up in case files, forgetting everything else until the smell of stroganoff filled the house. *Good choice, Keir.* When the front door opened and closed, I assumed it was Olivia leaving, but forgot that also meant that Keir would be arriving within minutes.

"Something smells good." I was startled by Keir's voice and jumped a little. He chuckled. "You forgot I was coming? Should I be offended?"

"I did not forget you were coming. How could I? It's just… these files."

His gaze slid to the stacks on the table. "Compelling?"

"Good word for it."

"Can you break away for dinner?"

"Ha. Ha."

I left the file I was reading open and pushed my chair back. When I stood up, he looked down at my bare feet.

"You even have pretty feet."

Well, there was something I didn't hear every day. Or ever. I wanted to avoid the cliché of looking down and really tried, but eventually I succumbed to the impulse to see what he was seeing.

"How about you?" I teased. "Do you have pretty feet?"

Without hesitation or sitting down, he pulled off one boot then the other. One sock then the other.

After examining his feet, I said. "Do not ever compliment me about a physical feature because then I'm going to compare myself to you and you're always going to win. Aren't you?"

He laughed silently and reached for me, but I ducked out of the way and headed for the kitchen.

"Nuh-uh. Stroganoff isn't good cold."

"I'll take my chances," he said, following close behind.

I turned into the kitchen expecting to see pots, pans, and a basic table setting. But what I found was the most romantic setting imaginable. Olivia had gone all out making good use of the china, crystal, and heavy silver courtesy of Maeve. While I don't have a dealer's expertise, I found the choices to be exquisite.

An old-looking silver candelabra sat off to the side with seven while tapers rising in an arc. Perhaps the biggest surprise was that Olivia had gone to the florist and picked up a table arrangement from Lily; scarlet red roses packed tightly amid wispy trailing tree fern. It couldn't have possibly been more romantic, which meant two things.

First, Olivia presumed my dinner guest was coming for a tryst.

Second, Lily's involvement meant that everyone in Hallow Hill would know about it by the time we sat down to eat.

Ah well, I thought. Might as well get used to small-town life. And why should I be ashamed of garnering interest from a heart-stopping beauty like Keir Culain?

Speaking of my luscious dinner companion, I looked his way. "I told Olivia I was having a dinner guest. And that's *all.* This ambush is all her."

"Ambush?"

Staring at the table, I said, "It looks like a seduction."

"It does," he chuckled cheerfully. "Let's eat."

The stroganoff had been left in a silver chafing dish on a rolling cart next to the table. The salad, waiting in a large wood bowl, was tossed but not dressed. The vinaigrette was in an elegant little pitcher with a dragon's head handle.

"I'm serving only because this is my house and not because I'm setting a precedent for domesticity," I said.

"Noted. Want help?"

"I know you're good in the kitchen," I said as I oiled the salad. "Probably better than I am. But I can manage putting salad on a gorgeous small crystal plate."

He looked down. "I guess this is pretty."

"Your mom has good taste."

He sputtered. "My mom?"

"I don't know what else to call someone who 'makes' a person."

"I take your point. 'My maker' sounds too sci-fi. Like I'm a robot." He smiled. "Sure. Mom works."

"She certainly acted like a protective mother. About me, I mean."

"Did she?" He did his best to look clueless.

I narrowed my eyes. "You know she did."

WE CHATTED ABOUT movies and townspeople and court meets while Keir made yummy sounds and complemented Olivia's version of stroganoff multiple times.

"Is it as good as the Russian Tea Room?"

"Oh. Let's don't ever let them know about Olivia," he said.

"I gave her the townhouse."

He stopped eating. "You did?"

"Yeah. I wanted to give it to Maggie, but she insisted that she 'wouldn't get the good out of it'. She said Olivia might like a place of her own."

Because we'd been dinner companions long enough to be comfortable with each other, long enough to be friends, it felt completely natural to eat and chat as we normally did. But the romantic setting, the circumstance of being alone with Keir Culain, and the promise of an 'audition' kept my thoughts returning to the after-dinner portion of the evening's programming.

When the last of the stroganoff was consumed, he turned his sexiest smile my way.

"Dessert?" he asked, causing innuendo to drip from the word in direct proportion to the speed at which juices were gathering elsewhere.

"Um..."

"I didn't get a good look at our bedroom this morning," he said as he stood, reaching for my hand and pulling me to my feet. He leaned close and whispered so that his warm breath was in my ear.

"*Our* bedroom? Isn't that yet to be determined?"

Keir Culain responded with the most arrogant chuckle imaginable. He clearly didn't have performance anxiety. "I'd like another tour."

At that moment I might've agreed to anything, even flying around in a starlit sky.

"Um..."

Without waiting for further invitation, he drew me into the bedroom. Seeing goosebumps raised on my arms, he said, "Light the fire." I looked around for matches, kindling and the like. "What are you doing?" he asked. When I told him, he grinned and said, "Just say the words. Fire. Light."

"You mean like talking to Alexa?"

"Yes. Except that what happens in your house stays in your house."

I was nodding, "An improvement to be sure."

"Try it."

I looked at the fireplace. "Fire. Light." Flames jumped to life. "That's pretty amazing. I mean participating in magic like, um, you can do? And the fire. It's not too little. Not too big. It's *just* right."

"That's because you saw the fire you wanted when you said the words."

"Oh."

"The house is yours. It responds to you. Maeve, I mean Mum, should have mentioned that." He looked around. "I like it here." Then he turned a smoldering look my direction. "I like *you* here. You know what I want?"

"What?" I asked breathlessly. Whatever it was, I wanted him to have it.

"One of your soul-searing kisses." *Soul-searing kisses? Oh my gods.* "No. I want at least three dozen of your soul-searing kisses. For starters. Starting right now."

Our bodies remembered the state of arousal we'd left at my townhouse door and picked up right there. We went from a civilized veneer of composure to tearing at clothes in sixty seconds.

I barely registered clothes flying every which way. I barely registered decorative pillows tossed aside and bed coverings being drawn back so that nothing remained but virgin-white, real linen sheets lit by firelight alone.

What I did register was Keir's physique, which exceeded every fantasy entertained by human women since the beginning of time. Quick to follow was self-consciousness about my own body, flawed by the passage of years, childbearing, and the joys of food and wine. This is not to mention neither time nor money for such frivolities as gym memberships. Keir was so in tune with my moods that he caught the shift the moment I began to withdraw emotionally.

"No," he said. Pulling my hands away from my body so that I was forced to stand with arms outstretched, he said, "You're exactly what I want. Not too little. Not too big. Just right."

I smiled at the repetition of my review of the fire. And all thought of anything except copulation with Keir left when he pressed my body into his. The responding groan, which was almost a growl, gave me all the self-confidence I needed to know that I was in the right place at the right time. And maybe Esmerelda was right. Maybe the Powers That Be had decided to throw love into the package as the cherry on top.

It wasn't a surprise that Keir was a skillful lover. The day we met Maggie had unartfully suggested as much by alluding to his reputation. What was a surprise was my body's response. I hadn't realized that I'd never had a sexual encounter with a man who knew what he was doing until I was in the midst of such an event.

Oh. My.

Copulation with Keir Culain was eye *and* leg opening. Every time I'd think a more frenzied arousal wasn't possible, he'd deliver a new maneuver that made me crazier and more vocal. I was glad I wasn't in the townhouse because I was sure I would've been heard by all the locals nearby. It was a wonder that my screams of pleasure didn't set off Romeo's alarm system.

Three orgasms and the equivalent of a Peloton workout later, I fell to my side facing him and said, "You're hired."

He chuckled. "So, I can move in now?"

"No wonder you weren't worried about your audition."

"Was that an answer?"

"Couple of details."

"What?"

"We're exclusive. Right?"

"All the way."

"What about your gatehouse? Don't you keep an eye on things?"

"That's not an issue. There are plenty of eyes on Tregeagle whether I'm around or not."

"The, um, faerie mound thing?"

"Yes." He smiled lazily as he began stroking my side at the smallest part of my waist.

"I need water. Do you need water?"

"Is there more stroganoff?"

I laughed. "No, but I wish there was because I'd like to see where you'd put it. You ate enough for four grown people or one sixteen-year-old boy."

"You mean four grown humans."

"Well… yeah. Or onr teenage boy, also human."

"Still waiting for an answer."

I took a big breath. "Okay. If I said you didn't pass the compatibility test, you'd know I was lying." His smile widened. "Are you sure it won't be a problem work-wise?"

"There's no one to question it, love."

"What does that mean?"

"I was made to have power over the fae monarchs so that I could keep the peace. You were chosen to have power over all magic kind to keep the peace. No one can stop us from being a couple except you or me."

After staring into his luminous eyes for a few beats, I whispered, "We're the power couple."

"Literally." He gently caressed the indentation beneath my bottom lip like he was fascinated with it. "What's the problem? I know you want me here because," he grinned, "My mum pulled it out of your house fantasy."

"I do want you here. Emotionally. But what's the point of being middle-aged if you're not any smarter than you were at eighteen?" Of course, it was silly to talk to Keir in terms of forty-odd years. "What I'm saying is that, until just a few weeks ago, I was half of a married couple. I haven't had time to get my feet under me as a single person. I think it would be stupefyingly foolhardy to jump into a live-in relationship so soon. I don't even know if my divorce is final." I made a mental note to ask Lochlan about that.

Keir sighed. "So. Sleepovers?"

"Definitely sleepovers." I nodded.

"Sleepovers every night?" he asked hopefully.

I laughed. "Let's don't push it and let's don't give it a

name. You're welcome to keep some stuff here. In your room. And your, um, closet. But there's no expectation. You can come and go. Just as long as you're not coming and going with other women."

He pulled me closer. "I'm not a fucking moron like your former mate."

I grinned. "Somehow I know that."

"Molly's intuition lessons?"

"Maybe."

"What is your intuition telling you right now?"

"That you want something else to eat."

"Right you are. What's my prize?"

I laughed. "Since I'm the one who guessed right, *I'm* the one who should get a prize." He took my hand and moved it to wrap around the cock that was again swelling to attention. I heard my voice lower and take on an almost unrecognizable sexy tone. "I can't think of a better prize."

He nodded just before nuzzling my neck. "Fuck now. Eat later."

We, or really, I decided that we wouldn't name our relationship. There was an inner voice that questioned my behavior, considering that I was still married. But I was beginning to sort out which aspects of my inner voice supported happiness, and which were bent on self-recriminations for their own sake. I chose the door with happiness behind it.

I SAT AT the library table in my study in silk pajamas and a somewhat ratty, old, red plaid robe. Keir had raided the refrigerator and used the toaster oven to refresh the leftover tapas and was now sitting next to me making short work of them.

"These are good," he said. "Why am I not invited to lunches?"

"Because I see you every night at dinner," I said absently. "So, I'm organizing this into priority stacks from left to right. The ones on the far left are cases that are no-brainers. I mean so far as making it onto the docket, not outcomes. These other three stacks are in descending order. Of course, I don't know what I'm doing."

I looked at his distracting shirtless form just as he shoved an entire spicy chicken tapa into his mouth. He chewed with a closed mouth smile while he reached for the one file on the far left. The no-question-about-it case.

As he began to read his smile fell away. He swallowed, turned the page, set it down, and looked at me. "I see why you put this in the serious stack."

"The serious stack," I repeated. "Yeah. I'm not an expert on magic kind, but this sounds bad. I looked Kelpies up in the book. Read about them. I couldn't pronounce the Gaelic so 'Kelpie' will have to do."

"What did you learn?"

"They're shifters that can appear as hot young women or water horses. They're associated with Scotland, but they're not exclusive to Scotland. Kind of like sirens in their womanly form, their goal being to lure young men and drag them to a watery death. In horse form they encourage people to touch their coats, which are apparently made of superglue. Either way, humans end up being dragged to a watery death." I looked toward the safe. "Hold on."

I retrieved the book that I'd come to think of as my magic-kind encyclopedia and found the section I was looking for.

"This is from a Robert Burns poem". I read aloud.

"...When thowes dissolve the snawy hoord

An' float the jinglin' icy boord

Then, water-kelpies haunt the foord

By your direction

And 'nighted trav'llers are allur'd

To their destruction...

"I guess it's common knowledge that their bridles are their weak spot. I don't know why they'd be created with a bridle, but I guess that's good and bad news. If somebody gets hold of a bridle, they'll be able to control that kelpie and all others."

"This really should be number one on the docket."

"You haven't seen all the files."

"I don't need to see all the files to know how serious this is. A fae prince who captured a kelpie and is refusing to let her go so that he can control her entire species?" Keir sounded horrified, even though we were talking about creatures who were far from sympathetic. He grabbed the file and reopened it. "The Bureau of Behavioral Oversight is bringing the suit. Good. They carry a lot of weight."

I closed the book, returned it to the safe, and sat.

"These things are beyond nasty."

Keir stared for a couple of beats before saying, "Humans would definitely think them monsters."

With a look intended to convey that I thought there was something *very*, *very* wrong about that response, I said, "You don't think they're monsters? One of the stories in the book? There were ten children playing on a river bank. A kelpie managed to get nine of them onto her back. When she tried to lure the tenth child, he touched the kelpie's nose and his finger stuck, but he cut it off to save himself. This is a species of magic-kind who live to kill humans in a grisly way, bodes never to be found. Every one of them is like the worst case of serial killer ever because they don't die. They just continue with the murdering. Forever."

Keir drew in a slow, deep breath. "I can see why that would be your first reaction. But the alternative view is that every species plays a role. Take Lochlan's wolves for instance. If Lochlan was in trouble, they wouldn't hesitate to sacrifice their lives to come to his defense. They wouldn't debate it. There'd be no inner conflict. Why? Because it's *what* they are. It's not up to us to decide if that's a good thing or a bad thing. It just is."

"Tell it to the mothers of the children who never saw them again. There aren't two sides to this question, Keir. Killing innocent humans simply because they came too close to a stream, or river, or lake is a bad thing. There is no alternative."

"You're thinking like a human."

"Well… that's my jam."

"Not anymore. Now you straddle the worlds of magic and mundane. Like a bridge. Let's start with this. How do you know those stories are true? How do you know the humans were innocent?"

I felt a link of chainmail slip from my righteous armor. "You're saying that…"

"That book you have? I'm not saying it's not informative. Certainly the illustrations are fun to look at. But it was written by humans and, just like all sacred books written by humans…"

"There are inaccuracies."

The ghost of a smile said Keir was pleased with the dawning of my enlightenment. "An understatement at best."

This job was going to be a lot harder than I'd thought. "But Robert Burns…"

"Was a poet whose purpose was to entertain."

Sitting back against my chair, I thought about that. Of course, Keir was right. Burns was the James Cameron of his day. I couldn't trust that book to be any more reliable than fairy tales. Fantasy, loosely based on fact, and distorted to shock or titillate.

"I'm not the right person for this job," I said quietly. Keir reached out to pull a lock of my hair through his fingers and smiled. "Don't say…"

"I wasn't going to say that."

"What were you going to say?"

"Too bad." I liked him more every minute. "Job is yours now. You're the guardrails for a race that can be, shall we say, morally ambiguous." He looked at my preliminary piles. "What else?"

"So, you're the Enforcer and the Advisor?"

He laughed and shook his head slightly. "Lochlan's the advisor. I'm just the bloke who's sleeping with the judge." I raised an eyebrow. "And, yes, it's new. I've never had a physical relationship with a magistrate."

I cocked my head and assessed him thoughtfully. "Can I trust you, Keir? *Really* trust you?"

The look on his face resembled shock and his response was barely above a whisper.

"Yes," was all he said. "Your well-being comes first with me. It always will."

WE TALKED ABOUT a few other cases.

"Lochlan will go over this, but the first day is usually reserved for evidentiarily-minor cases that won't require a lot of presentation."

"Open and shut." I summed it up. He nodded. I looked at my pile system. "So I need to organize my piles according to importance and order."

"If you want to get a jump on it. Up to you."

The leprechaun whose pot of gold was stolen as a prank, but the loss, though temporary, had caused him such distress that he cursed the adolescent pranksters with a magical form of leprosy. Despite pleas from the parents and offers of more pots of gold, the little hothead refused to withdraw the affliction. Pile number one. First day.

The phoenix who'd been captured and kept for the

entertainment of a fae princess who liked to set the bird on fire and watch it struggle back to life from ashes. Pile number one. First day.

One of the fae queens was jilted by a lover a few thousand years ago. He'd forgotten all about it when he requested an upgrade to his palatial residence, but she hadn't. She cheerfully accepted the commission and just as cheerfully acted out her woman-scorned feelings by trapping him in a "Groundhog Day" scenario. For a century, he relived the same day without being able to leave his house until relatives realized there was a problem. He wants restitution. Pile number one. First day.

A young gargoyle had been taken along on a shopping spree to Paris by a fae noblewoman. She told him to wait at Notre Dame where he'd likely go unnoticed. Unfortunately, she forgot about her pet and left him there, stranded in the human world. The gargoyle chieftain, who is the kid's great-uncle, wants the noblewoman stranded in Paris for seventy-six years, the exact time the kid lived in fear of discovery.

At that I threw the file down. "You got a lot of irredeemable personalities in the fae world," I said in disgust.

Keir had been sitting with his arms crossed over his anatomically implausible abs. In response to my outburst, he reached up to rub his bottom lip with his thumb. After evaluating my statement, he said, "In your life as a human, how much time did you spend as an observer in the courts?"

"None." He waited. "Okay. I see where you're going with this. You're saying there are plenty of unsavory characters in the human world as well, but out of sight, out of mind."

"Well put." He smiled. "Let's go to bed. You're tired and filled with righteous indignation. I can take the edge off that."

I harrumphed. "Sure. Maybe now. But not in the middle of Court Week when I want to personally strangle people or hang them by their thumbs."

He barked out a laugh. "Hanging by thumbs. I haven't heard that one for a very long time. You should keep it in your tool kit."

"Why? It seems like every case is resolved with some kind of fine."

After a small grunt, Keir said, "That may be partly tradition and partly laziness. This job is yours to make of it what you will. You'll bring your own personality and creativity and… Well."

"You were going to say it."

He laughed. "Guilty."

THE NEXT MORNING there was a timid knock at the door at eight thirty.

Keir had already gone. Apparently.

I dragged myself to the door and peeped through the thoughtfully-provided hole, before opening it.

"Olivia. What…?"

"I need to tidy up, Mistress." *Mistress?* "You might be having company." She looked over her shoulder.

"What kind of company?"

"I was told it's a human tradition. Housewarming?"

I looked down at my rumpled nightclothes and opened the door wider. "I'm getting in the shower."

"I'll make the bed and some treats for your guests."

"Um, sure. That'd be great."

"Shall I admit them?"

"You mean let them in? If they arrive before I'm

ready? Geez, Olivia. Now that you're finally talking, you're not going to start sounding like a butler are you?"

Her blank expression told me she had no idea what I meant. "Okay."

"Sure. Why not? Everybody here knows everything about everything." At that moment I was finally gripped by both guilt and good manners. "Oh golly. I'm sorry for acting like that. Got no excuse except that it's early, I haven't had coffee, and I'm working through the new info that I'm really not a first-thing-in-the-morning surprise party kind of person."

"Okay."

"What I meant to say is that dinner last night was scrumptious, the table was divine, and you were so thoughtful to get here first and make things presentable. I'm so lucky to have you."

Her uncertainty turned to a radiant smile and I made a mental note to treat Olivia like a delicate flower since she was expressing every indication of typical feminine sensitivity.

I HAD JUST stepped out of the shower when I realized that I

had interacted with Olivia, in her true, magical form. And I was barefoot.

It seemed the thing my guides had predicted, that the magic would 'settle on me' had come to pass. I could see without the shoes. I was dying to call Keir and tell him the news.

I thought I heard strains of "Der Kommissar" while I was brushing my teeth, but decided it was my imagination. I wound my damp hair into a messy bun, pulled on at-leisure pants and a long sweater then took a last look in the mirror. I hadn't put on makeup, but I looked pretty good without it. Not younger so much, but… slap me for saying this. Glowing. Maybe the great health I was promised was making me look presentable at nine in the morning with no coffee, much less breakfast.

The living room was practically full when I stepped in. Brad, Lily, Dolan, Molly, Jeff, Esmerelda, Lochlan, Ivy, Keir and the mayor were milling about, commenting on this and that.

When my guests looked up and saw me, they yelled, "SURPRISE!" in unison.

I smiled and waved. "What's this? It's not my birthday."

Maggie said, "Housewarmin'. Your present's in the kitchen."

"Well," I said, "let's go see what it is."

Olivia handed me a mug of coffee as I entered the kitchen, which smelled like homemade donuts. *Gods Bless Olivia.*

My little crowd followed along into the kitchen and gathered around my Arthurian table recreation. I had time for three sips of coffee before turning my attention to my impatient company.

The package wrapping was sublime enough to be called magical. And probably was.

I tore through paper, ribbons, and outer boxing to reveal a true treasure. A vintage tea kettle that was also a replica of a train engine. If it was like the one I'd seen as a child, it would whistle like a train and the wheels would go faster as the water heated.

Looking around at the expectant faces of people who wanted me to be pleased, I suddenly felt very lucky.

"How did you know?" The same way they knew everything else I supposed. "I always wanted one of these and was never able to find one in decent condition. I LOVE it!"

My 'guests' gave each other self-congratulatory looks then moved on to sample home-made donuts. I handed my gift over to Olivia.

"Would you rinse this out and fill it with water? Let's put it on the stove and take it for a spin." Olivia smiled at my joke as she took the kettle. It was a good day indeed.

As Keir returned from admiring Romeo with Dolan, I leaned into him and said, "Did you know about this?" He smiled. "And you didn't warn me?'

"What fun would that be?"

I shook my head and went off to find Maggie. Pulling her to the side, I said, "Did somebody think to invite John David?"

She pulled back like she hadn't heard me right. "Why no. No' so far as I know."

"Why not?"

"It did no' come to mind. He keeps to himself, ye know."

"He keeps to himself because he's been marginalized by this community. I want him here for this."

"I do no' know if we can get him here in time. We all

have businesses to open shortly." She looked toward the light coming in from the windows. "If it was dark, I could fly there. As a blackbird."

"Orrrrrr we could just call him." I paused to make a point. "On the phone."

"Oh aye. That's the thing to do."

"I would've thought taking care of that awful hobby-lobby thing would've changed the way he's regarded."

"Hobknobbit. Aye. You're right. I should've thought to invite him." She shrugged apologetically. "Old habits."

Fearing I may have made my concern sound like a rebuke, I said, "Thanks for doing this. It's wonderful." I knew that including the vampire in social gatherings would be a change for the locals, but I'd made up my mind that he would be a regular fixture at luncheons until he was thought of as 'one of us'.

After stepping into the master, I found my phone where I'd left it on my closet island and called John David's landline. He might've gotten a mobile phone, but I hadn't talked to him for a few days.

I was both surprised and relieved when he answered after seven rings.

"Who's calling?"

I made a mental note that we needed to scrub the rust off his social skills.

"It's me. Rita." Deciding to give as good as I got, I added, "Who else would be calling?" I was immediately sorry for being petty. "Listen. I'm having a few friends over for an impromptu housewarming. Right now. And it'll be over in forty-five minutes. Can you make it?"

"Yes," he said.

"Well. Good. I'll hang up now."

He beat me to it and ended the call before I did.

Twenty minutes later I heard,

Don't turn around, oh oh

(Ja, ja)

Der Kommissar's in town, whoa oh

It was a song that never failed to make me smile even though I had no idea what it was about. Another thing Maeve must've pulled out of my 'messy' head.

"Was that my doorbell?" I asked Olivia while trying to make the world's best donut last.

"I believe so, Mistress."

Okay. I saw in our future, Olivia's and mine, a sit-down about what I could stand to be called.

"Huh," I said. "Thinking it was weird, but not disliking it."

I opened the door to John David and a me-sized statue of Eros sitting on the porch.

"Happy New House," he said.

I looked at the statue and laughed. "You brought me the statue I made you buy? John David, you've got a sense of humor." He gave me the enigmatic smile I would've imagined is a vampire staple. "Did you hate it that much?"

He stepped back a few inches and regarded the love god. "Actually, I was growing fond of it. What sort of person would I be if I gave you something I dislike?"

Well, that was charming.

"That makes me treasure it. Thank you. And please come in. We're having homemade donuts."

For the second time I mentally crossed myself in case inviting vampires in really was a horrible idea. I'm not Catholic any more than Maggie, but as she says, sometimes it's good to appropriate things that just fit.

"Look, everybody, my friend John David is here." The

noise stopped abruptly like that old stockbroker commercial and everyone stared. It was clear that a social punt was called for. "Did you know that John David saved us all from certain ruin last week?" Clearly, they hadn't all heard. "He disposed of an artifact that was up to no good. He's the only one of us who could do it unharmed. So," I looked at each of them with a schoolteacher's warning face, "we owe him a debt of gratitude."

The least likely attendee got the message and came forward.

"John David, "Esmerelda said. "I understand you buried that abomination in salt?"

He looked as pleased as is possible for a socially-challenged vampire. "Yes," he said. Then without further prompting, he went on to explain all the steps he'd taken beginning with digging out a special cellar in the floor of his basement.

By the time he was finishing the story, most of my guests had gathered around to listen. I hoped that was a breaking of the ice both around John David's heart and around the socially-closed population of Hallow Hill.

"Almost perfect," Esmerelda said. She turned to the

little crowd, "I saw the thing. It was nasty." Turning back to John David, she said, "If you're open to it, I'd like to come by and seal the site. Just to be sure."

John David looked as stunned as if he'd been struck by lightning. When it seemed that he was unable to speak, I rushed forward.

"He'd love that, Esmerelda. As we all would."

"I want to come," said Lily. "I've always wondered what that big house looks like on the inside."

Several others murmured their hopes for an invitation.

"John David," I said. "Do you have an operable kitchen?" He nodded mutely. "Good. Monday we'll all close up and go to John David's house for lunch. Olivia will cook. Everybody's invited except for Keir." I looked to him. "I guess somebody needs to 'guard' the village?"

Keir's scowl told me that he was either angry about being left out, or disappointed about being left out, or unhappy with the attention John David was getting from me. "Why don't we just have Esmerelda ward the village?"

"Well," I said, "I didn't know that was an option. I thought Esmerelda was a weaver." I heard hushed murmurs and tittering laughter. "And part-time soothsayer?

But whatever. Sounds good to me. Esmerelda?" I looked at Esmerelda with a question on my face. She nodded. "Good then. Monday twelve o'clock at John David's house for lunch and a tour."

I tried to get him to agree verbally, but the vampire still looked shell-shocked. He nodded.

Good enough.

"Romeo can carry three besides me."

When attention returned to donuts and watching the spinning wheels on my tea kettle, I pulled at Keir's sleeve. "I may need help getting my statue inside. It looks heavy."

"I'll get it," Keir said. "Where do you want it?"

"I don't know. What do you think?" I turned a wicked smile his way. "Maybe your room?"

"Ha! No. There's only one place for the god of love." He wiggled his eyebrows with a comical leer.

I chuckled and gestured toward the master. "You know the way."

Keir set the Eros statue near the fireplace and gave it a quarter turn so that the angle was just right. And I'll be damned if it didn't finish the room and add something I hadn't known was missing.

"Holy cow, Keir. You could've been a decorator."

He admired the placement of the statue with me. "Add it to the very long list of things I do extraordinarily well." His hand was slowly creeping from my waist to my derrière. I caught it before it reached its destination. We weren't alone and I was very straight-laced when it comes to public displays of pleasure. He was unfazed. "You think I should consider a career transition?"

My head jerked to see if he was serious. "Is that an option?"

He laughed. "No. Not at all. I was created for the job. Not the other way around."

When I reemerged from the bedroom, I saw John David heading out the front. I rushed over. "Hold on. Are you trying to escape without saying goodbye?"

"Things to do," he said. "I need to get my man to undrape furniture, open curtains, clean the corners. Polish up a bit. We have only three days."

It would've been impossible to miss the underlying anticipation.

"I hope it wasn't too presumptuous for me to throw a luncheon at your house. Everybody seems excited about being invited. Me included."

"It will be ready." His expression didn't match his words. He looked a little worried.

"I have no doubt. Olivia will come around nine thirty?" He nodded again. "Do you have enough place settings or should Olivia bring some?"

He laughed again sending the message that my question was ridiculous. It was the second time I'd experienced vampire joy and it confirmed that John David's mirth is a spectacular event. Not to be missed.

"Yes," he said. "I counted thirteen. There's plenty."

"When was the last time you entertained?"

The answer was a gleam in his eyes as he said, "Long ago."

"I'm sure it's like riding a bicycle."

He looked confused. "How is it like riding a bicycle?"

"Um. It means you don't forget how?" He blinked. "Okay then. See you Monday."

Without further adieu, John David was gone.

Keir, who'd been observing this exchange, weighed in. "What are you doing?"

"Helping out. What are you doing?"

He smiled. "So, you're including the vampire in your social registry, but not Aoumiel."

Without hesitation, I said, "I don't like her."

"I think everybody grasps that."

"And I suspect I'm not the only one. I noticed that no one suggested Aoumiel 'ward' the village on Monday. She's supposed to be the witch. Esmerelda is supposed to be the weaver."

With an abrupt change of subject, he said, "The donuts were good. I especially liked the ones that tasted kind of like gingerbread."

"Why aren't you asking why Thomasin Cobb wasn't invited? I'll tell you. Because you already know the answer. Nobody likes him and it's his own fault." I narrowed my eyes. "Are you going to bat for Auomiel? With me?" I frowned. "Do you understand baseball metaphors?"

"Have you seen the wall of sports monitors in my room?"

"Right. Silly question. The second, not the first. Still waiting for an answer on the first."

"I have no doubt that she did something to incur your ire. Knowing you as I do, I strongly suspect you're justified in your feelings."

"I am. Be sure and tell Olivia you like the donuts. She thrives on compliments."

"I will."

LUNCH AT JOHN David's house was a big success. He was real gentry. The house would've been a major tourist attraction if it was on the map and charged admission. The size of the place must have aggravated his feelings of loneliness and I felt sad for him all over again.

There was an oil painting of a person that had to be John David holding the bridle of a dapple-gray jumper. There wasn't a plaque with a year, but there was no mistaking that the painting was old.

He gave us a tour of the premises and showed us into one of the dining rooms. The table was set for dinner with a head of state. I'd seen why he'd laughed when I'd asked if he had enough place settings. On the tour, between the immense kitchen and various dining rooms was a butler's pantry the size of a two-car garage. The walls were lined with breakfront cabinets with glass doors that displayed collections of china, crystal, and every manner of silver tray, bowl, platter, and compote.

If someone hadn't been keeping up with the polishing, he would've had to hire a temporary service to get the tarnish off in three days.

Everyone left except Keir and Esmerelda, who were riding with me. Esmerelda had brought along a tote with supplies for sealing the hobknobbit. She laughed when I called it her bag of tricks.

On the way back to Hallow Hill, I said, "I really hope this breaks the ice, finally, for John David. All creatures need to be with others. Well, except for Howard Hughes. But he's dead. See what happens when you're alone?" I was babbling, but I wanted Esmerelda's reassurance and didn't want to ask for it outright.

"He's going to be fine," she said from the backseat. "Magic kind are standoffish. But now we know him."

I felt relief on John David's behalf. He was going to be okay.

I FELL INTO a routine that agreed with me so much I felt, in some ways, like life had begun when I'd arrived in Hallow Hill.

After breakfast, I stopped by the shop to see what had arrived overnight. Sometimes pieces were ready for sale. Sometimes they needed refurbishing. In some ways, those were preferable because it added to my sense of purpose. I suppose I'd always liked making things better, for people, for things, but that had gotten lost in the daily grind of trying to keep my ex happy. Dolan was either the genius Maggie had once described or else he used magic to repair things. Either way, there was no arguing with results.

After looking in on the night's haul, I walked with Lochlan and the wolfdogs, as I'd begun calling them. As fall progressed, I bundled more to remain comfortable even in the crisp breezes encountered at the top of the hill, but Lochlan always seemed comfortable in any clothing, in any weather.

We talked in-depth about the cases I was considering. At times he would tell me about similar situations in the past and how they'd been resolved.

"So, would you consider these precedents?" I asked.

"Certainly, they are precedents, but that's not to mean that your decision is guided by what's gone before. Each new magistrate is appropriate for the time. Things change."

On weekdays, I had people in for lunch. On weekends I had lunch at the pub.

On returning home, I'd nap for a bit and then return to poring over the files.

My original intention, for Keir to be an occasional sleepover guest was forgotten when he walked me home from supper every night and slipped inside before I closed the door.

Sometimes we made love on the rug in front of the fireplace amid briefs spread everywhere. "Watch the glasses! I don't want to be the first magistrate to soak files with wine."

Sometimes we made love in the big, beautiful bed. "I used to make fun of people saying stupid stuff in movies like, 'I wish we could just stay here forever'."

"But now that doesn't sound so stupid?" Kier asked. I nodded, my cheek rubbing against his chest where I rested my head. He loved hearing that I enjoyed his company, in and out of bed.

Life was good.

It got even better when, one day, as I was saying goodbye to lunch guests, I saw Lochlan across the way waving frantically. I jogged across the road.

"What is it?"

"Puppies," he said with excitement.

My stomach immediately filled with butterflies. "Puppies?"

"Well, come in."

Angus wagged his tail as I passed him in the hallway outside the mud room. I stopped long enough to acknowledge the proud pop.

"How many?" I asked.

"Three. Perfect and healthy. Of course, they would be. They're magic, you know."

Aisling didn't lift her head when I entered but looked my direction and I saw the tiniest tail wag.

As Lochlan had said, three pups, eyes closed, weighing about one pound each were sleeping as soundly as if they didn't yet know they'd been born.

"Which ones are mine?" I whispered. Since I had come into my magical sight, I no longer saw the dogs in their Border Collie forms. Even though I continued to call them dogs, or wolfdogs, there was no getting around the fact that they were big, bad wolves.

Two of the pups had the same coloring as Angus and Aisling. One was a darker gray.

"These two." Lochlan pointed to the two that looked like their parents. "You can touch. Just a soft finger stroke. You can't bond too early."

"You sure Aisling will let me?" After a go-ahead nod, I squatted down and gave each of the babies the lightest stroke of one finger. Mine. "What about this one? Where is, um, he or she going?"

"He's going to an old friend. Fae nobleman I grew up with."

"So when will they be coming home with me?"

"They'll grow faster than you'd think, but it will still be after Hallowstide. You're welcome to come and visit every day while they're still with Mum."

I stood. "It's a great day, Lochlan. I feel like celebrating."

He chuckled. "Understandable. So far as I know, no human has ever owned magical beasts such as these."

I didn't know what to say to that. "I didn't know that. An unexpected honor. I will love them. You know that.

Right?"

"Of course, I know." He laughed. "You don't think these marvelous animals would go home with just anybody!"

Chapter Nine

Jack O'Lantern Junction

THERE WAS NO getting away from the fact that Hallowstide was fast approaching when the village became one giant Halloween decoration.

"I've never seen Jack O'Lanterns made from turnips. The cute ones are fun. The others. Well, they could be the most hideous things I've ever seen. They look like shrunken heads."

Maggie laughed. "Well, this part of the world does no' grow the pumpkins this time o' year. Before air travel, it would've raised considerable suspicion to have a village full of pumpkins. Now we can just pretend we paid a precious premium."

"I'm guessing that means you didn't pay for them at all."

"Gift to Hallow Hill from the queen of the clan that occupies Tregeagle."

"There must be thousands," I said. "I mean it's festive and fabulous. But it might also be overkill."

"If ye mean to say less is more or some such rawmaish, we'll be partin' ways on the subject."

I chuckled. "I concede. It's great fun to have the village decked out."

That meant window displays weren't nearly enough to contain the enthusiasm. Every storefront, including the Hallows, had a gorgeous variety of pumpkins and gourds along with bright fall flowers. There were a few Happy Hallowstide signs and a couple of special seasonal items on the pub menu.

Shortly after the luncheon at John David's house, he'd called.

"Hello?"

"It's John David Weir."

"Hi."

"Hi. I'm calling from a mobile phone."

"Oh good! Is this the number I should keep for you?"

"Yes. It is."

He went on to ask what I thought about a murder-mystery dinner. It crossed my mind that the notion of a vampire staging a murder-mystery dinner was very Tim Burton. But for once, I was mature enough to school my features and keep that to myself. When he explained that he was thinking about hiring actors from Stratford and would try to persuade Olivia to cook, I said it was a smashing idea then crossed my fingers and hoped the locals would indulge him.

The gods never miss a chance to remind me how little I really know and that was never truer than in the case of John David's party. The residents of Hallow Hill acted like the *real* Santa Claus was coming to town.

I suspected that most Octobers talk would be centered on the upcoming Court Meet and festivities. But everything took a back seat to the excitement about John David's party, complete with 1930s-glam dress code. Even I fussed and fussed about what I'd wear and couldn't wait to see Keir in a dinner jacket. I thought about taking up smoking so that I could use one of those extensions designed for keeping over-the-elbows white gloves clean and stray bits of tobacco away from lush, red lipstick, the kind I swore I'd never wear.

Life is strange. I would go as none other than Rita Hayworth playing the title role in *Gilda* and was sure that no one there would get the joke.

That, my daily visits with the puppies, and Keir Culain were the only things staving off panic attacks. At one point I'd thought there might be time to prepare for being a judge, but as the event drew nearer I began to think there weren't enough days in a lifetime to prepare for being a judge.

"WHAT IS IT that has you so worried?" Lochlan had asked on our morning moors walk.

"Doing the wrong thing."

"How are you defining wrong thing?"

I gave that a few minutes' thought as we walked in silence. "Punish someone who's innocent."

"Cross that one off your list. Your intuition will not fail you."

"It won't?"

"No."

"How can you be sure?"

He slanted his eyes toward me, and I knew what he was thinking.

"What's next on your list?"

"How can I know that my solution is the right solution?"

"Rita, if most of the judges in the world were concerned about such things, the world would be a much better place for humans."

I sighed. "No. It wouldn't. There wouldn't be any judges because nobody would take the job."

He laughed. "You simply need the confidence that will come from successfully presiding over Court Week. You'll see that you, and you alone, are the right person."

"I love that you're so sure."

"It's not part of my job to be…"

"A cheerleader?"

"Em, well, perhaps. I want you to understand that my faith in you is not false flattery."

"That's very kind, Lochlan. What would I do without you?"

"Well, you'd be working as an insurance adjuster, living in a sordid little motel, trying to find the funds to pay a third-rate divorce lawyer who would help your husband's attorney take you to the cleaners."

I looked at the ground ahead with wide eyes. "Wow, Lochlan. Go ahead and tell me how you really feel."

"I just did."

"By the way, how's the divorce coming?"

"Oh, it's been done for some time."

"Done. As in final? And you didn't tell me?"

"You were otherwise occupied with your life and your future here. As you should be. I thought you'd put it out of your mind."

It was hard to argue with that. Because I had. "Thank you for taking care of that. And for saving me from the, um, sordid little motel."

He grinned. "Too dramatic?"

"A tad." His playful grin lingered. "So where are we on the docket?"

"First day's full. I'm trying to schedule the middling cases for days two and three. We want to have those out of the way before we begin the case of the kelpie's capture."

"Say that three times fast."

"What?"

"Never mind. You're thinking that case may take two days to present?"

"I think it's a good idea to leave that. Building flexibility into the schedule is always a must. Some things will take longer than expected. Some things will be brief." I laughed at his pun, but the expression on his face told me it was unintended. He probably secretly thought I was a crazy woman who occasionally barked out laughter for no reason at all. "It's an important hearing because the young prince's family is very powerful. If you rule against him and they disagree with your proclamation of resolution, it could be tricky."

"Tricky how?"

He shrugged. "The sephalian might have to do something other than sit around and look pretty."

"Why, Lochlan. That sounded like you think Keir is two things. Pretty and lazy."

"I didn't mean it to sound that way. We all have our jobs. Certainly, I could not do his and, just as certainly, he could not do mine."

"Are you, in your sly way, suggesting that the office of the magistrate is political?"

"No." He scowled. "Not at all. That would be the undoing of the very system that sustains us."

"You're just saying that feathers can be ruffled and, when that happens, Keir has to be called upon to restore order."

"Just so. I'm not saying that will happen, mind you."

"And yet there are a lot of references to the sephalian in the journals." I looked out at the horizon and wondered what my new life would be without the various people who'd taken up permanent residence in my heart. "He can't be killed, can he?"

"I want to say no, but he, like any creature can be killed if a powerful force wants it badly enough." Sensing my unhappiness with that answer, Lochlan added, "The sephalian has been the Enforcer for a long time, even by fae standards. There's no reason to believe he won't continue until he chooses otherwise."

"Nine days. That's how much time I have left to prepare. What else needs to be done?"

"The magic has settled in. You've chosen the cases to be heard. The only thing left is to familiarize you with fae politics. Not because it should influence your decisions, but because it's background you need to understand things."

"Okay," I said slowly.

ON THE WAY to the Hallows for lunch, I stopped by Esmerelda's. She was working at one of her vertical looms, designing something out of this world, but stopped when I came in. She said nothing, just waited.

"Can I interrupt for a minute?" She nodded. "I need a witchy thing, but I don't trust Aoumiel." Esmerelda waited for more, her face giving nothing away. "If I tell you what I want, will you keep it a confidence?"

"Yes," she said.

"I want to fly. With, um, Keir Culain in his sephalian form. But I don't want to fall off and die."

I wasn't expecting laughter, but she'd found something I said extraordinarily funny. "Fly all you want, magistrate. You're not going to fall from the sky and die."

"You're sure?"

"If you didn't think you could believe me, why did you come?"

Well, she had a point.

"Thanks, Esme. Are you going to the murder-mystery dinner?"

She grinned. "What an unnecessary question! *Nothing* could keep me away."

"You can't cheat and read the actors' minds." She just laughed. "No. I mean it. You can attend as an observer. Not a player."

"Who put you in charge?"

"Finish that question."

She scowled for a couple of beats and then gave me a little smile of surrender. "Who put you in charge, Magistrate?"

"You did," I said triumphantly. I was getting used to this.

"Is that the thanks I get? For being your personal advisor?"

It was my turn to laugh. "Esme. Everybody in Hallow Hill considers themselves to be my personal advisor. Your counsel is compartmentalized to, um, fortune-telling. You're not my shrink."

With a shrug she turned back to her weaving. "Whatever you say."

"Oh, for crying out loud," I said with mild exasperation. When I reached the door, I turned back, "First dibs on whatever that is you're working on."

She smiled without looking away from the loom.

ON THE WALK back to my house I called Keir.

"Hello beautiful," he said.

"What are you doing?"

"Eating Brazil nuts and watching worldwide sports in my room."

"You mean the room at my house that may or may not be yours?"

"Yes. My room. Don't worry. I won't interfere with lunch."

"Don't be silly. You can have lunch."

"Oh. Well, since you asked." I laughed silently. "Why'd you call?"

"Something to ask you. After lunch. I wanted to know where to find you."

"A mystery. Tell me now."

"Don't be childish. I'll tell you when everybody's gone."

WHEN OLIVIA HAD finished cleanup and left, I knocked on the door to Keir's room.

He opened it wide, anticipation shining in his eyes.

"I've figured it out. What you want."

"What?"

"A little afternoon delight. I'm in."

He grabbed for me. I giggled like a fifteen-year-old.

"I'm always interested in you in that way, but that's not why I was looking for you."

He leaned against one door jamb at the entrance to his room while I leaned against the other. "Out with it. The suspense is killing me."

"Do you remember mentioning something about flying? Um, with me?"

The corners of his mouth eased upward into such a kissable smile I almost forgot what I'd wanted to say. But it didn't stop there; the anticipatory pleasure traveled further up his face, bringing the light in his eyes to life in the most mesmerizing way. With a little internal shake, I forged ahead, "I went to see Esmerelda. She says I will not fall out of the sky and die." My eyes widened. "I didn't ask about paralysis. She didn't say I wouldn't fall out of the sky and be paralyzed."

Keir laughed softly. "I suspect that was implied. Esmerelda likes you. If that outcome was possible, she would have told you. So. We're flying? Together?" I nodded before my bravado deserted me. "Why now?"

"I'm terrified of the idea. I guess I feel like if I can manage that, I can manage to show up at Hallowstide and say, 'That's right folks. You thought you were getting a real magistrate, but trick or treat, you got me instead'." He laughed again. "I guess it sounds funny. But it's not." I took a deep breath. "I don't want to walk in there looking as scared as I feel right now."

"You know I'm going to be right by your side. All the time. All the way. Forever. If you let me."

To me, that sounded like a proposal of more than a room, a closet, and sleepovers. I quickly decided my best response was to skirt the issue. "So how should we do it?"

"Do it?" I knew he was teasing.

"Come on. When? Where? What should I wear?"

He laughed. "That's unlike you. I would have expected what to wear to come before when and where."

"Ugh. Was that a criticism?"

"Certainly not. It was an expression of satisfaction that I know you well enough to know you view this event as something extraordinary."

"You smooth talker. Answer the questions."

"Tonight. Tregeagle. Bundle up. You'll be cold with the wind rushing past." I nodded. "But Rita. You will be safe with me."

"Then why were you trying to get a spell from Aoumiel?"

"To make you feel confident. Not because I believed you'd fall."

"Oh."

"In fact I prepared for this. Just in case you changed your mind sometime. I'm going to ask two of my brothers to come so that you'll feel triply safe. Between the three of us, no harm can come to you. Promise."

I thought back and remembered that Keir had told me Maeve created 'us'. I'd intended to ask him about that, but apparently, was too ADD to remember.

"Brothers?"

"Yes. Two are close by. One in Ireland. One in Scotland." He grinned. "You'll like them. Promise."

"Sounds like a whole lotta promisin' goin' on."

He pulled me into an embrace that had me wishing it was midnight in front of the fire.

"Promise. You'll always be safe with me."

AT DUSK I knocked on the door of Keir's gatehouse at Tregeagle. Between my excitement about flight and the fact that he looked so scrumptious when he opened the door, I almost knocked him down rushing in for a kiss.

Gripping my waist with both hands, he pushed me away, firmly, ending the kiss in an abrupt way that was nothing like Keir. I looked up to see the face I loved wearing a stern expression I'd never seen and noticed, for the first time, that he was wearing something suitable for a Robinhood's-Sherwood-Outlaws-theme party in a color that could only be called *Braveheart*-blue.

What the...?

The mad face growled, "Unhand me, Magistrate." It took a second to process that he was referring to my hands locked around his neck.

"Rita!" I heard Keir's voice and turned my head to see him moving toward me, looking luscious in a Henley, jeans, and an apron. "Kagan. Take your hands off my woman."

I took a quick step back at the same instant Keir's look-alike did the same, holding palms facing outward. "Not my doin', brother."

Keir looked at me, shaking his head. Pointing to another identical version of himself lounging in the big leather chair in a tweed jacket similar to Lochlan's favorite walking costume, Keir said, "This is my brother, Killian, the Party Animal." I blinked. Killian responded with a salute and a grin. "Seems you've already met my brother, Kagan, the Quiet and Broody."

"I, um..." I stammered, "wasn't expecting such a distinct family resemblance."

Keir scowled. "You think we look alike?"

With no idea what the right answer might be, I spoke with my usual quick wit. "I, um..."

He laughed. "Just kidding. But don't worry. I'm the only one who owns a cell phone and a pair of jeans." He leaned in and said, "The two of them are lost in the past."

When I found my voice, I said, "Hello Killian. Hello Kagan. Sorry about the..."

Kagan waved me off leaving the impression he'd prefer that I didn't finish the sentence.

"I had this made, just in case you ever changed your mind about a ride." Keir smiled as he held up a leather contraption. "It's a breast collar harness. I'll submit to wearing it in my altered form so you'll have something to hold onto and feel more secure."

It looked complicated, but if it would keep me from plummeting to an onomatopoeic death? I'm all in.

"Want dinner?" Keir asked cheerfully.

For the first time I noticed something smelled good.

"What do you have?"

"Fish stew."

"Peanut butter and crackers?" I asked hopefully and heard Killian snort.

"What's wrong with fish stew?" Keir said.

"On second thought, I think I'd better not eat before we, um…"

"Fly?"

"Yes. I have a bad history with amusement park rides."

"You're afraid you're goin' to chunder," said Killian.

I looked his way. "No. I'm afraid I'm going to yak all

over my boyfriend's beautiful wings and never be able to look him in the face again."

Killian laughed as he looked at Keir. "I get it. She's priceless."

Keir gave me the full monty smile before pulling his apron over his head and turning the gas off under the fish stew. "Then let's go!"

The moment at hand came sooner than expected and my courage was heading for the exit.

"Wait."

"What?"

"Maybe this is..."

Keir interrupted. "The best idea you've *ever* had." He grabbed my hand and pulled me out. "It's about to get dark."

"You're sure we won't be seen?"

Keir put one arm around me as he guided me up the hill. "The cloak that keeps us from being seen by Mundies will keep you out of sight." He leaned in and whispered, "Stop looking for an escape route. We're doing this."

We walked through the Tregeagle gardens, which I could now see without the red shoes, and stopped in the clearing near the entrance.

Keir gave me a brief kiss, a big smile, and changed into his sephalian form. Killian and Kagan strapped the harness over his shoulders, between his front legs and attached it to a smallish version of a saddle complete with stirrups. It had two substantial grips on the pommel for me to hold onto.

"Because of his wings, you're going to need to ride with your knees bent all the way forward. Like a jockey," Killian said. He helped me into the saddle and put my feet securely in the stirrups. It was surprisingly comfortable. "Hold on here." He pointed to the leather-covered handles shaped like giant staples.

"You don't have to tell me twice," I said as each hand took a death grip.

"Good," Killian said. "Lean forward until you feel more confident."

I did.

He nodded. "Off we go then."

Knowing Keir, I shouldn't have been expecting a warmup. I should've known we'd lurch forward in one giant leap and be aloft before I had a chance to either shriek or scream that I'd changed my mind and wanted to stay permanently grounded with two feet on terra firma.

The breath had frozen in my lungs. I couldn't say definitively if that was from fear or the cold temperature. Keir's body was warm between my legs, but he hadn't been kidding about the chill of wind rushing past.

By the time my brain had begun to function I realized I was flying a few hundred feet above the countryside on a bright, moonlit night, flanked by two of the most magnificent magical creatures in mythos. For reasons I may never explain, I wasn't afraid. I wasn't nauseous. I wasn't cursing myself for being stupid.

When we dipped low and flew over Hallow Hill, I felt inexplicably sentimental.

Home.

I wasn't sure Keir could hear me in the wind, but my face was close to his ear when I said, "Has there ever been a woman so lucky?"

Let the trials begin!

Now that you know Rita Hayworth and the strange, but fantastic world in which she finds herself, I hope *you'll continue with the series because there's sooooooo much more to come.*

Book Two begins with John David's murder mystery dinner and ends with Rita's ruling on the case of the kelpie captive. In order to fully understand all aspects of the case and arrive at a decision, she insists on personally traveling to the Northern Ireland faerie mound. The fae clain in question is grudgingly forced to admit her so that she can view the facility where one of the overprivileged fae princes has been holding the kelpie.

I know you get hounded for reviews for everything from sunscreen to refrigerators. I feel your pain. But reviews are enormously helpful to me personally. Please take a second and rate this book.

Victoria Danann™

NEW YORK TIMES and
USA TODAY BESTSELLING AUTHOR

Victoria's Website

victoriadanann.com

Victoria's Facebook Page

facebook.com/victoriadanannbooks

Also by Victoria Danann

PARANORMAL WOMEN'S FICTION (for *no-mercy* heroines over forty)

Not Too Late 1. **Midlife Magic**

Not Too Late 2. **Midlife Mayhem**

Not Too Late 3. **Midlife Mojo**

THE KNIGHTS OF BLACK SWAN

Knights of Black Swan 1. My Familiar Stranger

Knights of Black Swan 2. The Witch's Dream

Knights of Black Swan 3. A Summoner's Tale

Knights of Black Swan 4. Moonlight

Knights of Black Swan 5. Gathering Storm

Knights of Black Swan 6. A Tale of Two Kingdoms

Knights of Black Swan 7. Solomon's Sieve

Knights of Black Swan 8. Vampire Hunter

Knights of Black Swan 9. Journey Man

Knights of Black Swan 10. Falcon

Knights of Black Swan 11. Jax

Knights of Black Swan 12. Trespass

Knights of Black Swan 13. Irish War Cry

Knights of Black Swan 14. Deliverance

Knights of Black Swan 15. Black Dog

Knights of Black Swan 16. The Music Demon

***Order of the Black Swan Novels**

Black Swan Novel, Prince of Demons

THE HYBRIDS

Exiled 1. CARNAL

Exiled 2. CRAVE

Exiled 3. CHARMING

THE WEREWOLVES

New Scotia Pack 1, Shield Wolf

New Scotia Pack 2. Wolf Lover

New Scotia Pack 3. Fire Wolf

WITCHES and WARLOCKS

Witches of Wimberley 1. Willem

Witches of Wimberley 2. Witch Wants Forever

Witches of Wimberley 3. Wednesday

CONTEMPORARY ROMANCE

SSMC Austin, TX, Book 1. Two Princes

SSMC Austin, TX, Book 2. The Biker's Brother

SSMC Austin, TX, Book 3. Nomad

SSMC Austin, TX, Book 4. Devil's Marker

SSMC Austin, TX, Book 5. Roadhouse

Cajun Devils, Book 1. Batiste

Made in the USA
Monee, IL
09 May 2021

68089610R00275